It happened so fast, say people wh[...] sudden bursts of violence—but [...] drip and I can see every[...]

Black sneakers on our reclaimed tiles, old appliance manuals in the junk drawer, the RSVP to the wedding of my boyfriend's cousin, a small lace-trimmed envelope waiting to be mailed. The man's eyes are framed by the slit in his balaclava, a word I know from the tattered paperbacks I tore through in the rehab center's shabby library.

I take one step back, jam my hand into my shoulder bag, and rummage wildly for the pepper spray. But I've never used it before, and it's buried under travel Kleenex packs and lip balm and generic ibuprofen and noise-canceling headphones and laptop and charger and moleskin notebook and tampons.

His hand closes around the Jesus candle my boyfriend bought from the bodega by the train station. Señor de los Milagros de Buga, $3.99 plus tax. It's the size of a relay runner's baton, glass as thick as a casserole dish and filled to the brim with solid wax.

My fingers brush the pepper spray canister. There's a little rim of plastic that acts as a safety—I just have to flick it to the side. *Too slow, Sydney.* The candle comes at me in a fluid sideways arc.

Half ducking, half flinching, I twist away. His sidearm swing smashes the candle into my left ear. There's an unbelievable volcanic *thud* inside my head, a searing, blinding flash, and time's not a slow drip anymore, it's a film reel with missing frames.

I am holding myself up, clinging to the door.

I will stay on my feet.

THE

SEVEN

VISITATIONS

OF

SYDNEY

BURGESS

ANDY MARINO

REDHOOK

Redhook Books/Orbit
Hachette Book Group
1290 Avenue of the Americas
New York, NY 10104
hachettebookgroup.com

First Edition: September 2021

Redhook is an imprint of Orbit, a division of Hachette Book Group.
The Redhook name and logo are trademarks of Hachette Book Group, Inc.

The publisher is not responsible for websites (or their content) that are not owned by the publisher.

The Hachette Speakers Bureau provides a wide range of authors for speaking events. To find out more, go to www.hachettespeakersbureau.com or call (866) 376-6591.

Library of Congress Cataloging-in-Publication Data
Names: Marino, Andy, 1980- author.
Title: The seven visitations of Sydney Burgess / Andy Marino.
Other titles: 7 visitation of Sydney Burgess
Description: First edition. | New York, NY : Redhook, 2021.
Identifiers: LCCN 2020056119 | ISBN 9780316629485 (paperback) | ISBN 9780316629461
Subjects: GSAFD: Suspense fiction.
Classification: LCC PS3613.A7485 S48 2021 | DDC 813/.6—dc23
LC record available at https://lccn.loc.gov/2020056119

ISBNs: 978-0-316-62948-5 (trade paperback), 978-0-316-62946-1 (ebook)

Printed in the United States of America

LSC-C

Printing 1, 2021

For Anne

THE

SEVEN

VISITATIONS

OF

SYDNEY

BURGESS

THE FIRST
VISITATION

1

The man in my house is wearing a mask. Even so, I can tell he's as surprised to see me as I am to see him. It's in the way his shoulders jump and erase his neck when I open the door with a triumphant shove, driven by the promise of a rare night alone. With my boyfriend and son camping upstate, I'll be picking the movie I want to watch, ordering Thai food with the spice level cranked, starfishing out in the middle of the bed, dozing off with the windows open to let in the breeze off the Hudson—

"What are you doing?" I blurt out as if I know him. As if I've caught the neighbor kid prowling around the side yard again. He's wearing gloves and a black tracksuit. The drawers of the front hall credenza are pulled out. He steps toward me.

It happened so fast, say people who have lived through sudden bursts of violence—but for me, time's a slow drip and I can see everything at once. Black sneakers on our reclaimed tiles, old appliance manuals in the junk drawer, the RSVP to the wedding of my boyfriend's cousin, a small lace-trimmed envelope waiting to be mailed. The man's eyes are framed by the slit in his balaclava, a word I know from the tattered paperbacks I tore through in the rehab center's shabby library.

I take one step back, jam my hand into my shoulder bag, and rummage wildly for the pepper spray. But I've never used it before, and it's buried under travel Kleenex packs and lip balm and generic ibuprofen and noise-canceling headphones and laptop and charger and moleskin notebook and tampons.

His hand closes around the Jesus candle my boyfriend bought from the bodega by the train station. Señor de los Milagros de Buga, $3.99 plus tax. It's the size of a relay runner's baton, glass as thick as a casserole dish and filled to the brim with solid wax.

My fingers brush the pepper spray canister. There's a little rim of plastic that acts as a safety—I just have to flick it to the side. *Too slow, Sydney.* The candle comes at me in a fluid sideways arc.

Half ducking, half flinching, I twist away. His sidearm swing smashes the candle into my left ear. There's an unbelievable volcanic *thud* inside my head, a searing, blinding flash, and time's not a slow drip anymore, it's a film reel with missing frames.

I am holding myself up, clinging to the door.

I will stay on my feet.

There's an electric current buzzing through my teeth. The front hall is full of bad angles, a nonsense corridor in a dream. The coats are swaying on their hooks. I raise the pepper spray, but my arm can only aim it in the direction of the baseboard, the off-white trim that doesn't quite touch the tile, a haven for crumbs and lost earrings. In the gilt-framed mirror next to the closet door, I see a gloved hand holding the candle up in the air. The man is very tall, and the tip of the candle hits the ceiling before it comes down.

The walls are tinted red and the whole house roars like the ocean. There's a hot-penny tang I can taste in the back of my throat, a cocaine drip that fills my mouth and overflows. Tissue packs and hair clips are scattered across the tiles, coming up fast.

I shouldn't be here. These words can't really form because the darkness is thick enough to stifle thought. It's more like a sharp sense of injustice wrapped in the fear that throbs somewhere in the void. An impression that I have been cheated by circumstance.

I shouldn't be here.

2

Y ou're a lucky woman," says Dutchess County Sheriff Mike Butler.

I ride a wave of displacement. Lucky? I don't feel lucky. I feel like I want to unzip my skin and wriggle out of my body and into another. By what metric is he measuring my luck? I suppose he means that I'm luckier than a woman whose attack has resulted in her murder. I want to tell him: *lucky* is what you are when you win the lottery.

I calculate how much time has elapsed since the attack. Ten, eleven hours at most. Now I understand all those survivors' stories on *Dateline* and *20/20*. It happened so fast. It's amazing what can be compressed into mere seconds of a human life.

Butler takes off his hat and rocks on his heels. I know his face and name from a campaign billboard near my town's highway off-ramp. On the billboard, his face is somehow both jowly and chiseled, as if the features of a hardass drill sergeant were superimposed onto a mall Santa. In person, Butler's the kind of guy whose middle-aged weight gain makes him look even more powerfully built, his barrel chest and gut filling out his uniform without seeming flabby.

Behind his shaved head is the classic hospital corner-mounted television. Wan light comes through vertical slats in the blinds and paints staccato lines on the wall. *Saturday morning*, I think—words that conjure up Pilates for me, a long run for my boyfriend, Matt, and an extended gaming session for my son, Danny. And then, like a ravenous, plundering army, we take our reward: brunch. When my boys and I brunch, we brunch hard. Pulpy juice straight from the gleaming contraption, huevos rancheros, black beans, avocado, crispy bacon, home fries, strawberries from the little roadside stand...

Butler clears his throat. "Okay," he says. Then he puts his hat back on and studies the cup of water on the bedside table like it holds the key to cracking this case wide open. I think, perhaps unfairly, that he has no idea how to talk to a woman wrapped in bandages lying in a hospital bed. I am his mother, his sister, his wife. My victimhood disturbs him. It's not what he signed up for.

He takes a step closer to my bed. "You took quite a shot," he says. From this angle, I can see the landscape of razor burn under his chin. "Lucky lady."

It's almost funny, in an existential nightmare kind of way: trapped in a hospital bed while a man reminds me how lucky I am, over and over again.

He glances at my freshly bandaged wrists, and his eyes travel across my older scars, exposed by my short-sleeved hospital gown. Then he looks me in the face. "I was just at your house. That's quite a thing you did."

For the first time, it dawns on me that my house is a crime scene. It's probably crawling with cops and forensic techs. I think CSI is called something different in real life, but I picture a team in HAZMAT suits, spraying luminol. In reality it's probably two local cops in rubber gloves poking around our dressers and desks, combing through the front hall, the guest room. Suddenly I'm laser focused. I can feel a manic surge begin in my toes and course through my body. The jagged mosaic of sights and sounds from last night comes together in the man's cold eyes framed in a tight oval of black fabric.

I manage to hold on to it for a second, but then the mosaic goes out of focus. Cobbled-together images of things I didn't actually see run through my mind. A man in a tracksuit and balaclava walking down the sidewalk in broad daylight. His arms are long, too long, and his shadow pours like oil down the street, up my driveway, through my front door...

"I can come back later," Butler says. He sounds far away. I realize that my eyes are half-lidded. It's not just my thoughts that are drifting. I refused the Vicodin regimen the doctor wanted to put me on, three hundred milligrams every four hours for the pain. Opioids were never my thing—I was a fiend for the rush, not the nod—but I've seen addicts with decades of sober living fall off because of back pain, grizzled old alkies who figure what's the harm in a few pain pills if they're prescribed by a doctor? Or at least, they pretend to think like that. I'd wager most of them know exactly what the harm is, they're just falling back on the oldest addict trick in the book: self-delusion.

And so, all I'm on is ibuprofen. Four gelcaps. It's barely enough for a stress headache. I might as well be taking vitamins.

"The doctor wasn't too keen on me talking to you now," Butler says. "But I'd really like to take your statement sooner rather than later, if you're up for it."

"It's okay," I say, gathering my strength. "I'm good. I want to help."

"Anything you can remember, then."

"I wasn't supposed to be there," I say. "Home, I mean. I was supposed to be camping with my boyfriend and my son, up at Cedar Valley. Taking a long weekend. But I got called in for a last-minute pitch at the agency I work for. In the city. Matt and Danny"—my heart quickens as I try, and fail, to sit up—"the park's a total dead zone, there's no way to call them, they won't know—"

Butler holds up a hand. "We've got state police out of Poidras Falls tracking your family down."

Your family. There's a deep, sweet hurt behind those words.

"Tell me about the man in your house."

"He was tall," I say, flashing to the candle hitting the ceiling before it came down and the house roared and the walls turned red. "Taller than Matt, and he's six-one." I pause. "Taller than Trevor, too."

"Who's Trevor?"

"My ex. Danny's father."

"Okay," Butler says, flipping open his notebook and jotting something down. He's not using one of those standard-issue cop notepads, but a green moleskin.

"I have one of those," I say.

"My daughter works in a coffee shop in Poughkeepsie," he says. "They sell these things by the register." He shakes his head. "Kid drops out of SVA, down in the city, after her freshman year, says school is sucking the life out of her painting. So now, you know what she does? Brings home a bag of the day's used-up coffee grounds, smears them on canvases. Not my thing, art-wise, but she's saving me forty grand a year, so I can't complain."

I don't know what to say to that. In the moment of silence, I can feel myself drifting again. "Gray eyes," I say.

"Gray?"

"They were cold. Like the winter sky."

"Winter sky," he says.

I suddenly recall hurried questions from a different cop in the more immediate aftermath. A woman. Severe pony-tail, wine-dark lipstick. My neighbor, the pediatrician, who found me on his lawn, hovering awkwardly in the background, holding a mug in two cupped hands. I am disturbed by how the memory comes on: from nothing to something, a bucket of paint splattering a blank wall.

"I remember," I say, "I told all this to somebody at my neighbors' house."

"You were in shock," Butler says. "This isn't going to be like it is on TV, where you give your statement and you're on your way. It'll be a process. You'll remember new things days, weeks from now. But this is a good time for us to talk. Most people…" He trails off with a frown and lowers the notebook. "Most people would be doped to the gills after what you just went through, but the doctor said you refused the heavy-duty painkillers."

I hesitate. I don't hide the fact that I'm an addict in recovery from anyone, but I don't ordinarily talk to county sheriffs. It feels like I'm planting an asterisk in our conversation, something for Butler to come back to later, casting a pall over everything I tell him.

"I've got nine years clean," I say. I know that this is admirable, that I have nothing to be ashamed of. But talking to cops twists my thoughts. It's like putting my bags through the scanner in airport security. Of course I know there's nothing in there, and yet still, after all these years, anxiety engulfs me and my heart pounds and I think, *what if*—what if they find something?

"Good for you," Butler says. He sounds different now—guarded, maybe. I wonder about his daughter, behind the counter of that coffee shop. Is she an Oxy fiend? Is Butler's father an alcoholic, dying of cirrhosis? Addicts orbit everyone's life, and a person's reaction to addiction in general—whether they believe it's truly a disease or just an excuse to stay high all the time—tends to be reflected through the lens of their own experience.

Is Butler himself a clandestine pill-popper, a raider of confiscated evidence?

His eyes flit once again to my scars. I don't volunteer any information about them.

"So, I'm sticking with ibuprofen," I say, trying to end this conversational tack. But I can see something in his hooded eyes, and a knot forms in my stomach. I know what Butler is thinking. He might not even know it yet, but the kernel of an idea is forming.

Nobody's as clean as they say they are. We're dealing with a drug thing. Some dealer who didn't get paid, some old city debt getting settled up the river, darkening our quiet suburban doorsteps.

I keep my mouth shut. I don't want to protest too much, before he's even brought it up. But the way my mind is working now—telling me I have to manipulate, steer the conversation—makes me feel like I'm a suspect being grilled in a stuffy, windowless interview room.

There's a sharp pain in my head, a cold needle piercing the dull, pounding ache. The edges of the room are fuzzy, lenses smeared with grease.

Butler glances over his shoulder at the door. When he looks back at me, his gaze is unclouded. "The doctor also said you refused a rape kit." His tone is as matter-of-fact as ever.

"I wasn't raped."

"No sexual assault."

"No. I told you guys what happened."

"You told Deputy Carlson, back there at your neighbors' house."

"Right. I remember. Sort of."

He consults his moleskin. "Approximately seven forty-five p.m., you open your front door and interrupt a robbery in progress. The perp bashes you in the head with a"—he flicks his glance to me—"Jesus candle. The next thing you know..."

3

The ground has swallowed me. A great physics-defying hole stretches up through the house. The pain in my head is pure compression, like I'm being squeezed in a vise clamped over my ears. A high-pitched mosquito whine surrounds my head.

I'm swamped by a rush of bone-deep shame—the feeling when you wake from an uneasy dream convinced that you've cheated on your boyfriend, crashed your mother's car, covered up a horrible crime. *I have done it again.* Clean for nine years, seven months, twenty-two days. Detox, rehab, halfway house, then meetings like clockwork. Almost a decade of building a real, solid life for Danny and me. Ditching the old cycles of manic pleasures and hurts for hard work and discipline. And now, in one colossally stupid night, all of it has been erased.

They're going to take Danny away from you.

I shudder. That's as much movement as my body will allow. I try to retrace the steps that brought me back to this place— the time-smeared bewilderment, the icy-hot gasp of my body clawing its way to the surface. Coming back from an overdose is still a familiar sensation, even after so many years. Whom did I call to get drugs? It should have been impossible. Forget

about cocaine—I don't even know where to get weed anymore. Was it somebody from the agency? Did we go out to
celebrate after the pitch? Where did I get a rig? But maybe I
didn't take a shot. Maybe I just did too many lines. That makes
more sense—social cocaine, ad agency cocaine, upwardly
mobile cocaine—not shooting-up-in-a-stairwell cocaine.

The problem is, for me it's all the same. And I am insatiable.

I reach in a direction I believe to be up. My arm weighs
a ton, but my hand is strangely weightless—the balloon on
the end of a heavy tether. I manage to curl my fingers over
the rim of the impossible hole. I'm deep within the guts of
my house, a between-place, and my thoughts flash wildly to
the special effects in *Doctor Strange*, Danny's favorite Marvel
movie. I remember watching it with him and being a little
nervous that he favored the trippy visuals of that film over
the straightforward heroics of Thor and Captain America.
He'll be in middle school next year, walking the halls with
kids who have already started smoking pot and drinking and
probably dropping acid.

They're going to take him away, away, away from you . . .

Danny in a foster home, Danny all alone.

Danny with a new mother.

I cry out and a gurgling sound escapes my throat. There's
a metallic taste in my mouth, a rusty mélange of blood and
saliva. I try to hook my fingers as best I can over the rim of
the impossible hole. My arm feels unwieldy and wrong, and
I think it must be more than just a malfunction in my motor
control.

That's when I realize that my "arm" is actually both my
arms bound together—hence the heaviness. My fingers are
numb. My thoughts grind helplessly against this new confusion. *What is this around my wrist?*

Duct tape. The gray kind that screeches when you pull it from the roll.

I blink and the rim of the impossible hole gets closer. I am rising up through the between-place. High above, a ceiling fan is a small black cross in a vast white sky.

I am on the floor in the downstairs guest room.

With dizzying clarity, the memory clicks into place: the man in my house, the candle, the red walls, the floor tiles.

Is there a name for the feeling of being relieved and terrified at the same time?

I haven't relapsed and overdosed and taken a blowtorch to my life with Matt and Danny. I've been attacked. And now my wrists are bound with tape.

I clamp my eyes shut against a wave of nausea, a queasy conspiracy between my head and my stomach that makes it impossible to think. At the same time, I hear a man's voice in the hall and some part of me screams *MATT* even though I know it's not him, it sounds nothing like him, and anyway I can't scream, I can only gurgle wetly.

The man's voice is raised in anger. He's talking to someone else.

"Because there wasn't supposed to be anybody fucking home!" he says. And then, less vehement. Chastened. *"No. I've been over every inch of the place. It's not here."* Pause. *"I know. I realize that. And I'm telling you, it's not."*

Something like despair presses down on me. It's not here. The black cross shrinks to a dot and then disappears into all that endless white. I'm sinking softly back into darkness. I try to fight my descent, clawing weakly at the rim of the hole, but it's too far away and my arm weighs a ton. The white sky diminishes to a distant point of light and blinks out.

4

Butler looks startled. He lowers the notebook. "There was a second person in your house?"

I try to slip inside my memory, to let the man's voice come through, but the sounds are all part of the cracked mosaic. The voice is garbled and indistinct, like a back-masked recording, *Abbey Road* played in reverse. *Paul is dead, Paul is dead, Paul is dead.*

"I don't think so," I say. "I only heard the one voice. I'm pretty sure he was on the phone."

"He took a call or made a call?"

"I don't know. I woke up and he was talking to someone."

"What was he saying?"

My heart races. I wonder if it would be okay to ask for some Xanax. I made a deal with myself long ago that a strict No Benzos policy would be part of my recovery, but surely these are extenuating circumstances. I let the man's voice unspool through my head. I'm back on the floor, and he's out in the hall.

"He was looking for something," I say.

"He said that over the phone?"

"*It's not here.* Something like that."

A three-note chime rings out and a tinny bluegrass guitar begins to play. Butler mutters under his breath, fishes in his pocket, and pulls out his phone.

"I hate this thing," he says, as if we are on the cusp of the great mobile phone era and he has just been forced to get one of the infernal devices. I wonder if he says that every time his phone rings.

He answers it with a terse "Butler." Then he holds up a finger, gives me a nod, and goes out into the hallway. My heart surges. They caught the guy! Or they found a clue—a dropped wallet, an abandoned car, a mask and gloves in a dumpster.

Of course, it could be Mike Butler's daughter calling to let him know that the cat puked on the kitchen counter again, and no way in hell is she cleaning it up this time. The moments that send our lives off course—the traumas it takes us forever to come to grips with—are the moments that cops and doctors brush up against in a normal workday. They're scoffing at political memes on Facebook and texting friends about the bar last night between encounters with shell-shocked people who will never be the same.

I test my ability to sit up. The ringing in my head sharpens, the point of the needle extends, and I lie back against the pillow. My wrists sting when I move them, little jolts of pinprick pain that float atop the bruising. I will myself to heal. Surely my junkie days left me with freakish resilience, some kind of mutant healing power. I vow that I will not let my son see me like this. I will tell the nurse to notify me when Matt and Danny have arrived. I will get up from this bed and walk out to them in the waiting room. They will see me on my feet.

I press the call button and wait. The ambient noise of the ward drifts in. Some things never change: the clacking footfalls of harried staff, the ceaseless chirping of machines nobody ever seems to check. It feels like a hundred little alarms are going off at once, and nobody's running to hit snooze. My head is aching. I close my eyes.

Fucking hospitals.

I open my eyes to find Sheriff Butler sitting in a chair, which he's pulled up close to my bed. One hand is wrapped loosely around a Styrofoam cup, the other cradles his phone in his lap. We lock eyes and he shifts in his seat, a big man in a tight space.

"Did you find him?" I say. My voice is a croak. Butler picks up a water bottle with a plastic straw, like you'd stick through the bars of a hamster cage, and puts the straw to my lips. Gratefully, I suck down a little water.

"We—yes," he says. But there's a hitch in his voice, an odd hesitation, like he's not quite sure. Seems pretty binary to me: you either caught the guy or you didn't.

"Where?"

Butler sets his coffee cup on the floor and leans forward in his chair, elbows on his knees. He lets out a long, audible breath. "Ms. Burgess..."

"Sydney."

"Tell me exactly what you did after you regained consciousness."

5

I'm out of the impossible hole. Awake. I don't know how long I was out, but the man is still talking on the phone in the hall outside the guest room. I lift my head and wince at the pain. I take a moment to focus my eyes. It hurts.

The squat little stained-glass lamp I bought in a furniture shop in Cold Spring is on, casting its orange-and-green autumnal glow from atop the dresser. I scan the room through what looks like a fish-eye lens. The damask curtains are drawn across the big picture window that faces the water. There's a rolltop desk, a framed print from Lobsterfest, an old iMac we're going to donate one of these days, the collapsible drying rack where Matt drapes his sweaty running clothes because throwing them directly into the hamper breeds bacteria.

"*That's out of the question,*" the man in the hallway says. He's sort of whisper-screaming into the phone. I'm staring at Matt's limp blue shirt with corporate logos on the back, swag from a 10K he ran last year. My brain wants to make some kind of connection, but it's like the power lines are down in my head.

"*I'm not doing that,*" the man says.

Then it hits me: the guest room is where Matt's entire running wardrobe lives. He hangs his windbreakers in the closet, keeps his spandex tights in the dresser, slides his shoes under the guest bed. Among those shoes are his racing flats. Screwed into those racing flats are metal spikes.

"*You want that done—no, you listen to me, all due respect—you want that done, you do it yourself.*"

Panic spurs me into motion. I glance up at the open door to the bedroom and try to place the man by the sound of his voice. He's maybe twenty feet away, in the kitchen's second entrance. He could pop his head in here in a matter of seconds.

"*Because I'm not fucking stupid.*"

I try to move without making a sound, and that's when I notice that my ankles are also bound with tape. I tamp down a scream of frustration. My heart's galloping along, and I can feel panic stealing my thoughts, turning me into the frantic mess I tried so hard to beat into submission with yoga and Pilates and SoulCycle and weights—any form of relief that doesn't come in a little square ziplock full of white powder.

"*You know what? Fine.*"

The decorative lamp can barely illuminate the mess under the bed. Pockets of secret clutter serve as the release valve for our visibly neat and orderly house. Our closets and crawl-spaces look like bachelor pads from movies about schlubby guys getting with inordinately attractive women. Straining my shoulders, I reach my bound arms under the bed, past old socks and dead guitar pedals and a thick coding manual.

The man's voice is louder.

"*I'll take care of it. But this is on you.*"

There's an air of finality to this last bit of conversation.

He's coming. No time to rummage for shoes. I pull my arms out from under the bed and plant my palms flat on the floor. On my knees, downward dog, I push myself to my feet. I'm wobbly but I have no choice. The sound of his footsteps tells me that he's plodding toward the guest room. No point in trying to be quiet. In a few seconds it won't matter. I hop around the bed, bending my knees and using my arms as a fulcrum to spring myself as far as I can. Past the dresser, to the door, straining with the effort.

For a split second I see him, ten feet away, coming down the hall, one of our Gusthof carving knives glinting in his right hand. He sees me, too, and starts running. With a ragged shout I slam the bedroom door shut, just as he reaches it, and turn the lock on the doorknob. At the same time, he slams his big body against the door. The whole frame shudders. I jump back, my mind serving up insane flashes of the blade slicing through, *Heeeere's Johnny.*

He tries again, hitting the door hard, the dull thud harmonizing with some crossed wire in my brain, the whole world pulsing and throbbing. You'd be surprised at the amount of involuntary screaming that you're capable of. Screams are the great equalizer—men, women, children, all of us a bunch of shrieking automatons when situations move beyond everyday panic and into the realm of true mortal terror.

The next blow to the door is sharp and focused, and I hear a splintering sound. He's changed his strategy—he's kicking it.

I've made no progress. I'm just standing here, next to the drying rack and the iMac. The brief hint of normalcy that surrounds these things nearly brings me to my knees. How can this possibly be happening to me? But I pull myself together and rush to the dresser. I stand on the side opposite the door and brace my palms against it and push. It's a solid piece of furniture, not the usual IKEA particleboard you tend to find in guest rooms, the last vestige of apartment life. This dresser is a block of real wood that once belonged to Matt's parents. It's not full—besides running clothes, the drawers hold things like wrapping paper and tape and Halloween decorations—but I can barely move it. Shoving it like I'm doing lunges to stretch my hamstrings isn't going to work.

The next kick elicits a *pop* from the door frame. I can almost see the dent where the man's foot stove the wood in. I hear him moving quickly down the hall, toward the kitchen. He's going to give himself a running start. I flash to true crime shows about the victims of knife attacks. Words like *defensive wounds* surface in my throbbing head. I have the sickening impression, almost like it's already happening, of the carving knife shredding my palms as I hold them out reflexively, a last-ditch effort to keep the blade away from my face, my neck, my heart.

I bend my knees and jam my bound hands underneath the lip between the floor and the base of the dresser, in the space created by the four squat legs. I strain, tilting this absurdly heavy piece of furniture with a strength I know I wouldn't possess under ordinary circumstances. The dresser lifts off the floor. Footsteps race down the hall.

With one last cry I heave the dresser past its tipping point and step back. It falls and lands on its side with a great crash, blocking the lower half of the door, which bursts open as the man throws himself against it. The door bashes the dresser and stops, stymied by the barricade. I hear the man cry out in surprise as something he can't see and didn't expect repulses his charge. Because of the slight angle of the dresser, there's about an inch of space between the blocked door and the frame. It won't take him long to use his leverage to widen the opening.

I scramble back down to the floor and lie on my side. There, from this vantage point, Matt's Asics racing flats are easy to spot. I reach in with my awkward club-arm and grab one shoe by the laces and pull it out.

"Fucking bitch!" the man yells. He batters the door without mercy. The dresser holds.

I say a silent *thank you* to the running gods: Matt's last race was a 10K around the perimeter trails of Griffin Park— no blacktop, no roads, no sidewalks. Just dirt and grass. The half-inch spikes are still screwed into his Asics. I turn the shoe upside down so they're pointing up at me, eight little mud-encrusted needle-teeth.

I have no time to judge a safe angle or saw gingerly at the tape. Without a moment to brace myself, I stretch the tape as tautly as I can and bring my bound wrists down hard on the spikes. The pain is instant and immense as the spikes pierce the tape along with my skin and grind against the prominent bones just behind the soft cartilage of the wrist itself. Again and again—three more times—I lift my arms and bash the tape against the spikes. Blood spurts across the rubbery maze of the sole of the shoe.

Behind me I hear the dresser begin to slide. He's figured out the proper place to push to move it inward. I wiggle my wrists and the blood-slickened tape loosens. I grit my teeth and wrench my arms apart. The tape gives way and my heart nearly explodes. My hands are free. I claw at the tape around my ankles, unwrapping myself like the world's most spastic mummy, and then I'm on my feet, throwing aside the curtain. Outside, through the trees, the moon glitters on the river's placid surface, and it's the most beautiful thing I've ever seen. I pop the screen off its frame with a single hard shove and glance over my shoulder. The man is squeezing through the widened opening. His cold eyes bore into mine.

I slam my hands down on the base of the windowsill and lift my body and vault out of the window. This is a move I had no idea I was capable of. My bare feet hit the soil of the little strip of garden that's flush against the house in the back and side yards. Adrenaline is a funny thing: it's propelling me onward in a dead sprint toward the dark trees that separate our house from the next-door neighbors', but it can't do anything about how wobbly I am. I feel like my center of gravity's been diverted way off course, into my throat or my knees. My breath comes in an audible pant that would sound forced coming from a character in a movie.

The elms and oaks are thick and very old, but there aren't that many of them—I'm through them in half a minute, barely feeling the wood chips and twigs that trouble my feet, and then I'm sprinting across a manicured lawn. I trigger my neighbors' sensor-activated floodlights affixed to the side of their garage.

I cut the angle across the blacktop and out onto my street. The houses are generously spaced, but they aren't set very far back from the road. And it's not that late. Plenty of living room lights are burning.

I don't know what the man who attacked me is willing to do. I don't want to lead him straight to an unsuspecting neighbor's doorstep.

I want the whole neighborhood to see what has happened. He can't kill us all.

I scream for help. I wave my bloody arms and flag down a passing car, but I don't even stop when the wide-eyed teenage boy screeches to a halt and gets out and tries to talk to me. I hear doors opening and people calling out to me, to each other. I pass a dozen houses before someone reaches the street and plants himself in my path. It's David Winters, a pediatrician I met exactly once at a neighborhood barbecue.

"*Sydney!*" he's saying, over and over again. "*My God, Sydney.*"

I don't know how he gets me to stop running. My mind isn't processing reality as a linear point A to point B experience. I just know that I'm sitting in the grass of his front yard, which smells freshly mowed. There are people milling about, looming over me, looks of frightened concern on the faces of my most casual acquaintances, all of us dropping our cheerful neighborly masks, probably forever.

You're safe now, someone says. But I just shake my head.

No, I say. I don't know why. He's right—I am safe now. I have escaped.

And yet: *no*.

6

Butler rubs his temples and lets out a long breath.

"Sydney..." He shakes his head at some internal disbelief. "Look. I believe that you were in a bad situation, okay? I want you to know that. I'm not sitting here saying you brought this on yourself. Nothing like that." He glances at the door again, like relief might be waiting in the wings.

"What are you talking about? Just tell me what happened with the guy."

"I was hoping you could tell me."

"I told you everything already."

"Right. Okay then." He sits back in his chair and slaps his palms on his thighs. "The man who broke into your house is dead."

I have no idea why Butler is trying to spare my feelings—I don't have any bleeding-heart love for the guy who almost sliced me up. My movie-saturated brain conjures up a high-speed chase, a hail of bullets. "You guys kill him?"

"No," Butler says. "You did."

I let out a clipped laugh of disbelief—unseemly, I know, but it's a reflex. "What did he do, slip on the front steps?" I imagine some kind of twisted liability clause, one of those wacky news stories where the guy's parents will sue Matt and me for not properly installing a railing on the house their son was burglarizing.

Butler shakes his head. "He was stabbed with a kitchen knife. Multiple times." He picks up his notebook from the bedside table and reads from a page. "Twenty-eight, to be exact, localized primarily around the neck and face. Severed jugular. Severed *head*, almost."

The Gusthof cutlery set was a gift from Matt's parents. My first Christmas with them. Danny was eight and couldn't get over how big their tree was. It was a monstrous fir, fat as a garden shed, wired to an exposed beam in their vaulted living room to keep it from falling over.

The knife's unlikely path etches itself in my mind, a dotted line on a map beginning with Matt's parents in a high-end home store: Judy Melford selecting the priciest set, dots looping through fastidious Owen gift-wrapping the box. My own hands ripping apart the paper, revealing a brand I've never heard of but assume to be very fine. Those same hands dicing tomatoes and onions for brunch scrambles, slicing up butternut squash for hearty fall soups...

"And you think—" I roll through my churning thoughts. The mosaic pieces itself together. I remember the dresser, the thud of his boot against the door, the feel of the cool night air on my face as I vaulted over the windowsill. "That's impossible."

"We found him on the floor inside the guest room. The place was all torn up. It looks like you struggled."

"He was twice my size."

"Adrenaline does crazy things to people."

"But—no. That's impossible. Sorry."

"The thing is, Sydney, with something like this, it looks

personal. Especially with the face...It's the kind of thing somebody does when they know the other person. Not when they're defending themselves. You really took your time with this guy."

"Wouldn't I have been covered in blood if I stabbed somebody twenty-eight times?"

"You were."

I lift up my bandaged wrists.

Butler shakes his head. "Look, if you're playing the lost-memory card for my sake, you can drop the act. I really do believe that something terrible happened to you, and you had to react."

"Something that was my fault, though, somehow."

"I'm not saying that. I just want to know exactly how it went down."

"I told you."

He gives me an inscrutable look. "You've got a domestic on your record. A couple of disorderlies."

I wonder if it's standard procedure to dig up the criminal record of a survivor on the night of her attack, or if being an addict affords you this special scrutiny.

"I was a totally different person then," I say. "A kid in a shitty relationship." There's a pleading edge to my voice that I hate as soon as the words come out. *Sorry about the mess I used to be. Sorry that you have to spend your weekend investigating my attempted murder.*

"This is with your son's biological father?"

"Yeah. Trevor Erwin." It's been so long since I've spoken the full name out loud, the four syllables are like some foreign conjugation.

"He still in the picture?"

I let out a short, sharp laugh, and my brain rubs against

my skull. Fresh tears well up. "He went nine years without ever trying to get in touch, so the short answer is *hell no*. I'd always figured rock bottom caught up with him, he pulled some half-assed scheme on the wrong person, whatever."

"But?"

"But then a few weeks ago I saw him outside Danny's school."

Like seeing a ghost, I almost add, except the cliché doesn't really apply. It was more like catching a scrap of an old dream, some windblown thing that drifted into my waking life. A man whose voice I barely remember and whose ruined face, viscous and wet-looking even after all this time, sprang from the same awful night as the scars on my arms. Trevor Erwin, leering from the window of a rusted F-150, flicking the ash of a Swisher Sweet onto the pavement of the horseshoe pickup lot.

"What did he want?"

"No idea. He drove away when he saw me coming at him."

"You two have custody issues?"

"No. I always figured he was glad I took Danny off his hands."

"He on the hook for child support, anything like that?"

"This isn't a person with a bank account we're talking about here. It would have been pointless. I'm doing fine."

The moleskin comes out again. "You know where he's been staying?"

"My guess is the back of his truck."

"He have any reason to hurt you?"

"Not in my mind. Maybe in his." The black TV screen blurs the edges of the sheriff's head and I blink his face back to distinction. "It's been a long time."

"He still using?"

"I don't know—we don't hang out. Like I told you, I'm clean. For real." The extra emphasis that slips out makes me cringe, the doubling down of a guilty teenager. "All this is another life."

"I understand," he says, "I'm not saying this is a drug thing. But—look. I've got thirty-plus years in law enforcement. I'm not easy to shock and I don't judge people for what they do in the privacy of their homes. So if you're seeing someone, if you've got some other blast from the past, if this involves some kind of sex play that got out of hand—"

"*Sex play?*"

"Okay"—he holds up a hand—"okay. That was just a for-example. Calm down. We can talk again later. My guys can reconstruct the order of events from the scene. Maybe that'll help jog your memory."

I try to pull on a thread in my mind that might lead back to a feeling of savagery, of the kind of primal rage that could inspire such blinding ferocity. I could almost believe that I did it, if the man had been stabbed once or twice. I think I would be capable of something like that out of pure self-preservation, although I don't know for sure. But the sheer will to drive a knife into another human being's body twenty-eight times, to slice through flesh and sinew, over and over again—that is a monstrous act, no matter the circumstances. It would put me in a certain tier of humanity where I do not belong.

"Can you show me a picture?" I ask.

"I don't know if that's a good idea right now. Why don't you get some rest, and when you wake up, your family will be here."

The emotional whiplash is dizzying. Soon I will touch

Danny and Matt with my hands, the same hands that the sheriff is telling me just cut a man to pieces with a Gusthof carving knife.

"Show me," I say. "Maybe it'll help."

Frowning, the sheriff swipes at his phone. Then he holds it out horizontally in front of my face. My first instinct is to look away, like I do whenever gory crime-scene footage comes up in something I'm watching. It's not that I'm squeamish, exactly—I just decided after I got clean that the fewer images of humanity at its worst I see during my short time on this earth, the better. And I don't want Danny growing up thinking it's normal to watch beheading videos or whatever. But right now, I force myself to look. I have to know.

There's the door to the guest room, halfway open, the dresser at an angle against it on the floor. Just beyond the dresser is the body of the man in the tracksuit. He's lying faceup, his arms and legs splayed in the odd, haunting angles of the dead, like he's reaching for parts of his body he'll never be able to touch. Dark blood soaks the carpet underneath him. It's nearly as black as his clothes, as if his tracksuit leaked its pigment. Next to his left arm is the knife, a long silver triangle stained with blood that looks like rust in the washed-out photograph. Next to his head is the mask. The killer pulled it off to mutilate the man's face and neck, a rugged landscape of torn and lumpy flesh. There are few discernible features—flaps of skin have been ripped out and resettled in patches, obscuring his eyes and mouth. I think I can make out his nose, a twist of putty roughly in the middle. Deep lacerations crisscross his forehead and scalp. His long hair reminds me of a surfer's hair in a movie, and it's speckled red as if a fine mist of blood settled over him, spritzed from a spray bottle.

Sheriff Butler pockets his phone. I blink and the image of the dead man is burned into the back of my eyelids. There's an acute horror to seeing a victim of such brutality lying on the carpet of the room where I go to rummage for sewing needles and sheet music. But the picture on Butler's phone doesn't jog my memory. This is all I know: The man was forcing his way into the room as I vaulted over the window-sill. I saw his eyes, and that was it. I was gone.

"It wasn't me," I say as firmly as I can.

"Okay," Butler says, too easily. Humoring a child. "We can circle back to this later."

He picks up his coffee cup and leaves the room. Too late, I realize that I want him to stay. I want to keep talking, to convince him of my innocence and of the randomness of the attack, to unravel threads until we arrive at the truth. But all I'm left with is an impression of the dead man's ruined humanity, his obliterated features. I try to conjure up the feel of the knife in my hand. Nothing. The pressure in my head is tied to the nausea that roils my guts. My eyes drift to the button that will bring waves of relief, of calmness and forgetting. I look beyond it to the window, fighting to quell the dry-mouthed fear that used to choke my thoughts like wisteria during a post-bender crash.

The tremors of not knowing what I've done.

THE SECOND
VISITATION

7

Fernbeck, New York, is a fifty-five-minute train ride from Grand Central Station, straight up the Hudson River. It's a classic commuter town with a modern soul, John Cheever with juice cleanses instead of gin-soaked melancholy. Although I'm sure there's plenty of the latter in the twilight garden parties of the old-money folks whose Tudors dot the hills.

Matt drives slowly, steering carefully around the notorious pothole at the entrance to our wooded subdivision. Over the summer Danny started running with Matt—a mile here, a mile there, looping around the cul-de-sac at the end of our neighborhood. As Matt takes me home from the hospital, I think of my boys that way, disappearing over the crest of our street's gentle incline, Matt in his borderline-obscene short-shorts and Danny in his baggy Brooklyn Nets gear, a pair of mismatched scamps heading for some crazy adventure just over the hill.

The life I've built once again seems miraculous.

Any well-being I salvaged from the past forty-eight hours evaporates when we step inside the house. The place has been turned inside out. We explore in a mute daze, picking through the mess like hushed spelunkers coming upon ancient ruins. Contents of drawers and cupboards are strewn across the floors of the kitchen, the living room, the bathrooms. Our mantel has been swept clean of its keepsakes: framed photos of the three of us in Yellowstone, little pewter bears from Matt's parents' cruise to Alaska, a bouquet of dried peonies.

I peek into our bedroom. It's a riot of open drawers and crooked pictures. The vanity is askew. Our bedside clocks have been turned facedown.

It's not here.

In the kitchen, my eyes go on autopilot to the knife block with its single blade missing.

I never thought about it before, but of course it's not the cops' job to clean up once they've processed a crime scene. It will be up to us to put our home back together. I tell myself it's really not so bad. It's just stuff in disarray. It could have been worse. *Lucky, lucky, lucky . . .*

I put Danny to work getting his bedroom in order, flaring with a hot, indignant rush at the thought of the man rifling through my son's Lego sets, his games and toys, his underwear drawer.

I stand with my arms folded in the doorway of his room, watching my son apply himself with quiet efficiency to picking up his things. Love pours out of me like it does a thousand times a day, when I'm watching him draw in his sketchbook at the kitchen table or assemble byzantine Lego cities on the living room floor, or carefully slide his books into his backpack according to a sorting scheme only he understands. But there's a different tenor to it now. It's like the last cloud parting after a storm. Quick dark fears come back—that I'd overdosed, that I was going to lose him—and the sheer relief that settles over me at the sight of his sun-burned face, his messy brown hair, his big searching eyes, makes my chest feel hot and tingly.

Eleven is a funny age for a boy. Puberty hasn't yet dragged his voice down an octave or two, and he's still got the earnest, slightly spacey, yet dialed-in focus of a little kid inventing new games to keep himself occupied. At the same time, I'm beginning to see the teenager he's going to be in everything he does, a shadow outline of a self-conscious boy who will be slightly smaller and gentler than his classmates. There's always the possibility of a growth spurt, of course, but in my heart, I know he will never fill out enough to join the ranks of the hale and hearty.

"This place is trashed," he says, shaking his head in a dis-approving way that strikes me as absurdly grown up.

It's astonishing how thoroughly the intruder picked through our drawers and closets. He clearly thought he had all the time in the world. Which means he must have been sure we were gone for the weekend. Which means he was watching, listening, waiting.

I can't help it: I turn and look over my shoulder into the hallway. It's brightly lit. I've been turning on all the lights.

"Wow," Danny says, regarding the tiny drawers of the jewelry organizer I gave him to store his Shopkins—little rubbery-plastic figures of anthropomorphized food, gnomish creatures, and other, weirder items that were all the rage among the fourth-graders last year. The drawers have all been pulled open.

My instinct is to make this whole situation into some kind of game with a ridiculously complex backstory to shield Danny—at least for a little while longer—from what really happened. But he's not six, he's eleven, and he doesn't need me widening the disconnect between his impressions and the truth.

"The guy who broke in here…" I say, without completing the thought. *Won't be doing this again.*

"Ah!" Danny says, pulling his Nintendo Switch from beneath a nest of cords and chargers. "Phew." He holds it up so I can see. "It's okay." He sets it down on his desk and begins picking up the basketball cards that litter the floor. His weird industriousness begins to worry me—shouldn't he be standing here, overwhelmed, maybe even crying as he tries to process the unreal chaos that used to be his safe, orderly bedroom?

"What are you thinking?" I say, immediately feeling stupid.

"It's foolish to be a burglar and make a huge mess," he says with no hesitation. "Then your fingerprints are all over everything."

"He was wearing gloves," I say, wondering when Danny started calling things *foolish*. He sometimes comes home from afternoons with Judy and Owen deploying new phrases, hinting at a more refined way of being. I have, at times, imagined parties full of kids in private school ties sipping punch ladled by servants, dragging Danny out back for impromptu croquet. Some elaborate orchestration by Matt's parents to mold Danny into a buttoned-up youngster more befitting their orbit.

"Gloves." Danny studies a hand as he considers this. "That makes sense."

"Hey. Danny-tello." (Guess his favorite Ninja Turtle.) "Seriously: you okay?"

He holds a sock up to the light. "Uh-huh."

I watch him for a little while longer. "I'm going to go help Matt for a minute, okay? I'll be right downstairs."

I leave Danny as he's gathering up fantasy paperbacks from a deranged pile near his overturned bookshelf.

I collect Matt from the den, where he, too, is placing books back on the shelf, and by some unspoken agreement, we head for the guest room.

Walking down the hallway from the kitchen gives me a prickly feeling. We're retracing the dead man's last footsteps. I wonder if he registered, somewhere at the edge of his mind, the framed vinyl record sleeves lining the wall: *Abbey Road*, *Led Zeppelin IV*, Mahavishnu Orchestra's *Birds of Fire*. How strange to be moving through the trappings of someone's life on the way to snuff it out.

The guest room door is closed. Matt puts his hand on my shoulder.

"Why don't you let me check it out first?"

I shake my head. "I want to see." I open the door. There's no dresser blocking the way—the cops must have righted it to clear a path. I flick the switch on the wall next to the door, and the overhead light comes on. No more than two or three steps inside the room is a patch of dried blood, staining the tan carpet black in an amoebic blob that seems far too big to have come from one man. Now that I'm faced with the entire three-dimensional scene instead of just a zoomed-in photo on the sheriff's phone, the extent of the savagery hits me hard. Blood spatters the wall behind the collapsed drying rack, feathery stains that mar the cream-colored paint in great crimson swoops.

My knees buckle—a real thing that can happen, it turns out—and Matt acts fast, blurting out a hilarious-in-a-different-context Keanu-style *whoa!* and grabbing my arm, holding me up. He supports me as we walk over to the bed and sit down, and I take in the room from this perspective. There, on the floor, marooned like a lonely ship on a bloody sea, is Matt's racing shoe. The bulbous antique lamp is lying on its side, plugged-in cord stretched taut, as if it tried to get away. The dresser is put back roughly where it belongs but angled out strangely from the wall. It looks solid and imposing, and I'm frankly stunned that I was able to move it an inch, much less topple it over.

Adrenaline does crazy things to people.

My eyes go, inevitably, to the dark stain. Matt contemplates it with me, and a sickly heaviness settles over us. It feels like one of those nights we spend tiptoeing around a crucial issue, something knotted into the fabric of our relationship which deserves to be voiced with the utmost care, and which we will avoid at all costs.

"I can't believe this happened," he says.

I put my head on his shoulder. The lean firmness of his body is comforting. He's a rangy six-one, strung together with the bandy kind of muscle that feels like the bungee cords we use to secure our Subaru Outback's hatch if we've overfilled it. He turned thirty-nine in April, and forty's looming presence has begun to simmer beneath his routines, upping the intensity of his morning runs, making him reach for a seltzer instead of an IPA after work, forcing his mouth to form sentences like "I'll get the Greek salad" instead of "I think I'll do the bacon cheeseburger." He even bought a juicer to make breakfast smoothies the color of toxic waste.

Matt begins to sob, and my head bounces on his shoulder. He takes a few deep breaths, forces himself to be still, and then lays a soft kiss on the unbandaged side of my forehead.

"I'm ready for my close-up," I say.

He shakes his head in wonderment. "I can't believe—I mean—you're okay. That's what the doctor said. You're going to be okay."

He tries to shore up his voice, to sound reassuring, but his words come out cracked and broken.

"I have no memory of doing what they said I did, Matt." I gesture toward the stain. "*This*. The sheriff even showed me a picture. Nothing."

"Listen," he says, taking my hands lightly in his. He swallows, gathers himself. "You have to know that you did the right thing. Whether it ever comes back to you, or you're just blocking it out, or what—I want you to know that you were incredibly brave, so much braver than I would have been. You saved your life, Syd. And…and…" His lip is trembling. "*Fuck* that guy." He lets go of my hands and grips his knees. His knuckles turn white. "I should have been here," he says, shaking his head.

The man's voice on the phone in the hall outside the guest room comes back to me in a dim flash. *I've been over every inch of the place.*

"He was definitely looking for something," I say. "That's why the house is all torn up. He was here for a long time before I got home."

Matt frowns. "As far as I can tell he didn't take anything. The stuff you'd think—I mean, my grandmother's necklaces and rings, the TV, the laptops—they're all here. He just made a mess."

"Yeah." I pause, remembering. "When I came to, I heard him talking on the phone to somebody else. It was like an employee who's worried that he screwed up, talking to his boss. He kept saying *it's not here.*"

Matt considers this. "What's not here? Money?"

I shrug. "What else do people steal?"

"Sure," Matt agrees, "but why us? I mean, we're not *poor*"—Matt runs a nonprofit that consults Fortune 500 companies on corporate social responsibility, and I'm a senior copywriter at Halloran Digital—"but we're not, like, *rich*. Look at basically anybody else's house on this street. It's insane that we would be *targets*."

"No idea," I say.

"Also, why would he think we'd have hoards of cash lying around the house? What normal person does that in the twenty-first century? It doesn't make sense."

Trevor used to smash the windows of parked cars to steal change out of the cupholders. And he once got arrested breaking into a split-level ranch while the family was inside, watching TV. Desperate people do stupid things.

"I don't know," I say.

"The important thing is that it's over," he says. He takes a deep breath and presses the side of his body against mine with great force, as if snuggling is not sufficient and he needs to burrow inside my skin.

"I still can't remember a thing about it."

"Listen to me. You did what you had to do in the moment, and it was absolutely the right thing to do."

He puts a hand on my knee. I look away from the stain on the floor, but it has burned into my retina. There's a dark overlay transposed on the wall, the drying rack, the old computer, the Lobsterfest poster.

"I was just trying to get away," I say quietly. "I honestly don't think I felt any sort of rage toward the guy at that moment. That's the funny part—you'd think I would at least vaguely recall the feeling of it, right? Some kind of crazy primal anger, seeing red, whatever? I mean, I was scared, but it—" I stop myself short of saying *it all happened so fast.* "It was pure flight response, you know? There wasn't any fight."

"Well, you definitely fought. You fought and you won."

"It doesn't feel like it."

"If you lost, you wouldn't be sitting here right now."

"It doesn't feel like I lost, either. It feels like..." At the border of the stain closest to the door is a small gobbet of limp flesh. "We're going to have to rip up this carpet."

Matt lets out a shocked little chuckle. "We're not really going to stay here, right?"

"What, tonight?"

He blinks like he can't believe that he has to explain this. "Not just tonight. I mean here. In general. This house."

"Are you talking about moving?"

The sharpness in my tone makes him put up his hands. "I guess it's too soon to talk about anything like that. It's just something we should think about."

I stand up. "I love this house."

While Matt was first getting to know all the corners his comfortable upbringing allowed him to cut, I was auditing night classes with Danny in my lap because I couldn't afford a sitter, learning to spot the teachers who wouldn't have the heart to kick me out. Scraping together half the down payment for this place—splitting it right down the middle with Matt—was a massive *fuck off* to the wasted, chaotic mess I used to be. And since then, every day of blissful normalcy for my son and me is another precious middle finger raised in the general direction of my past.

"I know you do," Matt says. "I love it, too. But even if we just stayed with my parents for a while, they have plenty of room. The upstairs is basically its own apartment, we could have our own space. You love the water pressure there— remember heaven-shower?"

The shadows of Matt's words take on a different shape: *my mother's offered and I've already accepted.* The mention of the shower oversells it. I tamp down a too-soft protest and make my case.

"I'm not letting this fuck up our lives any more than it already has."

I look out the window toward the evergreen tree line that separates our house from the neighbors'. There, at the edge of our yard, is the sapling we planted on Danny's tenth birthday. It was Matt's idea.

"Something beautiful to grow along with us," I say, repeating what Matt said as he patted down the soil around the spindly trunk.

He squeezes my hand. "That was a good day."

I have a sudden desire to help Danny clean his room, and feel guilty that I have left him alone, even for a few minutes, in this ravaged, off-kilter place that used to be governed by safe and predictable rhythms. I vow to do a better job under-standing where his head's at in the aftermath of all this. I need to establish an open line of communication that goes beyond *You okay?*

"You should get some rest," Matt says. "We can talk about all this later."

But I can't tear my gaze away from the window. I remem-ber the slap of my palms on the sill, the exhilaration of vault-ing free, my feet hitting wood chips and grass. My brain can't triage the thoughts that arrive in the wake of this mem-ory, and I spin through them anxiously.

I understand where Matt is coming from: we're living in

a *murder house* now, the kind of place that will inspire wide-eyed whispers among neighborhood kids for generations. Yet I feel like we could simply gut-renovate this room, turn it into a screened-in porch, something completely different to eradicate the horrible energy that's bound to linger. Intertwined with these plans is the meta-thought that's passing judgment on my character: How could you be thinking that far ahead when you still haven't accepted the fact that *you* did this. *You* massacred a human being, spilled his blood all over your guest room with apparent glee.

Look at the stain, Sydney. Fucking *look* at it.

A sharp pain glides through my head like an icy ball bearing. I rub my temples and stand up. There's a distant mosquito whine, a high-pitched ringing that originates both near and far.

"I have to go help Danny clean up." My voice sounds like I'm speaking into a plastic container.

"Okay," Matt says, getting to his feet. "Good idea."

"No," I say, with more force than intended. "I mean alone. I sort of failed at talking to him before. I need to know how he's doing."

"I'm sure you didn't fail." Matt puts his hands on my hips. "How about I come with? Maybe then we'd get a better sense."

"Of what?" Paranoia creeps in: Danny, guarded around me, open with Matt. A second Danny, the real one, growing up obscured from his mother.

"Well, I'd really like to see how he's handling this, too," Matt says.

"I know. But I think I need a minute with him first."
More for me than for Danny.

"Of course. Absolutely. Take as much time as you need.

I'll go check out the basement." His fingers inch up under my shirt. "I love you."

"I love you, too."

"We're going to get through this. I'm with you all the way."

"I know."

8

I keep coming back to the knife.

It's my first night home from the hospital and I can't sleep. What feels like five seconds after I drift off, my eyes snap open in the dark. I can tell it's much later without looking at my phone. Those of us prone to sleeplessness can always tell. We can read the great curve of the night as it arcs toward day. We've lived every minute of every dark hour in excruciating detail. Back when substances rocketed me into the dawn, the small hours—three, four, five in the morning— were purely of a piece with the night. As long as it was still dark, it was still *the night before*. But now these hours belong to some other slippery, enigmatic zone, not quite night and not quite day. It's proven to be when regret hits me the hardest, and when I know with dismal certainty that it's just a matter of time before I fuck up all over again. I envy normal people—people like Matt, lightly snoring at my side—who skip blissfully past these hours every night as if they do not exist.

When I'm awake during these hours, my thoughts inevitably turn to the day ahead: I will have to be up soon for work. I need to sleep in order to function. If I can't function, I will lose my job. That will be the first crack in the life I've built. Then it's only a matter of time before I let the old Sydney back in. The endless, familiar spiral. No amount of mindfulness can ever truly banish it.

But for once, I have nothing to do in the morning. I remind myself of this as I lie on my back, point my toes, and stretch my legs, clenching the bands of muscle in my thighs and around my knees. My job for the next week, at least, is to rest and heal. It's very quiet here. I let my legs go slack. I try to let my thoughts float like clouds over my town, imagining steam rising off the low hills in the wake of a rainstorm that might have been a dream. My heart begins to pound, at odds with the scene I'm trying and failing to hold in my head. It's okay, I tell myself. Don't fight it. Give in to the anxiety for now, and you can sleep again when it passes.

And yet the knife.

The knife is an absence around which I curl the fingers of my right hand beneath the sheets. Or did I massacre the man with my left? This whole thing is so improbable and insane. If the crime-scene techs determine that I sliced up the intruder with my nondominant hand it would scarcely come as a surprise.

The memory still hasn't returned. No flashes, no hazy impressions, no lurid strobing scene behind my eyelids. I grip the imaginary knife and slide my hand silently along the fitted flannel sheet that covers our mattress. Surely some hint of muscle memory remains. Stabbing someone twenty-eight times requires metronomic savagery. The vicious automation of a piston. But the movement, the thrust and the pull-back, has failed to imprint.

Next to me, Matt stirs in his sleep, makes a dry lip-smacking sound, and turns onto his side. His sleepy breath wafts over me and vanishes. I stare up into the darkness of our bedroom. Blackout curtains render the room a sightless void, and there's a weird expansiveness to it. With no hint of walls or a ceiling, I sometimes get the impression that I'm sleeping in a vast chamber, a secret hangar dug into the side of a mountain. I try to let the rhythm of the thrusting knife lull me back into a state close to sleep, but it's no use. I bend my elbow and my forearm skims the sheet. My bandaged wrists create a bit of drag. My fingers curl around nothing. Around the handle of the knife. Around nothing.

The icy needle slides behind my eyes and I squeeze them shut until the pain dulls. There's ibuprofen on the bedside table, along with a glass of water Matt set down for me before he turned in. I wonder what the harm would be in taking a single Vicodin. Just one, to get me through the night. Then, in the morning, I could forget about it. I could tell myself, with a wry shake of the head, that I *dreamed* I took a Vicodin. That wouldn't be out of the ordinary. I'm always dreaming about drugs. Nine years clean might as well be nine minutes for my subconscious, where old cravings fester and scheme.

I consider all this throughout the pain's slow ebb. The mosquito whine becomes a distant thing, no more obtrusive than the faint chime of a childhood hearing test. After a while, the needle recedes, and the whine is silenced.

In its place is a new sound. Familiar, yet I can't place it right away.

A blippy electronic melody coming from a small, cheap speaker, placed elsewhere in the house. Downstairs in the living room, perhaps. I rack my brain. There's an old Bose CD player down there somewhere, but I vaguely recall that it's been shoved into a cupboard with the seldom-played board games. There is, however, an off-brand Bluetooth speaker in the kitchen that's been known to go haywire.

The melody is impossible to tune out. Anyway, I'm already wide awake. I toss the covers aside, sit up, and slide my bare feet into the worn moccasins I keep by the nightstand. I don't worry about disturbing Matt—all the old jokes about people who can sleep through bombs going off apply to him.

Out in the upstairs hallway, the melody isn't exactly louder, it's more *present*. Thicker in the air. Mentally I catalogue Danny's handheld devices and games: iPad, Nintendo Switch, 3DS. I move down the dark corridor from the bedroom I share with Matt, past the bathroom and the linen closet, to the entrance to my son's room.

The door is slightly ajar. I stick my head inside. There, bathed in the dead-channel glow of a night-light, is the blanketed lump of my son, fast asleep.

I take one soundless step into the room, then another. Danny's mouth closes and opens and a small, meek noise escapes. I wonder how many hours of my life I've spent watching him sleep. I try not to be a helicopter parent, but I do hover. I'll admit it. When he's asleep, there's nothing wearying about him, and all the ways he can push my buttons or frustrate me amount to nothing. It's like my sleeping child is a restorative potion, a game changer. I wonder if I'll ever be able to tell him things like this when he's older—how much his simplest, most basic human functions mean to me. The fact that his little organs perform their various tasks correctly without prodding or corrective therapy or medicine. How fortunate we are.

My right arm slides up my thigh and down again, over and over, in slow controlled movements. My fingers curl around empty air.

I glance at the dim shapes of Danny's furniture, his desk and bookshelves and beanbag chair. It hits me all at once: I know exactly what the source of the melody is. I was the one to discover it in here. It isn't in Danny's room now, but it *was*, earlier in the day. Ignited by this memory, the afternoon unspools.

9

Together, Danny and I make serious progress cleaning his room. I leave the toys to him and begin folding the clothes strewn across the floor with the intention of putting them back in his dresser drawers, but then I have a change of heart. I think about the man touching these things—Wolverine boxer shorts, Spider-Man T-shirts, Danny's prized Brooklyn Nets jersey. I go to the linen closet and grab one of the plastic laundry baskets and toss in anything the man laid his hands on.

My wrists ache—I should probably be resting, but I can't just stand around. The ringing in my head comes and goes in Doppler waves.

Danny straightens up from a crouch, holding a pair of Brooklyn Nets bobbleheads to his chest. "Do I have to go to school tomorrow?"

"Nope," I say. "No school for you, no work for me. We're just going to hang out for a while."

I expect him to get motormouthed at the prospect of an impromptu vacation, asking about movies and dinner at Oretti's Pizza and whether his best friend, Loren Parker, can come over. Instead, he just stands there, holding the bobble-heads, looking at me.

"Your face," he says.

I set the laundry basket down. "It's going to be swollen for a little while. But I'm okay, I swear on the soul of Professor X."

I take a step toward him and he takes a step back. "It looks different now," he says. "And Professor X isn't dead. Or real. So, his soul isn't a thing."

I blink. *Missing the mark, talking to him like he's eight. Matt should be here, Matt knows how to get through to him . . .*

"No, Danny, trust me, it's just the swelling. It looks worse than it feels."

He shakes his head. "It's different than it was in the hospital."

I try to smile. "Mrs. Potato Head." *Shut the fuck up, Sydney.*

He's not buying what I'm selling. He clutches the bobble-heads tighter. The noise in my ears cranks up, a whole cloud of mosquitoes whining in the center of my skull.

I kneel down so that I'm eye level with Danny. He's watching me intently. I make a goofy face at him, but he doesn't seem to register it. He's sometimes struck dumb by worry and fascination, as if the object of his anxiety is worthy of deep examination. I recognize this trait and it breaks my heart that I have passed it along. *Just live*, I want to tell him, but that's useless advice. The inability to *just live* is what makes us who we are. I have never read about this in any parenting guidebook, but there's a distinct feeling of cosmic wonder at the knowledge that the little behaviors implicit in my DNA have made the leap to another human being, while at the same time wishing for them to be replaced by something better—more manageable—for Danny.

"I'm going to be fine," I insist. "We're going to put this house back together, and things will be back the way they were before you know it. Is that what you're worried about?"

He shrugs and fixes his eyes on a mess of Star Wars Lego, half a ruined *Millennium Falcon* out of which Han and Chewie have spilled.

"Danny," I say as gently as I can, "look at me."

Reluctantly, he turns his head my way. His nose is leaking snot and he wipes it on the back of his hand, then wipes the hand on his shirt.

"It's barely a scratch," I say. "It's not even as bad as the time you fell off the jungle gym." I smile ruefully. "Remember, we were living in the duplex? And you could hear the other people's TV through the living room wall, and it was literally *always* on? All they watched was *General Hospital*, like they recorded it so they could watch it round the clock."

He sniffles. Tears streak down from his red-rimmed eyes. I'm taken back to the first few months with newborn Danny, when every hour of every day delivered new bouts of self-recrimination.

You're fucking this up.

You don't know what you're doing.

You're going to be a terrible mother, what were you thinking?

I used to assure myself that people have been doing this for the entirety of human existence. People in the Dark Ages raised kids. Humanity perpetuated itself. And now we're living in a time when information and advice is more plentiful and accessible than ever before. Besides, look at all the trashy dipshits you know on social media, their kids don't just up and die.

"The complex had that jungle gym. And one of those

wooden playgrounds with the tunnels, and the steering wheels."

"I remember," he assures me softly. I don't know why I chose this memory, neither reassuring nor pleasant, but I've come too far to course correct. An intrusive thought screams: *you're making him into a weirdo, school shooter, animal torturer, recluse, a junkie like you.* I smooth out the edges of my voice.

"You were with Mrs. Vanderbaugh while I was at work." I shake my head. "I don't know why I ever thought that lady would be a good—well, you know, I couldn't afford a real daycare, and it seemed like she was okay with the other kids. It seemed like she was, I mean, not exactly licensed, but a person who could pull it off. I know you deserved better, but this was way before Halloran, before things started to fall into place for us, and I'm sorry if I acted out of desperation, or if I didn't step outside myself and really *think* about what was the absolute best thing for you. Like sometimes I just had to act. Bob Halloran calls it *building the plane while we're flying it*, have you ever heard that expression? Mrs. Vanderbaugh had that step stool you used to like."

Danny blinks.

"So, I was at the diner when I got the call, halfway through the regular-people breakfast shift, after the truckers. Mrs. Vanderbaugh's voice always sounded like she was about to bust out into show tunes, and it wasn't any different that morning. That was so weird, like, *Danny's had an accident*"— a strain of some brassy Bette Midler number in my voice— "*I called an ambulance.* When somebody says *ambulance* your heart basically explodes, because that's pretty serious. Also, I didn't have health insurance back then, and ambulance rides are insanely expensive, but I wasn't thinking about that at the moment. I just wanted you to be okay. So I don't even take off my apron, and time sort of skips ahead. I'm in the car and then I'm at the nurses' station, and then I'm yelling at Mrs. Vanderbaugh who's got all these other kids she had to bring to the hospital with her running around the hallway. And it's like, lady, if you all came here anyway, what was the ambulance for—because at that point I found out that you'd fallen off the jungle gym and essentially just skinned your elbow and knee. I guess she was worried about a concussion because that's what happened to her nephew. At this point I was totally thinking about the cost of it all, and I'd already been to see you, and you were basically fine. Right? Like me. I'm basically fine."

Danny shuffles his feet.

"Tell me what the number one thing is that's bothering you," I say, "and we'll solve it together, right now."

He shakes his head.

"Please, Danny. I promise I will help you."

"Your face," he says quietly.

"Okay. What happened when you fell off the jungle gym?"

"The gravel cut my knee and elbow."

"And it was pretty bad, right? It looked gruesome!" I make a face like, *yuck*. "You know, when I got the call, I stood there behind the counter and in my mind, I suspended you in midair and willed you not to hit the ground. Have I ever told you that? Like if I could just hold you there, suspended, dangling, frozen, then I could rush home and catch you."

He nods.

"Anyway, what happened after they patched you up, and put disinfectant on it?"

"It got better. I obviously know how healing works, Mom."

"Right. So, give me a week or two and I'll be the same old me."

"It's not that," he says. He's bolder now. I have drawn him out. Mother of the Year. And yet he's still holding something back.

"You can tell me anything," I say. "Always."

He swallows and wipes his eyes. I think he's got himself under control, and then his lip begins to tremble. "It looks too soft," he says. He brushes a fingertip against the skin under his right eye and swipes it along his temple. "Here."

"Puffy, you mean. Swollen."

He shakes his head and seems to recoil, a little, at the sound of my voice. "Too soft. Or, like the ocean. I don't know."

"My face is like the *ocean*?"

He winces and turns his head as if he's been slapped. "I don't know. It doesn't look right."

"Danny"—it comes out too sharp, my mother's voice rising inside me—"I don't understand what you mean."

He shuts his eyes tight. "It's soft and watery. It's moving around."

Gingerly, I mimic the movement of his hand on my own face. My finger slides across a raw lump of flesh, and pain stabs down into my jaw. My teeth feel out of sorts, buzzing, electric.

Indignance boils over. "I got *hurt*. I can't help how I look right now." Suddenly I'm desperate to be seen by my son. "Open your eyes."

He shakes his head. His hands clench and release. His right foot swivels restlessly, up on its toes. *He's going to piss himself*, I think.

I take a breath and soften my tone. "I'm sorry." I realize,

all at once, that my son is coping with fresh layers of trauma while I'm shoving my injuries down his throat. "Hey, Danny-tello"—I scoot back on the rug to give him some space—"I'll just be over here, okay?"

Warily, he opens one eye. The distance between us seems to satisfy him.

"Come on," I say, picking up the *Millennium Falcon*. "Let's put this ship back together and get them on their way."

I hold the flat, disc-shaped ruin out to Danny. He eyes it, then shakes his head. "I think we should concentrate on the cleanup first. Rebuilding Legos should come later."

I set the ship back down. "Genius." I grab an overturned plastic bin and gather up scattered Lego bricks. I follow a ragged trail of them leading over to Danny's bed. I swipe my hand underneath to collect any hidden strays, and my fingers brush the smooth rounded edge of some other toy. My hand closes around a palm-sized piece of plastic, about the size of an egg.

I pull my hand out from under the bed and find that I'm holding a lime-green Nano Pal—one of those old Tamagotchi rip-off toys where you "care" for the dog or cat or hamster on the rudimentary screen. I stare at it dumbly for a moment. Then my mind begins to cast about for an explanation. It must be part of the nineties-revival craze that's sweeping pop culture. Hipsters donning ill-fitting flannels and ripped jeans and going on cruises to sip Zima and be entertained by Smash Mouth and Candlebox. Binge-watching *Full House* on Netflix. Playing with Nano Pals and Pogs.

Danny has tons of random toys that manifested seemingly out of nowhere (aka Matt spoiling him when they go to the mall). Still, it's funny that he'd be interested in a clunky old gadget like this.

I hold it up so he can see. "They still make these, huh?"

He narrows his eyes at it from across the room. Then he shrugs. "I don't know."

"I used to have tons of them." I press the button to wake it up, but nothing happens. No crudely digitized furry friend blinks onto the screen. I give it a little shake. "Needs a new battery."

"It's not mine," Danny says, occupying himself with setting pencils and pens neatly into his desk drawer.

"Did Loren leave it here?"

"He basically only plays Fortnite," Danny says.

I turn the little pod over in my hand. The plastic casing is scuffed. The tiny screw that holds the battery compartment in place has been pretty well stripped. This is not some new comeback edition. This is a genuine series one Nano Pal.

My collection went up in flames nine years ago.

I get to my feet. "I'm gonna show this to Matt."

"Okay," Danny says, without looking at me.

10

Night. Danny's blank *okay* echoes dully as my moccasins swish along the hardwood floor of the downstairs hallway. I'm headed for the basement, where I brought the Nano Pal earlier today after leaving Danny's room, and where the toy still resides, as far as I know. The melody is all around me now, that cheery tune I haven't heard in nine years, *da da dee dee dee da dee*. A happy, well-fed pet.

Mother of the Year.

When I was a little girl I loved to "ski" in my footy pajamas, skimming the fabric soles along the linoleum in the kitchen of the apartment I shared with my mother. But there would always be some sticky bit of sauce or a patch of dried broth to trip me up. By contrast, the hallway in my house is smooth sailing. The floors are perpetually spotless. I Swiffer obsessively.

The decorative record sleeves are mounted in special frames and protected by thin sheets of glass. Moonlight trails me down the hall from the kitchen and shimmers across the frames, there and gone. I feel like I'm skirting the edge of some ritual I can't fully grasp, as if I've strayed from the path into a wild place marked off by crude and ancient totems. The door to the guest room is straight ahead at the end of the hall, the door to the basement off to the right. The melody pushes the icy ball bearing deeper into my skull and I pause, hand against the wall, while the fragile notes make it shiver and spin.

I squeeze my eyes shut and take a deep breath. Then another. Perhaps it's due to spending the past two days in the hospital, but I'm aware of the smell of our house in a way I haven't been since we first moved in. We all grow immune to our own household odors, yet stepping inside a neighbor's place we're hit with the baked-in redolence of hasty week-night dinners, the ghosts of spilled drinks and carpet cleaner, all of it swirling into a fragrance that's distinctly the Kleins, the Tanakas, the Baileys.

What, then, of the Sydney-Matt-Danny smell?

Eyes closed, I let it fill me. At first there's an earthy tang to it, like the rich loam beneath a wet pile of leaves. Then it becomes sharper, more metallic—the rusty chain of an old bike shoved into the back of the garage and forgotten. It stirs something within me. I hesitate to call it a memory when it's as indistinct as the voice of a childhood friend who moved away, recalled decades later—a copy of a copy.

Then, all at once, I grasp it—

Rusty, earthy, metallic. Organic yet weirdly alien, an interior thing corrupted by exposure to the world in a way that it should not be.

Blood.

The dead man's blood, the blood of the man I slaughtered.

I open my eyes to find myself in the guest room. The blinds spill thin bands of moonlight across the bed, the floor, the stain by the wall. The melody hangs thick in the air, the smell of blood even more oppressive. It's like the steamy wet heat of a sauna, a miasma of death-reek and the song's mad loop.

Across the room, the red digits of an old bedside alarm clock tell me it's 4:52 a.m.

I'm astonished. When did I move from the hall to the guest room? How long have I been standing here with my eyes closed?

In my past life, there would be nothing out of the ordinary about finding myself in some new place with no memory of how I got there. Sydney Burgess alone in a strange room at the break of dawn? Call it Tuesday. But now it feels just as *other* as the impressions of a mangled face on the sheriff's phone. I haven't lived that kind of life in a long time, and while I'm thankful beyond belief to have emerged on the other side, for the first time in many years I feel a faint, flickering pull toward that sordid, reckless haze. If I could slip into my past self again for just a minute or two, greet the dawn with a racing heart and a mind like a frayed wire, nip at a plastic handle in a mad quest to level off...

That doesn't sound so bad right now.

In that state, at least, the past few days would have been bearable. Even understandable. Can't remember killing a burglar? Shit, Sydney, you're lucky if you can remember your own name. You've been on benders that have stripped away every last bit of your identity, hurtling you into some egoless netherworld where your stinking room at the squat falls away to reveal the radiant clockwork heart of the universe (and later, picking wearily through the mess with a burnt mind and jittery hands, you come across a drawing of the experience that seemed profound in the moment: a few inky blobs and a ragged triangle sketched with a pink highlighter).

When I got sober for the last time and all my lost days and nights began surfacing in a horrific clip show, I could always shake my head and think *I was fucking crazy*.

But now I've been clean for nine years, and I can't let myself fall back on that convenient old excuse. Because I know I'm not crazy. This is happening to me. This is real. And I refuse to let it tear down everything I've built.

I rub my eyes, try to clear my head, but the stench and the song remain, twining around me, slithering into my nostrils and down my throat.

The bloodstain, an oily black pool, drags moonlight down into its depths.

(What *depths*? I think distantly.)

I suspect that if I stepped into it, my foot would fall through the floor to the between-place I was trapped in after the man bashed me in the head.

I turn away, but not entirely. I can only stand to look at the bloodstain out of the corner of my eye, but I don't want to unsee it. In fact, I'm desperate to parse what's there. There's something inside the pool (what *pool*?)—a presence so impossible and full of grace that for a brief weightless moment I'm left with the impression that my peripheral vision has been haunted by a dancing specter.

Later, I will imagine oil spill footage, fluffy birds soaked in crude, glistening black and struggling against the weight of catastrophe. But that's not correct. It's merely the closest analogue my mind can serve up. Something real and documented and *of this world* for me to latch on to.

I turn away completely, face the window, gaze out through the slats at the moonlight smeared across the river beyond the trees. At my back the bloodstain whispers to itself, or to what's inside its black borders. Nonsensical gibbering, words that aren't words, a language that hitches and skips with spectacular wrongness when it hits my ears, leaving me with nothing but the ragged ends of speech.

(What *speech*?)

I take a moment to gather myself. Then I leave the guest room, shut the door behind me, and follow in my earlier footsteps.

11

Nano Pal in hand, I leave Danny to his tidying and hurry down the creaky wooden stairs, past more of Matt's framed record sleeves—Derek and the Dominos, Elvis Costello, The Clash's *London Calling*. The basement is fully carpeted and drywalled, there's not a patch of dank cement in sight. Track lights run the length of the ceiling in two rows. Couch cushions have been tossed onto the floor, and the cabinet doors of the random old armoire we keep down here have been thrown open. Blu-ray cases are fanned out across the rug—it looks like Matt has been cataloguing them to see if they're all there, as if the man who broke in was after his director's cut of *Apocalypse Now*.

Matt appears in a doorway next to the bookshelf. "He didn't find the cave!" he says triumphantly.

In this house, we don't call it a Man Cave. It's an inclusive space where anyone is welcome. The walls are plastered with vintage tourist advertisements—Paris, London, Prague— along with a relic of Matt's late adolescence: a framed poster of *Attack of the Clones*, signed by Ewan McGregor and Natalie Portman.

Under the poster sits the mid-century sofa Matt appro-priated from his parents and reupholstered. Across from the doorway is a small reclaimed-wood bar with no taps or sink—Matt and I aren't really that handy, so we never bothered to install them. Also, there's an unspoken rule that while this isn't a totally dry house, it's not the kind of place where alcohol is fetishized. The stainless-steel mini fridge is full of soda, juice, and seltzer.

The TV is roughly the size of a display monitor in a war room in an underground bunker.

A shelf running the length of one wall holds Matt's sprawl-ing toy collection: wrestling action figures locking arms with the crew of the USS *Enterprise*, meticulously painted knights and footmen from some tabletop gaming phase he entered and exited long before I came into the picture, an army of squat pink monsters he calls "Musclemen."

In the corner is an Ovation acoustic guitar on a stand, with a small pile of sheet music—tablature books, mostly—beside it.

From here, the cave looks as it always does: neat and spotless.

"Wow," I say, grabbing the edge of the bookshelf and roll-ing it along its wheeled track, half obscuring the doorway. The shelf-on-wheels is as close as we could get to a secret passage. The original idea was that you'd tug on a book and the door would slide open, like a hidden lair in a spy movie, but we couldn't figure out how to build the mechanism. So, it's really just a sliding door. Apparently, it blends in well enough to be overlooked by a burglar. "Silver lining."

I follow Matt into the cave. He opens the fridge and hands me a grapefruit seltzer. I let the bubbles tickle my nose before I take a long sip. I didn't realize how thirsty I was.

"How's Danny?" he says.

"I don't know," I say, setting the can down on a coaster. I fold my arms and turn to the toy shelf. I have been down here a thousand times. I know that I have never seen a Nano Pal among Matt's collection. But I look anyway. Then I set the small plastic pod down on the bar.

"I found this in his room," I say.

Matt studies it for a moment, then lifts his eyes to me. He tries to stifle a laugh, but it comes out anyway. "I'm sorry, Syd, but the way you said that—it's like you found his weed stash or his woods porn or something."

"Woods porn?"

He looks puzzled. "Yeah, you don't know about woods porn? In the pre-internet days of my storied youth, there would always be some inexplicable stash of porn magazines on trails in the woods in people's neighborhoods. Just, like, sitting in the dirt, there."

"And you took them *home?*"

He blinks. "Uh. Once."

A wire-thin nail slips deeper into my brain. I wince at the sound of shrieking metal. I hold on to the bar until the woozy sensation and the noise die away.

"Danny doesn't have woods porn," I say. "Or any porn. He's eleven."

"I know," Matt says quickly. "I was being an idiot. Strike it from the record." He pokes the Nano Pal with a finger. "Haven't seen one of these bad boys in a long time."

"Danny says it's not his."

"It doesn't seem like something he'd be into." He looks at me for a moment without speaking. "Maybe you should sit down for a minute."

"I'm fine."

He cocks his head and studies my face.

"What?" I say.

"Nothing." He picks up the Nano Pal and presses its wake-up button. "Dead as a doornail."

"It's not yours?"

"No." He walks over to the toy shelf and places it carefully between Sulu and Scotty. "But I'll take it."

"So, where did it come from?" There's an icy edge to my voice that reminds me, once again, of my mother. I will it to crack, soften, melt away.

"What," Matt says, "you think a grown man dropped his Nano Pal while he was trashing our house?"

"I don't know."

He puts his hands on his hips. "Are you sure you don't want to sit down?"

"No. Stop asking me that. Do *you* want to sit down?"

He frowns. Elsewhere, triumphant, my mother laughs.

"I didn't mean to snap at you," I say.

I glance at the art nouveau tourist advertisement for Prague, next to the screen-printed Eiffel Tower. The man who broke in here didn't get to see these things. This is the only room in the whole house he didn't invade. A clean space for the nexus of our rebuild. Good energy spiraling out from the cave, seeping into every corner of the house. Terraforming the next phase of our lives together.

Matt's phone chimes. He makes a little throat-noise, as if he's just received the call he's been waiting for.

"Hi, Mom," he says. I lower my eyes to the seltzer, take an interest in the cursive on the can. *Naturally Essenced.* How about that. "Good, good. He's fine, he's getting his room together. Keeping busy. Yes. She's right here. Hold on."

He places the phone on the arm of the sofa and taps the screen.

"Owen!" Judy Melford's voice issues from the speaker and fills the room, the cartoon genie out of the bottle. "It's Matthew and Sydney! Come hear this!" She lowers her voice just enough to make me understand that she's now addressing us, not yelling for her husband into their Colonial's vast and stately depths. "We're on speaker, too," she imparts. Then she sighs, gathering herself. My thumb dents the seltzer can. Matt gives me a tight-lipped nod—the same one he gave me before we bungee jumped in Cedar Valley. *You got this.*

"Sydney," Matt's father says, after a moment. There's a crinkly rustling sound and I imagine a newspaper tucked under his arm. "We're so glad to hear that you're all right. Thank God."

"She's not *all right*, Owen!" Judy says. "The poor girl's been through hell."

"I mean physically," Owen says. "Mostly all right. Considering."

"How are you physically, though, Sydney?" Judy says. Before I can line up the words for a reply, she keeps on going. "It's such a shame they took you to Saint Mary's. Presbyterian is very highly rated for emergency medicine. It's our premier teaching hospital, not even just for the area—nationwide. We know Dr. Bledsoe, their head of radiology."

"Dr. Bleed Slow!" Matt chimes in.

Judy makes a sound. Somehow, she alters her voice, directionally, to aim it at me. "When he was younger, Matthew made up funny little names for our friends. I always said he ought to send them to *MAD* magazine."

"Garbage Pail Kids," Matt says.

"Hmm?" Judy says.

"That's what I was emulating with the names. I never read *MAD* magazine; I think that's more your generation."

"I remember buying you *MAD* magazines."

"You might be right," Matt says.

"It's the same kind of irreverent humor as the garbage pail," Owen offers.

"I'd be mortified if Dr. Bledsoe ever found out," Judy says. "His wife's on the board at Capital Repertory. But are you really okay, Sydney? I mean, Saint Mary's discharged you so early. Is Matthew being a worthy nurse?"

"Um," I begin. The mosquitoes inside my head, lying dormant, wake in a fury. Carbonation fizzles on my tongue and becomes a gummy slug in my throat. "Matt's been amazing."

Hearing this coats her voice in pride. I have answered properly. "I wouldn't expect anything less."

Matt points at the cushion next to him and mouths *Come sit.* I drain my seltzer, set the can on the bar, and head to the couch. He puts his arm around me and pulls me close.

"Sydney's doing great—like, inspirationally great," he says, giving me a squeeze. "She's a million times tougher than I would have been."

"We were all so worried," Owen says. "Sick to our stomachs."

"I'll say," Judy says. "It must have been awful. So *startling*, and then to be assaulted in your own home. What a nightmare."

"It happened so fast," I say.

"I can't imagine I'd ever feel safe there again," Judy says.

"We're still processing," Matt says.

"It's going to take time," Owen muses. "A thing like that."

A thing like that. At this, even Judy falls silent. Exhalations fuzz across the speaker, an edgy not-quite-silence that troubles the air in the cave.

Matt takes my hand and runs a thumb along my knuckles.

I meet his eyes. *What do they know?* I wonder, all at once. Are the strange torments I—supposedly, allegedly—inflicted on the man already common knowledge among the Melfords? What version has Matt given them? What *thing like that* are Owen and Judy imagining, right now, while their breathing crackles in my head, stirring mosquitoes into a frenzy?

I seek refuge in blandness. "I've got some time off work now, so..."

Owen coughs. Matt squeezes my pinky finger.

"Sydney," Judy says, as if detecting in me the eager student, not quite up to snuff, who needs merely to be coaxed. "I don't need to tell you how vital stability is for someone of Danny's background."

The wire-thin nail flares white-hot behind my eyes. Matt grips my finger like a baby with a ring-toss toy. The visible skin has gone dead-fish pale.

"Mom," he says. "Syd and I talked, and we don't—"

"I know," she assures him. The white-hot flare melts away. Did I miss part of the conversation? Was some portion sliced off, a counterpoint to the violent act that's also been scrubbed?

"Know what?" Matt says.

"That Sydney's not going to come stay with us. I figured you'd never be able to convince her."

"I'm right here," I say softly.

"What was that, dear?"

"I didn't try to convince her," Matt says. "Syd and I discussed it, together. We're a team." He gives me that nod again. *I got you.*

"Well," Judy says. "Owen and I think it's for the best, anyway."

"Oh," Matt says. "That's good. Thank you for the offer,

though—we both really appreciate it, this is just something we'd rather navigate from here." He nudges me. "But that shower really is hard to pass up."

"It's an Eytysson," Owen explains. "Scandinavian design. The whole remodel up there is them."

"Sydney." Judy sounds like she's beginning again, dispensed with some bullshit preamble, getting to the heart of it. "We understand this is the most trying of times, that you've just been through something beyond traumatic. And I know the temptation is just to let things be for now. I'll be the first to say that of course you need time to rest and recuperate." She alters her voice to pretend like she's treading delicately. "But letting things be hasn't always worked for Danny, in the past."

I shift on the sofa. Matt senses my anxious heat, a radiating uptick in pure stress. "Mom," he says.

Judy is undeterred. "Which is why we think it best that Danny comes to stay with his Nony and Pop for a bit. That way you can focus on getting well, without the nonstop duties of motherhood interfering. I've had an eleven-year-old, and I remember all the headaches. No offense, Matthew."

"None taken. But Mom, this isn't what we discussed, and it's not fair to spring this on us now."

I free my pinky and get up off the couch. The cave, by no means a small room, now seems as stifling as a closet. "What do you mean by his *background*, Judy?"

"Syd," Matt says, reaching for me. I twist out of the way.

"I'm sorry?" Judy says.

"You mentioned *Danny's background*," I say.

"We love Danny," Owen assures me.

"Sydney," Judy says. "It's not necessary to spell it out."

I cross my arms. "Would you mind spelling it out just a

little, Judy?" The mosquitoes surge. I blink back tears as my skull seems to tighten around my brain, closing like a fist around the frantic swarm.

"I'm going to call you guys back," Matt says.

"Don't hang up!" I say. The part of me I can't name wants to hear what Judy has to say, relishes the sting.

Matt's finger freezes an inch from the screen's red END.

"Danny's already had such a life of upheaval," Judy says, "we just want what's best for him now."

"What upheaval are you referring to, exactly?" The wire glides from one side of my head to the other, that foreign-object wrongness, a splinter you can't quite dig out. "The time when I took us both out of a bad situation and worked my ass off at shitty jobs while I went to school? The time when I got hired at Halloran Digital and saved up enough to pay for exactly half of this house, where he lives extremely comfortably? Or right now, when he goes to the best public school in our county and takes three vacations a year and goes camping in Cedar Valley and eats pizza and hangs out with his friends?"

Matt mouths *I'm so sorry* at me, shaking his head. Then he points to the phone and rolls his eyes: *she's crazy.*

"There's no reason to get worked up," Judy says. "You need to be resting. All we're saying is that there may be some psychological benefit to him being out of a chaotic situation for a while. A situation that must be terrifying for him."

"Mom," Matt says, "this is honestly a little bit out of line. Danny's okay, he's staying here with us, and that's the end of it. All right? Now we really have to go."

Judy speaks faster, racing her son to the end of the call. "Matthew, wait! The police think she might've had something to do with it!"

My heart wants to explode. Louder this time: "I'm right here."

"That house isn't safe, Matthew," Judy says, "for you *or* Danny."

"What did Sheriff Butler say to you?" I demand.

I wonder if the phrase *sex play* factored in. How Judy must have relished that—confirmation of my deviancy.

How is any of this legal, discussing the details of an ongoing investigation with my boyfriend's parents? I wonder who in law enforcement Judy and Owen count as part of their social circle, which local cops little Matthew gave funny gross-out names to.

"Do what's right for Danny's well-being," Judy says. "We're more than happy to come get him. Just say the word."

"Bye, Mom," Matt says.

"I'll text you!"

He ends the call.

"Holy shit," he says, exhaling hard, "I am so sorry. That was insane. She's gone off the deep end, clearly."

I barely hear him. Now this room, our home's only safe space, feels violated. Judy's voice lingers in the air, acrid in its judgment, thick with accusation. I turn my attention to a poster of Big Ben. The Union Jack unfurls behind the clock tower. The colors remind me of a World War II propaganda poster: bold, striking, aggressive. The tower is half in shadow, and the way it's set against the flag gives it a 3D pop. But something's gone wrong. I remember there being windows in the tower before, but now it's just a foreboding block of limestone. I step closer. The tower looks fat and squat instead of tall and proud, like it's been pressed down, smushed. It bulges against itself like it wants to slip its skin. I blink. It doesn't look like Big Ben at all.

"He was in here," I say. There's a sheet of glass covering the poster, and my reflection ghosts the tower. My ear is the color of a plum. "The guy was in here."

"I really don't think so," Matt says.

I take a deep breath. There's a cloying smell in the air, over-ripe fruit on the cusp of turning. I can feel my heart beating in my chest. Judy's voice dances, uncaught, madcap and taunting. Big Ben is a sickly color. I step to the side so the overhead light bounces off the glass, and notice that it's smudged with finger-prints. There are dozens of them on either side of the tower, as if someone tried to wrap his hands around it and rip it right out of the picture. The man who broke in was wearing gloves. So, who's been poking at the glass? Matt? Danny? Why?

I recognize my scattered thoughts for what they are— the beginnings of a slide into a full-blown anxiety attack. Twenty-two-year-old me wouldn't waste any time fixing up a fuck-you-Judy shot of cocaine and grabbing a plastic handle of cheap-ass vodka to dull the jagged edge of the rush. Even in rehab, people who ought to know better were floored by the idea of slamming coke to blunt anxiety and panic. After all, isn't it supposed to *induce* that kind of thing? But brain chemistry is so weirdly specific. People who don't have ADHD can't understand how Ritalin or Adderall can possibly help an afflicted person live a normal life, since it's basically just speed. But if you're wired a certain way, it's like mainlining pure focus.

Present-day me, thirty-two-year-old me, begins my usual post-Melfords breathing exercise: count to four as you inhale, hold your breath for a count of seven, exhale to a long slow eight.

A layer of dust coats the top of the poster frame. This room isn't as clean as we think it is. Matt sits down on the couch. He recognizes my 4-7-8 breathing and knows to let me do my thing. Early on in our relationship, he would try to help me calm down, massaging my neck and shoulders, telling me to *just relax*, which always made me more anxious. It's like telling a person with crippling, unceasing depression to get out of bed and hit the gym.

Big Ben is the color of runny shit in a diaper. How did I never notice this before? I close my eyes so I don't have to look at it. I'm having a difficult time being mindful. I fall into the trap of meta-thinking and it's inescapable.

You're doing a breathing exercise because you're anxious.

It's not helping.

It's ridiculous.

You're doing a breathing exercise because you're anxious.

I open my eyes. I have learned from countless sleepless nights that the worst place to be is inside my own unstimulated mind. I need images and sounds. I need the rest of the world. I take a fresh seltzer from the fridge and pop the top. It's flat and tasteless, like liquid cardboard. I set it down on the bar.

Matt is watching me from the couch. I look at him and then look away, over at the guitar. I feel no urge to go sit by him, to be draped in shallow comforts.

A completely unprompted surge of paranoia hits me. I will live the rest of my life as a person who slaughtered a fellow human being with a knife. It will drive me crazy. I will confirm Judy's first impression of me, which has never wavered, and turn to substances again, I've never been more sure of anything. I might as well start right now, because keeping them at bay is going to be a horrible, drawn out slog. And ultimately a futile experience.

Matt will leave me.

I will lose my job.

They will take Danny away from me.

I stare at the Eiffel Tower and try to think nice thoughts about Europe. There's a whole continent full of beautiful cities, and if I keep my life together Danny and I will get to see them one day. But even on vacation, I will still be me: sitting up sleepless in a hotel, staring blearily at my phone.

I curl my fingers around the handle of an imaginary knife. How did I strike the first blow? A slash to the neck? A forward thrust into the man's soft belly?

I will never know. I can't remember. This lack will always float between me and everyone else like a rank smell in the attic that nobody ever talks about. An absurd omission.

"I stabbed a man to death," I say out loud, trying to sound firm and convincing.

"You did what you had to do," Matt says. Already I am sick of this explanation, the way his mouth shapes and reshapes the same goddamn words. Such a generic sentiment, the kind of thing anybody would say—a coworker, a total stranger. *So brave, so lucky.*

The Eiffel Tower is amateurish—a rushed illustration that never should have been turned into a poster. I wonder where Matt even got these things—they're slipshod and cheesy. They belong in a freshman college dorm. They're probably from Bed Bath & Beyond.

"I tried to cut his head off," I say. "I sliced up his face. I stuck the knife into his cheeks and cut him open like a piece of meat. I sawed away at him. I stabbed out his eyes."

I'm no closer to believing this. Perhaps I'm not speaking with enough conviction.

"I got sick of him screaming and I cut off his mouth so he would shut the fuck up. There was so much blood.

It happened so fast. His eyes were so wide, like he couldn't believe what was happening to him. Then I fucking stabbed them out."

Matt gets up from the couch. I move toward him. "No, just listen to me. I took his knife away and I fucked him with it, you understand? I stuck it inside him and I pulled it out and I didn't stop. I just kept fucking him, even after he was dead."

"Mom?"

I turn to the doorway. Danny is standing there, holding the wrecked *Millennium Falcon*. His face is a mask of fear.

I'm breathing hard. Something inside me wants to lash out. *Do you know what FUCKING is, Danny?* I want to sneer at him, mess him up, just to see what happens.

My heart is pounding.

And then something gives way and I feel bereft of spirit. A dull horror creeps in: I'm incapable of helping my son cope with all this. Judy is right, she's always been right. I'm actively making it worse.

"Sorry, Danny," I say, dry-mouthed and hoarse. Tears spring to my eyes. "I didn't see you there. You ready to put that back together?"

My son looks to Matt for help.

"What do you think," Matt says, "is it warm enough out-side to grill the rest of that chicken?"

"I don't know," Danny says.

"Why don't we go see"—he shoots me a worried glance— "and we'll let your mom get some rest until dinner's ready, okay?"

Matt steps between my son and me, puts a hand on Danny's shoulder, turns him around, and scoots him out of the cave, leaving me—

12

—alone in the basement. The Nano Pal song is as shrill as a siren. I don't know how Danny and Matt—and our neighbors—haven't been rudely awakened by its loud carnival-tune loop. There's a scratchy texture to the notes, a blown-speaker static that claws at the corners of my eyes.

I make my way across the carpet, shuffling in imitation of my mother's Thorazine creep to avoid bumping into the couch. I reach the false bookshelf without incident and slide it open.

Instantly the room is the song, the song is the room. With just a pale hint of moonlight leaking in through the single window set high into the wall, the space defines itself by the melody bouncing along the bar, the toy shelf, the sofa, the TV. Entranced, I step into this dark echolocation and the Nano Pal's cheery notes slide along my skin. Here, at the source, the notes are stretched into a single tone with smeared, electrical harmonies above and below. I feel this new noise—a dissonant chord—slip beneath the bandages on my wrists to lap hungrily at my wounds. I laugh at its playful caress, as I think I may have also laughed when I slipped the knife (*my knife*) beneath the flesh of the man's face to lift and twist his skin into a map of ruin. I can feel the sound all around me now, pouring itself into my mouth and down my throat. It tastes like malt liquor and the cocaine drip, like every glorious squalid bender I've ever been on, and I drink up every drop.

And then it stops. The room falls silent. I'm standing on tiptoes, arms outstretched, mouth open, chin lifted as if poised to catch snowflakes on my tongue. I relax and my whole body sags. I'm swamped with exhaustion, and I know that I'll be able to sleep now for many hours, straight through the morning and into the afternoon.

The Nano Pal bleeps once, quietly, normally—and its black-and-white screen comes to life, a dim little oval of light. I go to the toy shelf to examine it. As it cycles through its booting-up routine, the name of the manufacturer—WonderCo—fades into a block of black pixels, and then the letters waver and re-form into something else. On the screen, the pet itself appears. I can't tell what kind of animal it is. It's like nothing I have ever seen. The creature on the screen is undulating and static, moving and not moving, dancing in place and perfectly still. Its limbs are boneless, and it has no face. Through the heating ducts I hear the bloodstain gibbering. This part of the basement is directly below the guest room and if I look up, I know I will see the underbelly of the black pool, glinting with swallowed moonlight. The creature, the dark specter, dancing, dancing...

I'm aware that I'm making a low keening sound. It's the wrongness of the thing that pushes me over the edge. It's rearranging itself on the screen and I can't bear to look but I can't turn away. It's a tragic animal, caught in a between-place, purely liminal, and its failure to resolve itself *hurts*.

My wrists throb and the pain is in concert with the wound on my forehead. The corrupted screen remakes itself into a familiar pattern. If I could somehow place the horrible picture on the sheriff's phone—the image of what I did to the dead man's face—over the Nano Pal, it would overlay perfectly. The pattern on the toy's screen is the latticework around the man's eyes, the slips and scores of a hundred tiny cuts.

I've seen this pattern before. I didn't recognize it for what it was back in the hospital, but here it's so plain, so obvious. It's being communicated to me in no uncertain terms and I accept it.

The wounds I carved weren't random savagery. They mimic a visual I know well: the labyrinthine screensaver on Matt's office computer, writ large across his oversized high-def monitor.

Tendrils of flesh, vectors of meaningless corporate design.

Some new darkness interrupts the pale rectangle of the window. As I turn toward it, my vision drags the pattern through the air to alight upon an old familiar face, that scrap of a bad dream.

Trevor is in the window, body contorted to press his face against the glass. His good eye catches mine and the moonlight sweeps back through damaged runnels of tight shiny flesh. One of his arms, dangling, sways back and forth, fingertips barely disturbing the grass that peeks above the window's bottom edge. He mouths words at me, breath steaming the glass, but I can't make them out. Swaying and grinning his permanent grin, lipless and moist. It looks like he's hanging from something just out of sight, the way you might sprawl in a hammock on a lazy afternoon.

We remain like this for a moment. The years spoil the air

between us. Then I run out of the cave, up the stairs, down the hall to the mudroom, and through the back door. As my bare feet hit the deck's weather-treated boards, I set off the floodlight's sensor. Patio furniture, stark and gleaming, throws long shadows up the yard. At the edge of the deck, I peer over the railing, down at the basement window. Trevor is gone. I lift my eyes to the evergreens and scream after him, thinking he must have followed my escape route from Friday night.

"What do you want from me?"

There's a moment of pure suburban silence followed by commotion behind me, coming from the house. I turn as Matt and Danny burst through the mudroom door. Matt is holding a baseball bat.

"Jesus!" he cries out as he stops abruptly and puts an arm out to block Danny from moving forward.

"Sydney," he says, "why don't you put down the knife."

"The toy," I say. "The Nano Pal."

Matt swallows. Danny's eyes are wide, his hair mussed with sleep, his face the color of blank paper. He grips Matt's arm as if it were the harness of a roller-coaster car, keeping him safe as long as he holds on tight.

"Sydney," Matt says slowly and with great care. "Put the knife down on the table."

I blink. *The knife.*

I glance down. In my right hand's white-knuckle grip is a Gusthof santoku knife, its curved blade meeting the honed edge in a sharp point. I must have taken it from the knife block in the kitchen and carried it down into the basement, and then out here.

The night surges and slides around me, threatens to dissolve into so much wasted flesh and memory. I lay the knife carefully on the wrought-iron patio table.

"I'm sorry," I say. "I'm ready to go back to bed."

Matt hesitates. "What are you doing out here?"

"I thought I heard a noise," I say feebly. "It's okay. It's nothing. I'm just jumpy."

Even in my current state I know better than to tell Matt what I heard and what I saw. *I've had a breakthrough, honey! I just realized that I carved a pattern into the dead man's face! It's just like the background on your desktop!*

Down that road lie doctors, medication, a gray-walled institution.

And to my son: *Hey buddy! Your father, the man I pray you can't remember? Well, he's been watching us! And if you think MY face is bad . . .*

"Syd," Matt says, "you were screaming."

"I'm really okay."

And yet the knife.

THE THIRD
VISITATION

13

We've ID'd the man," Sheriff Butler says. "Thought you'd like to know."

As if this visit to my house is a courtesy and not an interrogation. As if he stopped over as a friend, off-duty, to shoot the breeze. I consider offering him a cup of coffee, but the words *sex play* flash in my mind and I decide that what I'd rather offer him is jack shit.

It's morning, two days after the Nano Pal's siren song dragged me out of bed and down into the basement. Yesterday Matt worked from home, sequestering himself in his office, taking long phone calls, stepping out only for bathroom breaks and a bite to eat. Not nearly enough time for me to have a secret rendezvous with his computer.

I can't get it out of my head: the desktop image, the Nano Pal's mad design. The savage topography of the dead man's flesh.

I still haven't mentioned any of this to Matt. I believe this strange communication, this haunted missive, is for me alone. Anyway, how would I even begin to broach the subject?

I didn't dare creep out of bed to sneak into his office, either. The last thing I need is for Matt to catch me stalking the halls of our house on a second consecutive night. What if I slid another knife oh-so-silently from the block in the kitchen? He's already on eggshells around me. He believes his eyes shine with concern born of love, but I sense in them the kind of nervous, raised-hackles fear that grips us near the ranting subway menace, the street-corner crazy. When I catch him glancing at me sidelong, I expect him to see what Danny saw, back there in his bedroom. When for the briefest of moments (*your face*) my son's body went rigid with terror. The involuntary clenching of his jaw, the widening of his eyes, the sudden pop of pure fright, the self-conscious shift of his gaze away from me.

This morning, Matt took Danny to school on his way to the corporate headquarters of one of his clients. Something about a public relations crisis with the division in Shanghai. I was just heading downstairs to Matt's office when the doorbell rang.

Sheriff Butler. How nice to see you.

Now he's settled his bulk down on the living room sofa and rested his hat on the arm. I sit in the Eames chair across from him. There's a nice leather satchel at his side made by a brand I don't recognize, more startup hotshot than upstate cop. I recall the daughter, the art-school dropout, and assume it's a gift from her. I have a sudden desire to see her coffee-smeared canvases, to pretend to understand and admire them to Butler's sheer bafflement.

"His name's Kyle Portnoy," he says.

The name means nothing to me. When I don't react, not even with a frown or a shrug, he reaches into the satchel, pulls out a thin manila envelope, and tosses it on the round glass tabletop between us. The base of the coffee table is the rough-hewn stump of an oak, lightly lacquered. It doesn't match any of our living room furniture. It's *aspirational*, according to Matt. One day it will sit proudly in the den of our future lake house.

I lean forward to open the folder and wince. The bandage has come off my forehead, but the lump is unmistakable, and the lancing pain comes and goes.

"You taking anything for that?" Butler asks.

"Tea and ibuprofen."

I wait for him to remind me how lucky I am, for his words to curdle so very casually into sarcasm. In my past life I was a wretched addled girl at the mercy of cops and their games. Now that I'm playing with a clear head among the trappings of middle-class normalcy, an arsenal of weaponized Pottery Barn at my back, the field has been leveled considerably.

And yet I can't help but wonder what he thinks of me. All these years and I still crave strangers' approval—the acknowledgement from the straight world that I'm one of them now. That I'm capable of the kind of fierce protective love that binds Danny to me forever. That the only hints of the person I used to be are the scars on my arms.

Butler unsnaps his breast pocket and pulls out a crinkly packet of peanuts. He opens it with surprising grace for a thick-fingered man, takes out a single peanut, and pops it in his mouth.

I flip open the folder. There's a glossy sheet of photo paper right there on top. A heavy-lidded man in a mugshot stares back at me: Kyle Portnoy. I recognize the eyes. The rest is new to me, the smooth reconstruction of a face I've only ever seen ruined, a seamless assembly of the horror I wrought.

His cheeks are lightly acne-scarred. The bridge of his

nose bulges right, shoved aside by a knuckle-sized con-
cavity. Stringy blond hair hangs to his broad shoulders. It
doesn't give off surfer vibes, as I'd perceived it on the sheriff's phone. The impression here is of a hard-living character
actor, a man whose addictions and bar brawls and trouble
with women haven't prevented him from clawing his way
into a few minor roles.

Here I am, making up a backstory for a life I obliterated.
My right elbow bends, my fingers curl, and I have to force
my arm to be still.

I stare into Kyle Portnoy's eyes, take in the S curve of his
nose, the tuft of brittle hair poking out of his right nostril.
The only sound as I force myself to look at the man I can't
remember killing is the sheriff selecting his peanuts one by
one. Outside, a dog yaps its head off.

Portnoy's forehead is high and barren, as if he's received
too much Botox. But I can't believe a guy like this would get
cosmetic enhancements. Either way, it's totally at odds with
the rest of his countenance. I shudder with the sensation of
the world gone suddenly wrong—and then it clicks back into
place and he looks perfectly normal. Forehead proportional.

I linger for a long time over the photo. Then I close the
folder and slide it back across the table.

"I've never seen him before in my life."

"Well," Butler says, slipping the peanuts back into his
pocket and brushing his fingers across the thighs of his uniform pants, trailing salt, "that's not technically true."

I rephrase. "I never saw this man—nor was I aware of his
existence—before he broke into my house last Friday and hit
me over the head and duct-taped my arms and legs."

A tiny smile tugs at the corner of Butler's mouth. He kills
the impulse.

"His priors are for possession with intent to sell," he says, "bad checks, some paraphernalia thing from way back. Another possession rap. No B and E, anything like that."

"You've got thirty years in law enforcement. Junkies have been known to steal."

He grunts. "Your boyfriend. I'm sorry, I forget his name."

"Matt."

"Matt. Right. I've got a cousin named Matt; you'd think I would've remembered that." He pauses. "Second cousin, I guess. Anyway, Matt claims nothing is missing from the house."

The universe of people Butler has spoken to about the incident—about me, my past, my personal life—fades in like the cosmos in a planetarium as the lights go down. Matt, obviously. Judy and Owen. How about Danny? My coworkers at Halloran? Bob Halloran himself?

Sex play.

A drug thing.

This universe abuzz with gossip. Anybody can say anything about you to the police, and you'll never know enough of it to ease your mind. I want to latch onto Butler now, beg him to tell me what he's gleaned from perceptions of me. Instead, I respond in as few words as possible to the matter he's currently poking at.

"That's right," I say. "As far as we can tell."

This universe's Judy-star flares in smug satisfaction. How she must have relished unloading all she knows about me onto Sheriff Butler. He must not have been able to scribble in that notebook fast enough. His pen probably ran out of ink.

"But you mentioned that he—Portnoy—was looking for something."

I fold my arms. "That's how I remember it."

"It's funny, isn't it. The things you remember and the things you don't."

I point to my head injury.

"Let me put it another way: the things you do and do not choose to talk about." He pauses. "Why did you mention your son's biological father, when we spoke in the hospital? You didn't report seeing him outside Danny's school, the day it happened."

Now it's my turn to pause. I'm starting to get a handle on Butler's personal brand of Cop Game. *Am I an aw-shucks rube or a clever motherfucker?* I want to tell him that shtick was played out by the early nineties. "I don't know, it's not like he was committing a crime. He was just kind of *there*."

"We haven't been able to pick him up." He pulls his moleskin out of the satchel, flips it open, and glances at a page crammed with scribbled notes. Then he looks at me expectantly, like he's waiting for me to say something. I don't open my mouth.

"So, this is the story you want to stick to," he says. "This man, Trevor Erwin, pops up a few weeks before you kill a *different* man in your home."

I can't figure out the precise angle of Butler's zeal. What's driving him? This should be an upstate sheriff's wet dream of a case, an open-and-shut self-defense killing. Suburban mom turns the tables on the lowlife who broke into her house, let's close the file on this one and get to happy hour, boys. I can't tell if he's really looking to trip me up, catch me in a lie, nail me on something, *blow the lid off the investigation*.

"I saw him again," I say quickly. I had never intended to report the face at my window to Sheriff Butler, but the need to be understood—and believed—compels the story out of me. A counterweight to the universe of opinion that hangs between us.

There's an almost imperceptible narrowing of his eyes. He brushes salt from his pant leg. "You saw Trevor Erwin a second time." It comes out bland, devoid of any particular tone.

"Two nights ago, I caught him peeking in our basement window."

Butler shuts the notebook and shoves it back into his satchel. "You're just telling me this now. Again, you didn't report it at the time."

"No, I didn't."

"A man you claim is stalking you."

"I didn't say—I don't know what he's doing. You have to understand, for Danny's sake, I've always been vague about his father, and about what happened. What do you tell your kid about a guy like Trevor?" I shake my head. "I know he has questions, and he's going to have more as he gets older, but things have been going well for us. Matt's the father he deserves. Even *talking* about Trevor lets him back in, in a way I'm not ready to allow. He doesn't just get to orbit our lives, after all this time, and intrude whenever he feels like it. I won't let that happen to Danny. So, I'm going to take care of it myself."

"Like you took care of Portnoy."

I don't bother responding.

"You're not scared of this guy," he says.

"No."

The barest hint of a smile, some private joke. "I would be."

"I saved his life, you know."

Butler raises an eyebrow.

I rest my arms on either side of the chair, palms up, so

that he can see the old scars snaking up out of the bandages. "Trevor used to stay awake for days at a time. We both did, I guess, but he had this heroic streak, like anybody's war story about some crazy binge he had to make it his mission to one-up. A whole week without sleep wasn't that weird for him. One time he pushed it to ten days. The record's eleven. You can look it up. That was when he started hearing shit in the walls."

"They all start hearing shit in the walls."

"It's a classic. So, one night he goes out and comes back with a Big Gulp full of gasoline, starts splashing it around. I assume there was some kind of insane strategy to it—the non-logic, back then, was always pretty spectacular. Gonna burn the fuckers out, right? I could only ever go a few days before running for the benzos to make myself crash, so I was passed out for the start of it. Until this immense choking heat wakes me up. The whole trailer's burning— curtains, the rug, the edge of the futon I'm sleeping on—and there's Trevor, just standing there, looking down, watching the flames running up his legs like he can't believe they're real. Then he lifts his arms above his head, like that's gonna keep them out of the fire. He says, *Sydney*, all calm like he's about to ask me to grab him a beer from the fridge. And then he just instantly *catches*. His whole body goes up and he starts screaming and flailing around. I run to the cabinet under the sink where we've got this old miniature fire extinguisher. The cabinet door's burning but I pull it open anyway. My arms catch fire and it's the worst pain I've ever felt. I manage to spray him down, and then we're sort of hugging each other so I can soak up the foam, too, and we're both screaming, and all I can smell is the cooked meat of his skin.

"Danny was just a baby at the time, so I push Trevor away and run to the bedroom. He's fine, thank God, just crying and coughing a little. I scoop him up and get the fuck out. Trevor's already outside, rolling around in the dirt even though he's not on fire anymore. He spent two weeks in the burn unit after that. I came to see him the day before he was supposed to get discharged. I told him to take care of himself, and then I took Danny and never looked back."

"Huh." Butler stares at me, chewing on his lower lip, weighing whether or not to speak.

"Here." I thrust my scarred forearms toward him. "See? I'm not hiding anything. Anything else I can do for you?"

With the tip of a finger Butler grazes the salt that clings to his pant leg. He takes in my scars, those frozen rivers of charred skin. Then his gaze drifts up and out into the room, and I imagine him glimpsing the same constellations that have been feeding my own anxiety: Judy, Owen, Matt, Danny, nameless, faceless others in my orbit, all of them unloading the sins of my past on the man who holds my fate in his hands. After a moment, he opens up.

"About a decade back we had three people go missing up here. Set of brothers and their older cousin. Looked like it was gonna be a long-haul type thing, but we got lucky—not four, maybe five days into the investigation, a hunter stumbles upon some shallow graves up by the Seven Rivers Nature Preserve. And there they were, all three of 'em. Sliced up just about as bad as your boy Portnoy, there. Beyond recognition and so forth. Dental records used to ID 'em." He pats his breast pocket and I hear the plastic wrapper crinkle. Satisfied that his peanuts are safely tucked away, he continues.

"We get a handful of murders a year, almost all of 'em

in Poughkeepsie. Drug dealers popping off, robberies gone wrong. That type of thing. This was something else. We didn't know—did we have a serial? Are we gonna find more vics up in Seven Rivers?" He shakes his head. "Nope. Turns out it was all in the family. The third brother, the oldest, had been pimping out his stepdaughter. I guess some of the relatives decided they were entitled to freebies and big brother disagreed. Strongly."

"Let me guess," I say. "Meth."

"Among other things," Butler says, "yeah."

"Well," I say. "That's pretty horrible."

When he doesn't reply, I add, "I'm sorry."

I cringe internally as the words leave my mouth. Every day my hours are marked off by a litany of apologies. It's as if the ninth of the Twelve Steps, the one where you apologize to the people you fucked over, has metastasized inside me. At work: I'm sorry to have to make this polite and reasonable request that you perform your job tasks. On the train: I'm sorry to ask you to move your bag from an empty seat so I can sit down. At home: I'm sorry the grocery delivery service didn't bring you the right kind of yogurt.

To Sheriff Butler: sorry about this sickening decade-old crime you chose to tell me about...why?

My voice comes out like cracked ice. "So, you stopped by this morning to draw some kind of fucked-up parallel between a bunch of meth freaks and me."

"That's not what I'm saying, Sydney. Calm down."

"How else am I supposed to take it?"

"Shit." He sighs. "It took me a long time to get that one out of my head, is all. And now it's—I don't know—*surfacing*."

"That's not my fault."

He looks at me like it probably is.

I laugh, incredulous. "Don't they have cop therapy for this kind of thing?"

He shakes his head. "I don't need a shrink." He leans forward, rests his elbows on his knees, and looks me straight in the eyes. "I need to take another look at where it happened." He's almost pleading. "I need to see the guest room."

14

Sheriff Butler is gone. I'm sitting at Matt's desk in his home office. The curtains are closed, but they're made of sheer fabric, and the room is bathed in junkie light. That's what I call the desolate midday glow when everyone in the straight world is at work but you're alone in a dead-silent room, having faced down your dawn and survived, and now, sick or well or somewhere in between—somewhere liminal— you sit among the empty bottles and burnt spoons, simply existing.

I'm still trembling from my encounter with the sheriff. Men have bared their obsessions to me before, and I've been the object of several—but never like this. In the first sober years, especially, men seemed entranced by my nearness to catastrophe. It was as if I emitted special ex-addict pheromones that advertised a propensity for recklessness, a miasma as telltale as cigarettes and stale booze. A man meets a woman with track marks and scars and a fragile plan to better her life and he thinks, *I could fuck her, easy.*

But Sheriff Butler? For him I'm both subject *and* object. Victim and perpetrator. He can't resolve it in his mind—he can't get me to overlap myself without the edges blurring. In much the same way, his investigation—obsession, whatever—has already diverged from mine, though we're picking at the same scab. Sitting here in front of the black screen of Matt's ridiculous monitor, fingers poised over the keyboard, about to wake it up, I'm pursuing a lead the sheriff will never even know about. He'll spin his wheels on this case for the rest of his life because I'll never tell him—or anyone—about the message I've received.

Who would believe me?

My face stares darkly back from the blank screen. I study my reflection, but right now there's nothing out of the ordinary. There's only me.

I hit the space bar. The screen comes to life. Matt's desktop blinks into place. There's the pattern, the Nano Pal's nudge—a mazelike design, lines like the right-angled components of a circuit board, bisected by broad arcs that slice across the face of it all. A genome? A chemical formula? It's all very nineties-cyberpunk-meets-vague-medical-iconography. The lines seem to waver like seaweed in a gentle current. In the center of this quiet maelstrom is a black box with empty fields for username and password—Matt's work login.

I know the passwords for his personal laptop, his iPad, all of our streaming services. Our devices are more or less communal. But I've never had a reason to sign on to his office computer before. I try the usual passwords—names of his childhood pets mashed up with the anniversary of our first date, the day we closed on the house, my birthday, Danny's birthday. I'm typing quickly, tapping the keys harder than I need to.

"Come on," I find myself muttering after a while, "show me."

Part of me won't admit this, but I'm talking to the presence that hangs heavy in the house, drifting into every room and hugging the ceiling like smoke. I don't know if *it*—whatever *it* is—is the kind of thing that takes requests. I don't know if it *listens*, exactly. But I know it's been trying to tell me something. And after what happened with the sheriff today, I know I'm not the only one who can sense it.

Show me.

I take my right hand off the keyboard and move my arm in a quick sort of thrusting motion, trying to call up the sensation of stabbing. The desktop image shimmers like blacktop heat haze. The lines, the cuts, the ruin of the man's face take on a fleshy, three-dimensional curvature. The screen comes alive, even though it's a lifeless display—the death-image, as seen on the sheriff's phone, magnified a thousand times and *bulging*, growing out of the screen like something oven-baked and rising. The razor-thin vectors splitting into raw wounds, wetly protruding.

And just like that, the veil is lifted on the memory of what I did to Kyle Portnoy. At last, I am being granted a moment of recall.

I sense the oily, dancing specter as it twines around my arm. Soft black tendrils, wispy yet firm, guide my hand with fervent curiosity. I feel like I'm gliding effortlessly through a slick incursion into some enveloping state of matter. It parts to let me in. At the same time, it buoys me. It is both the oil and the water, and I complete the emulsion.

Kneeling over Portnoy's prone body, I edge the knife into the side of his neck like I'm filleting a salmon. I feel a slight tug as I sever his jugular. Blood spurts from the wound, soaking the guest room carpet. There's nothing metaphysical about the specter's coaxing—its guidance springs from eagerness, and the viscous suspension that coats my arm is coming into its own before my eyes.

Next, I go to work on his face, slipping the tip of the knife into the meat around his cheekbones and scoring neat grooves in the flesh. The skin here is tender and supple and the darkness threads between my fingers in delight.

The sensation is a curious one. As I sit at Matt's desk, I'm experiencing the memory fully, watching myself immersed in the gore of the moment. And yet I find that I'm not horrified or repulsed. I don't feel much of anything besides an academic interest in what I'm doing. As I slide the knife along the side of his nose and open up a thin laceration, I lean down to smell the wound as if it's a flower in sudden bright bloom.

After a while I become aware of the pattern that I'm carving—that I'm being guided to carve. Flaps of skin, strangely mutilated, lie at precise angles. My eyes go slack. I take my hand away from the man's face and at the same time pull back from the keyboard to find that I've entered the password and logged in.

There, on the screen, is Matt's desktop, cluttered with files.

I stare blankly for a moment. And then I'm pummeled by a wave of nausea. Acid burns my stomach. Pain flares in my wrists and forehead. I push myself up from the chair and stagger out into the hallway. Bathroom. I need the bathroom. I'm going to be sick.

Oh, God, the horrifying expertise with which I flicked and twisted the blade, like a conductor leading a symphony, that wasn't *me*, that couldn't have been me...

I move down the hall, past the basement door. I can feel the scorch of bile rising in my throat, hot tears blurring my vision. How could I have done such a thing?

Butchery. There's no other word for it. The dispassionate way I slipped the knife beneath his pliable flesh, over and over again.

The same hands clutched Danny tight as I carried him away from the wreckage of a dead-end life. The same hands changed his diapers and bandaged his cuts and set cloth after damp cloth on his feverish forehead.

How vast is the spectrum of what I'm capable of?

I'm not going to make it. My breakfast is coming up fast and I'm going to spatter the hallway right outside the—

15

—guest room.

"Here we are," I say to Butler. He walks to the center of the room, puts his hands on his hips, and turns slowly in a circle, taking it in like a prospective buyer.

"All right," he says after a while. He eyes the bloodstain. "You folks going to rip this carpet up or what?"

"We're going to renovate," I say, though Matt and I haven't discussed this plan since the day I came home from the hospital. Nor have we discussed moving out of the house. I know the silence can't last, but for now, as long as we keep the guest room door closed, it's like there's nothing for us to talk about. Though I suspect that Matt is talking to someone else about it. I've noticed that his bedtime prayers—which he has performed on his knees, elbows on the mattress, hands folded, since he was a boy—have become lengthier and more involved.

I never thought I could be with someone who believes in God, much less a practicing Catholic who slips a crisp twenty into the collection basket every Sunday. I used to jab at his faith from all the obvious angles, from the earthly—the

Catholic church shelters child molesters, yet women can't be ordained as priests—to the theological—what kind of God lets mudslides destroy villages and little girls get raped and murdered?

Matt never argued with me. After a while, I realized I sounded like a teenage nihilist trying to be edgy. He never once tried to convince me to pray with him, either—he never seemed to care if I believed in God or not. Religion is truly a personal comfort for him, and he's more than happy to keep it to himself, like when he listens to seventies prog rock with headphones on because he knows I hate it. And so his quiet faith actually became endearing to me.

"You're staying here, in this house, then," Butler says without taking his eyes off the bloodstain. He scratches the back of his head, where the skin bunches up like a bulldog's face. He's left his hat on the arm of the sofa.

"Our lives are here," I say. Part of me wishes he would leave me alone, while another part wants him to stay long enough for me to figure out exactly what's on his mind. "Why, what would you do?"

He frowns. At last, he tears himself away from the stain and meets my eyes. "If this were my house? I'd get the fuck out." The oddly pleading tone that snuck into his voice when he practically begged me to take him to the guest room has subsided. I'm starting to think I imagined it. He regards me once again with that curious, inscrutable expression. "There's almost nothing of this magnitude that won't linger. Whether it's in the mind or..."

"Or what?"

He shrugs. "You know, I was a rookie patrolman back in the late eighties. Brass actually had this guy, some PhD type from NYU or Columbia, come up and give a talk about rituals, and cult murders, all the *Dungeons-and-Dragons*-is-satanic kind of shit everybody was freaking out about back then. Before your time, but—"

"I've listened to the podcasts."

"Right. Well, it's interesting how the context frames the crime, is all."

I smile, a little, at his phrasing. So much for the *aw-shucks rube* act.

"Back then, if I'd have come upon this scene"—he indicates the guest room as a whole—"with Portnoy's face in the shape it was in, I'd probably have those satanic panic alarm bells blaring in my head. The ME would find a pentagram carved in him somewhere, whether it was really there or not. Now"—he shrugs—"there's nothing like that. There's just you. And the only precedent I have for this kind of mutilation is the most fucked-up family dispute I ever had the displeasure to investigate. So I don't mean to draw the comparison as"—he reaches for the word—"an insinuation. But it's on my mind. I guess it never left and all this is just drawing it out." As he speaks, he edges closer to the stain and peers into its depths. I don't think he realizes that he's doing it. "I just think..." He shakes his head. "I need you to come clean and tell me why you did him like that. I figure you manage to get free, you run like hell. Maybe deliver a kick to the nuts first. But you run."

"I did run. I *remember* running. I told you. I don't remember this."

He steamrolls over my words like I didn't say anything. "Or you maybe stab the guy once and take off. Incapacitate and flee."

"I don't know what to tell you."

He makes a sound of sheer exasperation. "It can't *not mean*

anything, what you did. You understand? It can't be for no
reason. Not with his face done up that way." He presses the
toe of his shoe against the edge of the stain as if he's testing the water at the edge of the sea. Then he looks at me.
"I can't have that," he says quietly. He cocks his head as if
noticing something about me for the first time. It's the look
you'd give a friend if you weren't sure if they changed their
hairstyle or not. He studies my face. "There's *unrest* here.
Nothing's settled. I know you can feel it, too. I can see it in
your face."

I shudder. *Your face.* The sheriff settles himself down along
the border of the stain, kneeling as if in supplication to that
dark blot, that hole in the world. I take a step back and fold
my arms across my chest. Between the slats of the blinds the
river is gunmetal gray.

I don't like the way he's staring into the bloodstain. I feel
a strange surge of possessiveness. *There's nothing for you here,*
I almost say out loud. The dog-faced wrinkles in the back
of his head are covered in the salt-and-pepper stubble of
his high-and-tight haircut. They go smooth as he bows his
head. My eyes dart around the room, avoiding the bloodstain. Items flash quick-hit associations. The nautical blue
duvet cover on the bed: the time Matt pulled me in here
during our housewarming party to fuck me while our guests
chattered just down the hall. The Lobsterfest poster: our
summer road trip to the Maine coast, Danny's first crusta-
cean feast, the mess of butter and fishy bits on his face. The
drying rack: Matt's sweaty running clothes, all those free
shirts from corporate 5Ks. These things, *our* things, steeped
in the passing memories of the everyday while at my feet the
Dutchess County Sheriff reaches out and skims his fingertips
along the hard crust of the stain, the rigid whorls and piles of

the old carpet, caked in darkness. He whispers something as he caresses the blotch as if it were the bare skin of a sleeping lover. If he were to sink his fingers in and pull, dried blood would come up in hard chunks.

My heart quickens. Just for a moment—a passing flash—a sharp wave of disgust washes over me. Not at the sheriff and his fealty to the unrest in this room, but at the sheer blandness of the things I've surrounded myself with. The proof that I have embraced with all my heart and soul the proper aspects of being a *mother*, a *partner*, a fucking *commuter*. All the time and energy spent scratching and clawing just to put myself in the position to scratch and claw some more, at upward mobility, like a normal person. I recall the reckless misdirected rages and euphoric highs of the wreck I used to be, and once again the craving hits—to slip into that younger skin for a moment, to sidestep the notion that the straight world has anything to offer me. To stay the fucked-up course.

I haven't felt the pull of these impulses in a long time.

I want to ask Butler for a cigarette. I want the two of us to sit on the edge of the bed and smoke and flick ash onto the carpet. The icy needle jabs my inner ear and then recedes. The wounds on my wrist flare with pain (*or is it my old scars waking up?*).

I can't make out what the sheriff is saying. It sounds like hushed, conspiratorial gibberish. I catch a familiar syllable, a nonsensical turn of phrase. His hands move back and forth with drawing-room elegance, thick fingers putting pressure on the caked blackness at seemingly random intervals. Bits of crusted blood stick to his fingertips. He's speaking the halting language I heard the night of the Nano Pal's summons. The hitching, guttural rasp.

I step closer, around the side of the bloodstain, and try to catch his eye. "What did you say?"

He doesn't look up. The bloodstain ripples. Corrupted air rises. The darkness puffs out stink like a bellows.

"Did you see that?" I say.

That seems to get through to him. He raises his eyes. They're red-rimmed and puffy as if he's been weeping.

"You butchered this man," he says, "and now there's a *sickness* here. You did this."

"Not on purpose."

"You're a liar," he says.

I take a step back. "I think you should go."

He lumbers to his feet and draws himself up, straight-backed and glowering, to his full height. I realize for the first time how linebacker-massive he really is. I should know by the sudden twist of his face that he's going to raise his voice, but it still catches me off guard. He lifts a finger and points between my eyes.

"You're a fucking liar!"

16

With the sheriff's voice ringing in my head, I clean up the vomit in the hallway, brush my teeth, sip some water, and then I'm back at Matt's desk. I scan the files on his desktop. Meeting notes, assets from the nonprofit's tiny creative team, spreadsheets full of client data. The magnitude of the search hits me. I don't know what I'm looking for. I've followed such an improbable path to get here. And now it's like I've been shoved out of a moving car alongside a desert highway to find my own way back through the wilderness.

But there's still the second investigation, the sheriff's divergent path.

What the hell? It's all I've got.

I do a system search for the name *Kyle Portnoy*. No results. Still, a tenuous, silk-thin thread begins to form in my mind. Portnoy was looking for something—something he thought Matt would have? It's possible.

I think of the way Matt downplayed and dismissed my memory of the man looking for something in the house. Even though the evidence proved me right—the place was ransacked—he hasn't brought it up again. *The important thing is that it's over*, he said. It's at odds with how Matt normally conducts himself. He's always been the personification of *supportive partner*. Filling my travel mug with light-and-sweet coffee from the gleaming machine every morning before I leave for the train, rubbing my feet when I get home, taking Danny running with him. Each day he drops these small gestures like breadcrumbs along the winding path that he and I are traveling together. I've learned that the proof of love often lies in the accumulation of quotidian things. But in love, how much is performance?

With a pounding heart—I'm now officially *snooping*, something Matt and I routinely mock lesser couples for doing—I open his Outlook and search his emails. Nothing. Same with the chat program he uses for work. I open his applications folder, look for some random clue I missed. It's neat and organized and mostly untouched—dozens of "useful" programs that come preinstalled on the computer. A few games, plug-and-play music recording, web browsers—

And the messenger backup. If it's anything like the one on my laptop, it'll be synced to his phone. His texts will be stored there, even the ones he deletes from his phone, until he comes here and manually trashes them.

It's worth a shot. I open it. I scan texts from me, his Stanford cross-country buddies, his cousin Wynn (whose wedding I'm expected to attend along with Judy and Owen), a few work friends—all of them the mundane stuff of tossed-off digital life—except for an exchange with someone he refers to as "KP." I open that thread. The most recent text is one from KP with no reply, dated last Thursday, 2:53 a.m.

it wants to be known, it wants more of itself, it wants to keep growing inside me

I scroll up through a litany of texts, moving backward through time, eating up several days. All of them go unanswered by Matt. As I scan KP's words, I become more and more convinced that it's Kyle Portnoy. He's definitely looking for something. It's pretty much all he's doing. And he's desperate.

It's not here.

Finally, I come to a message from Matt and pause my scrolling. It's from early last month, September 3, 9:28 p.m. For some reason my mind tries to pinpoint exactly what we were doing on that particular night, but of course I can't remember, not really. 9:28? We were probably snuggled on the couch, watching Netflix, phones in hand. I scroll up a little more to get the gist of the conversation and begin reading texts in chronological order.

Matt
You need to calm down. It's going to take time before you see results. Think of it as a learning curve.

KP
i dunno man somethings really wrong

Matt
Nothing's wrong. I promise.

KP
i can't explain it i just know it wants more it wants to grow

Matt
You're overthinking it.

KP
no i just need more it needs more of itself

Matt
That's not how it works.

KP
i can meet you anywhere

Matt
You have to understand, I have a good-faith arrangement with my client. I can't violate the parameters they set for the treatment. Remember how lucky you are to be getting it in the first place, and let it run its course.

KP
come on man you dont know how this feels it's fucking hungry

Matt
I'm sorry. Good luck.

KP
wait

After that, Matt cut him off. There are no more replies, just incessant pleading from Kyle Portnoy that turns to desperation as September rolls into October. Then, in the days before his death, it's like he's screaming into the void.

it knows what ive done and it wants me to see
it wants to know everything its always hungry
it needs more i need more it wants me to get more it wont
stop
make it stop talking it won't shutup

it knows about sharon it knows what i did. it gives her back
to me in pieces. it wants me to see.
i let her die oh god i let her die
you have to get me more. it wont rest till it gets what it
wants. its inside me its everywhere i cant sleep.
cant fucking sleep

I close the text thread and quit the application. I stare at Matt's
monitor until my eyes go slack. The desktop image wavers
and its proud angles bulge and squirm, slick with gore.

Matt has been lying to me. He's directly connected to the
man I killed. He's the reason that Portnoy broke in here in
the first place. He's known it all along.

He has been putting my son and me in danger.

How much of love is performance?

A lone desire sparks, flares, catches: I want to go numb.
I don't want to think about any of this anymore—Butler,
Portnoy, Trevor, Matt, Judy, Owen, the knife. I don't even
want to think about Danny. But I lost the capacity for
numbness when I got sober for the last time. Nine years of
squaring up to meet both tragedy and triumph head-on, of
learning what despair feels like uncloaked and naked, and
now I'm teetering on the precipice of saying *fuck it*. The
craving, reduced over nine years to a wretched speck of no
consequence, shakes off the last of the cobwebs that began
forming the day I turned my back on my old life. It throbs
with reckless suggestions. Vicodin for the ache in my head
and the pain in my wrists. Some quality blow to teleport me
to a warm cocoon, a new skin that quivers like a hummingbird, everything flying by so fast I can't feel a thing. A few
quick nips from a plastic handle of vodka to level me off,
take the edge off the rush, keep me steady yet insulated.

I close my eyes and try to slip into 4-7-8 breathing. It's laughable. Portnoy's misery is burned into the back of my eyelids, a white-hot scrawl in the darkness. *I let her die oh god i let her die.* Transference occurs, a water-dipped finger tugging on surface tension then pulling free, and his pain is my pain. I can crawl inside his want and feast on his need.

I can't stand for Kyle Portnoy to be a human being with his own unfathomable desires. At least when he was an anonymous corpse the element of the unreal was a bulwark against madness. But now he has a name and a voice—and now I have seen myself in the act.

I abandon my pointless breathing exercise and close the text backup folder. Hands shaky and nerves frayed, I re-scan Matt's client files. Global law firms, investment banks, insurance giants. *Treatment*, Matt called it. *A good-faith arrangement with my client.* There's nothing remotely medical here, except for a single company: Alverion Pharmaceuticals.

I open an incognito browser window and search the name. A moment later I'm navigating the blandest website imaginable, all Big Pharma clip art and corporate platitudes about Alverion's mission to discover new biopharmaceutical treatments and make them accessible to the widest range of patients. I click on a section titled "Innovation in Action" and find slightly jazzier copy touting their research and development across a variety of public health issues. I don't notice the pattern at first. It creeps up on me, even though I'm sure it's been there the whole time.

The design on Matt's desktop—on Portnoy's face, on the Nano Pal screen—is imprinted faintly behind the text of "Innovation in Action." It moves as I scroll down, quivering like raw meat in a hot pan, and I can't seem to get a good look at it.

Dizzy and sickened, I close the browser window, shut down Matt's computer, and leave the office.

It doesn't matter which room I exit or enter—I will always pass the door to the guest room. Right now, it's mercifully closed. It occurs to me that even if we leave our home forever—even if we move to the other side of the world—I will always be walking past this door. And behind it will be the specter and the stain, gibbering wetly, choking out nonsense.

I stand at the threshold of the kitchen and train my eyes on the door to the fridge. It's crowded with magnets, postcards, drawings from Danny's sketchbook. I catch my distorted reflection in the vaguely insectoid curves of the restaurant-style espresso machine. The wrongness of my face takes my breath away. The elements of our kitchen, the backsplash subway tiles and the Vitamix and the iPad docking station, conspire to nauseate me. I go to the fridge and open it.

There, behind the milk and the grapefruit seltzer, is a half-finished six-pack of craft IPAs. I've lived alongside Matt's beer for years and never once been tempted to crack one open. Alcohol was never my primary drug of choice. Booze was always a supplement, a way to even my keel, the downer that kept me tethered to earth when the coke tried to fling me skyward. Matt has offered again and again to ban six-packs from the house entirely, but it's never been an issue for me, and I didn't want to deny him such a simple pleasure.

A grateful shiver passes from my chest to my thighs. It's akin to when I grabbed his racing flats from under the guest room bed to cut myself free of the tape that bound my wrists. Before I even reach into the fridge, I feel my anxiety begin to subside. The mere promise of mild inebriation—the first sight of a substance—is enough to open up a dopamine drip.

But the sheriff's phantom bulk still surrounds me, a bad-trip trail of a man losing himself to what he can't understand. And Portnoy's words won't stop sluicing through my thoughts. The fact that Matt has known exactly who the intruder was, all this time, and perhaps what he was capable of...

What else has he been keeping from me? What kind of a consultant is he, really? What has he been doing for Alverion Pharmaceuticals?

I nudge a row of pastel seltzers, take a beer by its neck, and pull it out. I shut the refrigerator door and heft the bottle, ice-cold in my palm. My junkie brain's old calculator begins to whirl and spin. There's a moment of crestfallen desire—if only we had a bottle of vodka. I always preferred liquor. I didn't care about the taste. I wasn't trying to savor the intricacies of hops and barley and malt, I was trying to alter the properties of the coke I'd been mainlining, to make myself feel something different. Matt favors IPAs, and this one's 7.5 percent alcohol. I figure if I drink the first one down fast and then go straight for a second, I should be able to work up a decent buzz, especially after nine years sober.

So, I'll have a few drinks. Two or three beers. That's how normal people cope. And I'm a normal person now. Just ask the fucking backsplash tiles.

I won't count it as a violation of my sobriety. It's just beer. I don't even *like* beer. Therefore, I'm not giving in to any true craving. Not really. I try to twist the cap off, and it doesn't budge. The cap's little teeth scrape my skin. I need an opener. We keep our collection of bottle openers in the drawer with the measuring spoons, meat thermometer, and pizza cutter. Just a few beers. Three at most. There are only three left in the house anyway. I go to the drawer and rummage for an opener. Beer is nothing. It's water. It's not like I'm going to launch myself headlong into a crippling addiction to craft IPAs. I'll forget I even did this by tomorrow morning. And then I'll never do it again.

I come up with a Brooklyn Nets opener and fit it snugly against the lip of the bottle cap. I pause for a moment, wondering about the last beer I cracked—where I was, who I was with. How long I'd been awake.

Then I hear the front door open. Someone steps into the hall. I try to do two things at once—toss the opener in the drawer and lunge for the fridge—and in my haste the bottle slips from my grasp.

Our kitchen floor is unforgiving. The bottle smashes. My bare feet are marooned in a sea of glass shards and beer froth.

Footsteps come through the living room.

The weight of the day presses down on me. It's as if Sheriff Butler never left. As if he's before me now, swaying slightly in his big heavy boots, torn between rage and confusion, tongue-tied in perpetual accusation.

17

Sheriff Butler comes at me. All at once he's a looming presence, blotting out the duvet, the drying rack, the Lobsterfest poster. His mouth is flecked with spittle. His red-rimmed eyes bulge. He has lost himself in the depths of the stain, and what has been returned to him is fouled. Dried blood clings like iron filings to his fingers.

His bulk is immense, all-encompassing. I take a step back and hit the wall. To my right is the dresser, to my left a clear path to the window. Hands on the sill, vault to the ground, sprint for the evergreen tree line, the neighbors' yard, the safety of the street. The wide-eyed teenager will screech to a halt. David Winters, the pediatrician, will come out to his front yard to intercept me. *You're safe now*, someone will say. I will think: *no*.

And I will be right.

The closed loop is like a noose around my neck. The path of my new life, once a beeline toward a better future, is concentric and ever shrinking. The air in the guest room is damp and humid. I meet the sheriff's eyes and see in them a darkness as black as the stain.

I watch him struggle for control of himself. "Why?" he chokes out. His breath is dry and salty.

Mischief rises inside me. A reprise of the urge to sneer at Danny—do you know what *fucking* is? It's as if something is gripping my throat and squeezing the words up out of me. I double down on what's troubling him the most.

"No reason," I say.

It's as if I've hit him with a jab to the face. He appears stunned for a moment, opening his mouth and closing it again. Then he takes a step back.

Fear welling up inside a man unused to being afraid is a wonder to behold. He glances at the stain and then back to me. There's a frisson along its surface, a disturbance akin to a dragonfly skimming pondwater. I feel its there-and-gone rippling in my throat and my stomach. Butler clenches his jaw. His hand goes to the gun holstered just below his hip and pauses there, all potential energy. With great effort the sheriff makes his hand into a fist and moves it away from the gun. His body gives off the sour odor of an animal trapped in an unclean cage. Sweat soaks the armpits of his once-crisp uniform and makes an imperfect ring around his gut. Slowly, he unclenches his fist and brings his hand to his mouth. There, he begins to dart his tongue in and out to taste the flecks of blood on his fingertips.

"Oh, God," he whispers.

I fight the urge to flee the room and slam the door behind me, though I can clearly see myself doing it and how it will unfold. I will get to the end of the hall, the threshold of the kitchen, when the sound of the gunshot will freeze me in my tracks. Then there will be two stains in the guest room, one dry and cracked as sunbaked mud and one glistening wet. I can see, also, the way this room will elicit splatter from Matt in great swaths along the glass of the Lobsterfest poster frame, the shirts draped over the drying rack.

I see the duvet cover soaked in my son's blood.

The sheriff's face is pinched and strained. "What are you doing to me?" His voice is pitched toward an edgy, rising hysteria. He lowers his hand. Dried blood dots the corner of his mouth.

"We have to get out of here," I say.

Sheriff Butler laughs. It's a horrible sound. He shakes his head. "It's not the *room*, Sydney, don't you see? It's *you*."

"Sheriff…"

"It's your goddamn *face*!"

My fingers prod my cheeks, my forehead. I wince when I touch the raised, raw skin of the tender wound.

"There's nothing wrong with my face."

He backs up to the bed and sits down on the mattress. His big body sags like a deflated parade balloon. He rubs his eyes. "It's the air," he says haltingly, searching for the right words. "The air around you is wrong."

I go to the closet door and pull it open. Affixed to the back of the door is a long rectangular wall mirror. I lean in close and pinch the skin of my cheek and pull it away from my face, stretching the corner of my mouth into a grotesque smile. I poke my cheekbones, pressing hard, and watch the red marks fade as I lift my fingers.

A thought intrudes. Absurd? Yes. But I can't help but entertain it.

The air around my face has always been wrong.

When I was a little girl, a theory wormed its way into my brain and wouldn't let go: *I am speaking a different language than everybody else.* What comes out of my mouth is total gibberish. This is my disability. Everyone at school feels sorry for me, so they pretend I'm speaking English. Even my own brain lies to me, because I hear my own words as English. But really, I'm just babbling.

That's when I finally see it. Something flickers across my face, a blink-and-you'll-miss-it distortion, a transparent mask. It's as if a clear plastic bag has been crinkled and then smoothed out. I clamp both palms against the side of my head to hold the distortion steady, trap it against my skin. But it's no use. I can't bring it back. Is this what Danny saw the other day in his bedroom? An exhalation out of nowhere, rippling my features like linen on a clothesline?

"Was that it?" I speak to the sheriff in the mirror, moving slightly so that I can see his reflection sitting there on the bed. He's watching me, expressionless and distant.

"Yeah," he says. He looks uncomfortable for a moment, as if he's eaten something disagreeable. He glances at the bloodstain. Then he smacks his palms on his thighs, stands up, and walks over to join me at the mirror. I cringe, a little, at the closeness of his reeking bulk. His body odor has become potent.

"There," he says, reaching for the mirror. With the tip of his finger, he traces my reflection's cheekbones. Dried blood clings to the glass. I'm not sure I see what he's trying to indicate. I turn away from the mirror to look at him directly. He flinches and takes a step back. Cowardice, obviously an unfamiliar state of being, has twisted him into knots. His inability to make me resolve one way or the other has flummoxed him.

He swallows. "I have to go now."

"Okay."

He draws himself up to stand ramrod straight, salvaging what dignity he can. Still, he can't get his eyes to meet mine.

They look askance, over my shoulder, out at the gray smudge of the river through the blinds.

I think I hear the whole room sigh.

"Don't leave town," he says, regaining some of his authority. "And rip up that fucking carpet."

18

I'm bending to pick up the bigger pieces of broken glass when Danny comes around the corner, all live-wire after-school energy, and *thunks* his massive backpack down on a kitchen chair.

"Today Loren stood up in front of the whole class and—"

"Hold up!" I say. He freezes. There's a dry leaf clinging to his hair. "I just broke a glass in here."

"I've got shoes on," he says, but he stays put at the edge of the room.

He regards the mess at my feet with a curious expression. The IPA bottle was amber-colored, unlike any piece of glassware that we own. Between the shards, the little islands of foam, and the bitter hoppy odor, I'm sure that Danny knows exactly what it is that I broke.

Despite keeping Trevor shrouded—nothing more than a placeholder—I don't hide the truth from my son about the person I used to be. He knows what addiction is. I've planted a simple dichotomy in his mind: some grown-ups, like Matt, are capable of enjoying a few beers every now and then. These same grown-ups can take medicine for pain that's prescribed by a doctor because they understand that too much is bad—just like too much candy or soda is bad— and have the willpower to stop before they hurt themselves. Other grown-ups, like me, have a hard time stopping before they hurt themselves. Since they don't want to hurt them- selves, or anybody else, they don't ever take certain medi- cines or drink alcohol, not even one beer.

Still, the person I used to be is an abstraction to Danny. I tell myself that he was too young to retain the specifics of the squalor of his first two years on this earth, though I often wonder what fragments he carries with him of the mother I was—manic and exhausted in equal measure— and of the makeshift crib in which he lay, unbathed and unchanged, while the noises of my wide-awake nightmares came through the thin trailer walls. Better he live with the vague notion that his mother had a "problem" than with the specifics of daily neglect. And, arguably worse, with the cloying, overbearing attention I drenched him with to make up for the time-smeared days and nights when I could scarcely be bothered to change his diaper. I used to obsess over myself as I was, looming over his crib, eyes hollow and breath rank, begging for absolution in the desperate way I clutched him to my breast. Mercifully, I've learned to devalue those moments, to see them through Danny's present-day eyes as nothing but a dreamy haze.

That's why the fact that I'm standing in a puddle of beer I came very close to drinking is all at once shocking and a lit- tle sickening to me. Now that my son is here in the kitchen, the gravity of what I came within the pop of a bottle cap to doing—breaking nine years of sobriety—makes my knees go weak.

Danny looks me in the eyes, and I feel light-headed. Then

he flinches and shifts his gaze over my shoulder, out the kitchen window.

"Can you go upstairs and grab my moccasins, so I don't cut my feet?" I say. He jets away and I listen to him bolt up the stairs.

I bend once again at the waist and carefully pinch the biggest shard between thumb and forefinger. I lunge for the slide-out cabinet that hides the garbage bin, careful not to move my feet, and trash the glass. Then something catches my eye on the counter next to the espresso machine. Rather, its absence does. The knife block is gone. I try to think back to when I last saw it, but I can't remember. Yesterday? The day before? I haven't been cooking. Citing my need to take it easy, we've been living on whatever Matt whips up from our meal delivery service.

I open the drawer full of random kitchen stuff. Meat thermometer, check. Bottle openers, check. Grill tongs, measuring spoons, tea diffusers, check. No pizza cutter, no corn skewers, no egg slicer. All of the sharp objects have been removed from the kitchen. Even the blade from the Vitamix is gone.

Matt's not taking any chances. At first it seems like a wry little in-joke, a callback to what must have been an alarming evening for him. *Put the knife down on the table.* I can't say I blame him, really. But this sneaky little act very quickly brings to mind the texts on his computer, which sent me to the kitchen for this ill-fated beer in the first place.

Concentric, ever-shrinking loops. A tightening noose. I can't reconcile this version of Matt—the one who blithely goes about his days, playing the role of the attentive partner, after some secret business he's caught up in nearly got me killed—with the one I've known since we met across the table when my agency was doing some pro bono creative work on behalf of Matt's nonprofit. The man who taught Danny to quicken his stride and bring his elbows in when he's running. Who drives me to Rhinebeck and Cold Spring to hunt down antiques for our future lake house. Who brims with small acts of love and gives of himself so freely that I know it's not out of obligation but simply his own sweet nature taking the reins.

We're going to get through this. His words, the night I came home from the hospital. *I'm with you all the way.*

It occurs to me that there are two unbroken beers in the fridge. Once I get this mess cleaned up and Danny retreats to his room for homework and video games, it would be easy to drink them both before Matt gets home. He only drinks on the weekends these days. I could easily replace them by then.

"One order of moccasins!" Danny says, bursting into the kitchen, halting in his tracks, then carefully setting the slippers down at the edge of the foamy mess.

"Thank you, sir." I wiggle my feet into the house shoes, and then I'm free to walk to the drawer where we keep our hand towels KonMari folded and organized. I select the most ragged one for sacrifice.

"Did you miss a lot of stuff at school?"

"Loren picked up the worksheets for me."

"That was nice of him."

"They make somebody do that if you're out for more than two days."

"Well, it was still nice of him."

I drop the hand towel flat across the puddle and bunch it to sop up beer and gather bits of glass at the same time. Then I toss the entire bundle in the trash.

"I was cleaning out the fridge," I explain, grabbing a roll of paper towels from the counter, tearing off three of them and laying them across the remainder of the spill. Behind me, I hear Danny pull out a chair and sit at the kitchen table. I press the paper towels down with my feet, then trash the whole soggy mess.

"Reminds me of Digital Brooklyn," I say, a little too loud.

"I one million percent knew that was coming," Danny says.

"Mind reader." The linoleum is sticky and reeks of beer. In the cabinet beneath the sink, I spin the lazy Susan and come up with the organic plant-derived spray cleaner. "My God," I say, "you were eight!"

The numbers come to me: Danny at eight equals Sydney at six years clean.

"Good old Digital Brooklyn." I saturate the floor with the earthy spray. "It's funny how your life can turn on what seems like a totally random thing at the time, right?" I tear off a paper towel. *Wiping up expensive earth-friendly cleaner with wasted paper products*, Matt once said. *That's, like, modern society in a nutshell.*

"Do you ever think about that?" I prod Danny.

"Like if I miss the bus and it gets hijacked that day."

"Your bus is never going to get hijacked, but yes. Same idea." I toss the soaked paper and tear off another sheet. The room still smells like spilled beer. "Anyway, remember how the sitter canceled, so I took you with me, all the way to that weird little warehouse-y convention center by the water?"

"You wouldn't let me play with the iPad on the way."

"One, it was a brand-new thing I had to work extra diner shifts for, and two, it had my whole portfolio on it."

"I wouldn't have messed up your portfolio."

"So we walk in, right, and there's all these people buzzing around, and obviously you're the only eight-year-old. Everybody looks younger than me, and cooler, and relaxed. They all seem like they already know each other, so I'm like, what's the point of a networking event?" I give the floor one last spritz of cleaner. A glass shard catches my eye, then another, scattered in the sliver of space between the fridge and the counter. "So, I don't really know what to do—I'd never been to one of these before. Like, do you just start showing your work to people? My work at that point was just stuff I'd written for classes I'd audited—which I also brought you to all the time, remember?"

Danny yawns.

"And then—*dun dun dun*—we spy the fateful drinks booth. Which had?"

"Cokes in glass bottles."

I roll a paper towel into a tight wand and slip it between fridge and counter. "Special treat. So, we're wandering around, you're drinking your soda, I'm trying to figure out why there aren't booths—I expected all the ad agencies to have booths, like a job fair, so I could just walk up and show somebody my work, but it's not like that, it's just a little party." I use the tip of the paper wand to sweep glass shards out of the narrow space. "And then butterfingers over here…"

This gets a laugh out of him. Warmth surges in my chest.

"The bottle was shaped weird," he says. A clump of dust follows the glass bits.

"The next thing I know I'm apologizing profusely to this old guy whose really expensive-looking shoes are now soaked in fizzy soda. Who turns out to be Bob Halloran.

Who thinks it's hilarious that I brought my kid to this hipster party slash fake networking thing." I gather up the little pile of detritus. "And so you, Danny-tello, are the reason I got my portfolio looked at at all. And the reason Halloran gave me a chance in the first place. How awesome is that?"

As I'm tossing the last crumpled paper towel, I hear the telltale bleep of the Nano Pal. I turn around. Danny is seated at the table, hunched over the small green toy.

"Danny, stop!" I cross the kitchen and snatch it from his palm. He looks up at me, stunned at the fierceness of my intervention, and then once again averts his eyes. He pretends to find something intriguing about a piece of junk mail tossed on the table.

"Where did you get this?" I demand.

"The basement." He fidgets with the corner of the envelope.

"What were you doing with it?"

"I brought it to school to show Loren."

"I thought he only played Fortnite."

"I just wanted to show him."

"Danny. Look at me."

With great reluctance, he turns his head but can't bring himself to meet my eyes. His gaze is focused somewhere around my shoulder.

"Look. At. Me."

He swallows. Raises his eyes. And manages to look me full in the face, though it seems to require great willpower.

I hold up the Nano Pal. "This is not a toy."

He looks utterly confused. "I thought that's what it was."

I hesitate. The absurdity of what I just said strikes me slightly after the fact. I glance at the screen. There, undulating and twitchy, an emergent newborn taking its first halting steps out of its amniotic fluid, is the creature, the dancing specter. Its movements are purely liminal, neither here nor there, and I think: *the air around you is wrong.* Yet it's merely the precursor. I know what comes next. The pattern. Alverion. Portnoy's obliterated face.

"I don't want you playing with this," I say.

"It doesn't work anyway."

I know what will happen if I shove the screen in his face and demand to know what he sees. *Nothing!* he will insist. *The battery's dead or something.*

I don't bother showing it to him. Instead, I close my fist around the Nano Pal. Danny goes back to scrutinizing the envelope on the table. *Time Sensitive. Open Immediately.*

"Okay, kiddo," I say. "Why don't you go get started on those worksheets."

He gets up without another word, shoulders his backpack, and leaves the kitchen. As soon as he's gone, I open my fist and take another look at the screen.

A sickness, the sheriff said.

I plunk the toy down on the counter and rummage through the top drawer until I find the meat tenderizer. The consummate blunt object. Safe from Matt's scouring.

I'm interrupted by vibrations against my thigh: my phone buzzing in my pocket. I pull it out and take a look. It's a number I don't recognize. I put it on speaker, so I don't have to press it to my aching head.

"Hello."

In reply there's a confluence of murmurs, like a hushed theater crowd before the lights go down. I'm about to end the call when a voice rasps out, a pained, raw-throated whisper.

"I didn't mean to scare you."

"Jesus Christ, Trevor." I glance over my shoulder to make

sure Danny's not lingering in the doorway. "How did you get this number?"

"*It's not hard.*" Trevor's voice dopplers back and forth.

"Okay. I'm done with this." I lower my voice. "Listen to me, the cops know about you. I don't know what's going on in your head right now, but for your own good—clear out. Go live your life. Leave me alone."

I end the call. On the Nano Pal's screen, the dancing specter's tendrils are whip-thin braids. At least destroying it would be a form of resolution. I raise the meat tenderizer and catch sight of my face in the gleaming silver of the coffee maker, stretched like putty in the curves of the machine. The wrongness is breathtaking. I'm a distorted statue, poised with hammer raised high. Some kind of Soviet propaganda sculpture, Brutalist and hewn from the grayest rock imaginable. Yet I can't get myself to bring the hammer down. The Nano Pal is evidence, the first link in the fucked-up chain that led me to Matt's computer, to his connection with Kyle Portnoy. The icy needle digs inside my skull, the ball bearing quivers, and I grit my teeth against the deep freeze in my temples and the heat in my lacerated wrists. I can't help but lose myself in the little oval screen. Of particular interest is the creature's face. What I had first seen as a total blank, a pronounced lack of features, is actually a loose sketch of something almost human. It comes and goes like a video game glitch, an overlay, a blink.

The air around me.

The crinkle of nonexistent plastic.

The wavering of form in the mirror.

The oily tendrils twining up my arm, guiding my knife hand with great competence and glee.

Specter, creature, *thing*—it's not dancing, I conclude. It's *swimming.* And this swimmer, birthed in blood or something worse, wants to be known. It wants me to recognize it. Port-noy's words come back to me: *it knows what ive done and it wants me to see, it wants to know everything its always hungry.* On the screen, the swimmer twirls and capers. It grants me another flash of last Friday night—a slit in the meat of a thick upper lip, the tip of a knife driving through the gumline, splitting teeth...

I didn't mean to scare you.

I bring the tenderizer down on the Nano Pal, and its insides skitter across the counter. The screen is webbed with cracks. Quiet, blank, dead.

THE FOURTH
VISITATION

19

Matt doesn't come home. Instead, he texts me. The PR crisis with his client in Shanghai has become a full-blown clusterfuck. As the consultant to the team assigned to un-fuck it, he will have to spend the night at his client's Manhattan office. He sends a string of coffee emojis, apologizes profusely, and ends with a heart.

I try to remember the last time Matt had to work late and come up empty. Here's what I do recall: in the past month he took a sick day for an early tee time with some Stanford buddies, worked from home two Fridays in a row to binge-watch *Game of Thrones*, and attended a three-day industry conference in Miami from which he sent me a barrage of poolside photos.

Now that I know that Matt is capable of lying about things of much greater import, "crisis in Shanghai" sounds like total bullshit. It sounds like a flimsy cover story for a crisis of a different sort. I wonder if the client in question is Alverion Pharmaceuticals. I'm gripped by paranoia, wandering from room to room, while those two remaining beers emit a low-level hum I can't drown out. For years I'd scarcely noticed

Matt's six-packs in the back of the fridge. They were like a model house prop, technically *there* without being *real* to me—the set dressing of some oh-so-clever postmodern film. Now that I've shifted them into the realm of the *real*, I can't get them out of my mind. For the first time in my life, I have a specific craving for the taste of beer, triggered by the lingering smell of the one I spilled. When I do finally manage to outpace the hum, paranoia surges: what if snooping around Matt's computer set off some kind of digital trip-wire? It's the one he uses for remote work, after all—it must be linked to his actual workplace computer somehow. What if he knows exactly what I've uncovered, and is trying to figure out what to do about it before he faces me in person?

If I sign on again, would I find any trace of the texts from Kyle Portnoy wiped from existence?

I don't dare give it a try. Besides, I remember most of them. Portnoy's despair is part of me now.

There's one line I keep coming back to, sleepless and jittery, avoiding mirrors, avoiding my son: *it knows about sharon it knows what i did*

I sit in bed with my laptop. It doesn't take long to track down the story.

Sharon Portnoy overdosed four years ago at the age of twenty-eight. Fentanyl. Survived by an aunt, a grandmother, and a husband, Kyle.

I let her die

Someone made one of those Legacy obituary pages for her, the kind where friends and relatives leave comments about the deceased. (*You came up in my facebook memories . . . Miss you so much, Shar . . . You always lit up any room you walked into . . .*) With the fervor that only teeth-grinding sleeplessness can inspire, I pursue each commenter's name as if it were a hot new lead. I track the acquaintances of Sharon Portnoy across a landscape of social media pages, message board posts, public announcements of marriages, births, deaths, arrests.

The clacking of my keyboard mutes the hum of the beers. Hours pass. My thoughts unspool along each thread of the network of names and faces radiating from the focal point of Sharon Portnoy's death. Immersing myself in the lives of people I've never met but who are all loosely connected, in different ways, to one another, it's almost—almost!—possible to lean into the pleasantly adolescent state that society's unfathomable complexity can inspire. The mounting satisfaction as a foreign social circle cracks open before you, and you begin to get weirdly invested in it. Alyssa's tattoo sleeve looks nice. New Orleans is a cool place for a honeymoon. Tom quit his job to become a rafting guide, good for him. On a normal night it might even be possible to close the laptop and drift off to sleep, buoyed by vague notions of destiny and fate. No piercing of the veil, no wicked insights—just the mild buzz of knowing that people all over the world are weaving in and out of each other's lives. A night like that sounds so peaceful right now, I can feel myself lusting after it. But on this night, peace is hard to come by. It dawns on me that the true focal point isn't Sharon Portnoy at all, but me. Kyle Portnoy's killer. I wonder if anyone will make a Legacy page for him.

Sometime later I hit a rich vein in my online stalking. Kyle Portnoy begins to show up in recent public posts alongside one of the commenters on Sharon's Legacy page. A woman named Liza Jane Foster who was Sharon Portnoy's coworker at a hair salon in Wofford Falls, a town about thirty miles northwest of Fernbeck. Liza Jane Foster looks to be about forty years old, cuts the sleeves off her numerous band shirts, and doesn't seem to give a shit that her dark roots are showing even though she works at a hair salon. She's got the tanned-hide pallor of a heavy indoor smoker, yet her teeth are brilliantly white and straight. There are photographs from last year of Kyle Portnoy moving into her ramshackle house, carrying boxes and an end table over the threshold. I scroll through more recent shots of the two of them at a barbecue. They're both drinking Dr Pepper while everyone else drinks beer.

I cross-reference real estate listings for "Wofford Falls" with "Liza Jane Foster," but nothing comes up. Maybe the house has always been in her family, or maybe she rents it. After $79.99 and five minutes on one of those shady people-finder sites, I've got the current address and telephone number of Liza Jane Foster. 117 Farm-to-Market Road, Wofford Falls. I Street View the place and confirm it's the same house that Kyle Portnoy moved into last year, bird's-egg blue siding faded to a pale watercolor wash and a sagging front porch with a sofa and a swing.

I close the laptop and stretch out on the bed. It's just past four in the morning. I have to be up in two hours to get Danny ready for school. I close my eyes. I don't bother to set an alarm—I know I won't sleep anyway. My head is throbbing. I consider the beers, imagine myself getting up out of bed, going quietly into the hallway, down the stairs to the kitchen. I savor the fantasy of opening up the refrigerator door. I curl the fingers of my right hand around the ice-cold bottle.

Around the handle of the knife.

Around the bottle.

There are no more knives. The knives are gone. I wonder where he hid them. I imagine Matt digging a hole in the middle of the woods, lit cinematically by the headlights of his car, bugs flitting busily through the beams. Dumping a bag full of sharp objects, filling in the hole with the rusty shovel that leans against the wall at the back of the garage. I watch him as he walks out of frame and starts the car as the camera stays focused on the filled-in hole, mounded like a fresh grave. The light dims as the car backs up, then vanishes completely as the car turns and fades into the distance. The forest is pitch black, silent and still—but it's only a moment before the night is shot through with a deeper blackness. The swimmer has entered the frame, a presence so devoid of light that it's somehow silhouetted against the dark trees. It begins to grow and change.

I am awed by the swimmer's tragedy as I watch it unfurl itself. I recognize the confident slither, the aquatic grace, from the oily tendrils that guided my knife hand. Yet there's something halting at its core, a blinkered impression in the deep wooded night. The same fluctuation I've seen in motor-mouthed addicts, know-it-alls whose desperation to impress with togetherness belies an obvious fragmentation. Lost lives patched together with tape and frayed wire. Cries for help flung from confused origins, the smell of some Victorian-era sickness spritzed with cloying perfume to mask the imminence of death.

From this swirl of ink, the swimmer rises before me— magnificent, yes, and yet puzzled by its own existence and cravings it doesn't understand. Now it's so much more whole than the dancing, unlikely image on the screen. A density of pure absence from which trees bend away. I think of silk rubbing on silk as it twines up through the branches. Around its weird density, impressions solidify. There's complicity with my world in its movements—it feels everything, strives for acceptance, and learns from what it touches. And it touches everything. There are so many limbs reaching up through the night. I'm most interested in its core—the writhing rat king where the whip-arms coalesce—but that's hidden deep in the night. It slithers before me, preening, growing against the trees, stretching to reach for Matt's receding car in kinship.

Once, long ago, I ran hand-in-hand through the woods with a girl whose name might have been Melanie. The two of us were best friends that night, and afterward I never saw her again. This memory, bounding context-free and so, so high in pursuit of some whim—a kiss that I had completely forgotten about until right now—strikes me as more meaningful than anything the straight world has ever offered me.

The swimmer's existence echoes my own. I begin to cry for the person I lost—the girl I used to be, whose raw nerves tingled as they scraped against the world as it really was. What is the swimmer, I think as I watch it twist itself into shapes that mimic the branches and leaves that surround it—clinging to their undersides and pouring darkly through cracks in the bark—what is the swimmer but a declaration of self I cast into the void long ago, echoing back to show me what I've become? Darkness is coalescing into *something* and that something is the person I used to be, looming, eyeballing me from the tops of the trees, bent at an impossible angle in judgment of the fucking *yuppie* I've turned into. The swimmer knows exactly who I am and

it knows what ive done and it wants me to see

I sit up in bed, clawing at the sweaty sheets. Morning light sears my eyelids. I blink away a gummy crust. The alarm clock says 8:07.

I come fully alert in a split second.

Danny.

I rush out of the bedroom, down the hall, and into his room, only to find it empty. The bed is neatly made, hospital corners tucked in just like Matt taught him. His backpack is gone. Downstairs in the kitchen, there's a bowl and a spoon in the sink. I grip the edges of the counter. A faint odor of stale beer hangs in the air. I remind myself that Danny's eleven years old. He's fully capable of waking up, getting dressed, eating cereal, and catching the bus without me prodding him. This is just more proof that I'm raising a reliable kid with a good heart. But I can't help thinking that he didn't bother to open my bedroom door to shake me awake and say goodbye because he can't bring himself to look at my face.

I catch my reflection in the coffee machine. The needle slides deeper into my skull. The edges of the kitchen are suffused in crawling darkness, something I dragged out of the woods and into the real world. I blink away the residue of my dream and blank my mind as best I can.

Shower. Clothes. Car keys.

Half an hour later I'm taking the off-ramp to Wofford Falls. The day is crisp and clear. Thick pines crowd Farm-to-Market Road and autumn light spills along the pavement in brilliant camouflage. The houses are spaced far apart and set back from the street. Mostly all I see is mailboxes, and 117 is no exception. The mailbox is a homespun contraption, all hammered tin and carved wood. Vague steampunk overtones, probably unintentional. I turn down a gravel driveway that winds uphill and ends at the front porch of the house. I park next to a boxy old Chevy two-door the color of a ripe plum.

Outside with my feet on the gravel, I hesitate just long

enough for doubts to surface. Liza Jane Foster might not be
home. She might not open the door for me. She might open
it just wide enough to stick a shotgun in my face.

I have to chance it. I can't get Kyle Portnoy out of my
head. I need to untangle this thread before Matt gets home
so I can confront him with more than just a string of enigmatic texts and the name of one of his clients. Those things
are so easily justified, explained away, downplayed into
oblivion until I'm once again the one doubting myself.

The porch creaks. Something scuttles underneath the
boards. There's no bell so I knock. Half a minute later, Liza
Jane Foster opens the door.

For the first time in several days, another person meets my
eyes without looking away.

20

Shot of vodka and a Bud Light."

The bartender is a moonfaced, hollow-eyed woman in her late forties. Big hoop earrings dangle to her shoulders. One of her hands is slightly larger than the other. There's malevolence in the way she pours. The barstool is angular and uncomfortable—a prank of a seat. The interior of this place, the Cat's Paw, barely tolerates my presence. The walls bend away from my glare as if they know what I've done. A bigmouth bass by the bathrooms is warbling a mordant, drawn-out melody, a single broken note of lamentation.

I steady my hand and down my first shot in nine years without a second thought, before my beer is even placed in front of me. There's nothing left to think about. There's only what's in my head—the horror in Liza Jane's attic—and the urge to get it the fuck out by any means necessary. The bartender plunks down the beer. Her nails are chewed to frayed and ragged bits. I take a long sip to chase the vodka's awful passage down my throat, and the burn subsides.

The Cat's Paw is mercifully dim and smells of urinal cakes. A handful of customers are seated in a booth. They look like grad students. Their table is littered with torn-off labels and shredded napkins, as if they're building a nest. Bottles glint dully in an overhead stained-glass lamp.

As the vodka hits my stomach and spreads, I'm wracked by a full-body shiver that starts in my thighs and works its way up. My heartbeat is uncomfortably noticeable.

I should cry, I think. Or go into the bathroom like a character in a movie and primal-scream my guts out. Punch the mirror, sneer at myself in the shattered glass. Instead, I pour half the beer down my throat to drown any spike in emotion. It tastes stale and coppery.

Crying and screaming don't align with what I'm experiencing right now, anyway. I am here, in this bar—the first bar I came to after hauling ass out of Liza Jane's driveway, tires spitting gravel—because I want to *banish* feeling, not *express* it. The bartender jabs her fingers against the screen of her phone. I make some kind of noise to get her attention and she pours another shot without looking at me. Down the hatch. I gag at the rubbing-alcohol acuteness of the burn and take a swallow of beer. The second shot brings with it the early stirrings of...

What?

Not regret, not exactly. More like the matter-of-fact notion that the mechanics of sobriety will have to be reset. In meetings, I can no longer lay claim to nine years. Tomorrow I will get up and start over with one day. In the wake of this dismal thought comes a hazy sort of acceptance. Surely what I've just been through is an extenuating circumstance.

Nine years.

One day.

Everything bleeds into everything else—the fact that I was once a degenerate creature, a junkie on the margins, and that the old me can be set off diametrically against the person I am now, the "mother" and "partner," has never seemed so patently false.

The vodka has folded time back on itself and I know that I love this—the act of getting fucked up, the sensation of being fucked up, the things I think while fucked up—more than I have ever loved being a mother. I drain the beer and order a second.

The bigmouth bass ceases its strangled warbling. After an excruciating moment of silence, the jukebox kicks on. It's a Tom Petty song that I have never heard before, a B-side or a rarity or a song that has not previously existed. Poor, dead Tom Petty. I recognize snatches of melody, but they're quickly subsumed. It's a patchwork, a hybrid version, a dissonant collage of Tom Petty songs that should not be. The grad students laugh, the bartender takes up her phone and scowls.

Things are so much easier to deal with when your goal for the day is to get fucked up. The world narrows. Even when I had to score for Trevor and me both because he was out pulling a gift card scam or pawning stolen sunglasses, there was a single-minded clarity to the day. Get powder, cook, shoot, ride the rush, level off with booze, fuck (if he gets it up), gobble benzos, pass out, repeat. And then Danny came along.

I suck down the second beer. *Go away, Danny.*

A third beer-and-shot combo arrives unbidden. The bartender, no fool, hears the unspoken *keep 'em coming.* A few more sips and my phone comes out. This is how it began so long ago, back when I could still call it fun. Let alcohol dictate the next level of oblivion. Shore up your defenses against that sober-minded scold—that little voice—who gets off on drilling shame down so deep it feels like you've been rooted in it forever.

The third shot brings with it rationalization: tomorrow I'll be starting over at one day. No matter what I do right now, I can't change that fact. So, I might as well not waste these precious hours on light beer and vodka. I need something to mute the hostility of objects, and my phone is already in my hand. I pull up the log of recent calls and tap the number of the last one I received, yesterday afternoon, right after I sent Danny from the kitchen.

Go away, Danny.

At the back of my mind, the nagging creeps up—alarm at what I'm doing, distant and faint, a siren across the void. I swallow beer. *Fuck off.*

Trevor answers after half a ring. "Sydney."

I don't bother to explain or walk back yesterday's *leave me alone.* The cheeky coded language we used to share comes back naturally. "I need to get organized. You got anything that could help me out?"

There's a long pause. Finally, he comes back on the line. "Tell me where you are."

"Cat's Paw. Wofford Falls."

"Sit tight."

I catch sight of myself in the mirror behind the bar and a sense of loathing so profound I can see it in the air almost makes me vomit. Look at the way my hand curls around the glass. It would be so easy to smash it against the bar and take the jagged edge to the nearest grad student's face. I can see him in the mirror, tucked into the booth, all thick-rimmed glasses and jowls. His fat cheeks would dangle like meat on hooks, slit along the curve of the bone.

I close my eyes. Nothing changes. Open or closed, it doesn't matter.

I can't unsee what I've seen.

21

Liza Jane Foster doesn't know who I am. How could she? Yet on the walk from my car to the front door I'd imagined that she would, somehow. That her face would betray some immediate indication of how this visit is going to go for me.

"Can I help you?" I'd expected her to be weathered and exhausted, but her eyes are bright and alert. If I'm being honest with myself, I had her pegged as white trash. I try to stay mindful of judgmental thoughts. It's a trap that people with serious recovery time fall into, doling out holier-than-thou points of view from atop our sober high horses, conveniently forgetting our tenure among the scheming junkie underclass. In my defense, scrolling through a stranger's social media kicks up first impressions and not much else.

"Um," I say. An auspicious beginning. "Hi."

She narrows her eyes. "You a cop?"

The question catches me off guard. I'm completely unprepared for an encounter with this woman. The gulf between us grows in my mind all at once. How am I possibly going to explain myself?

"No." *I'm a copywriter, ha ha*, I almost add, which would be a truly asinine thing to say. "My name is Sydney Burgess."

Liza Jane blinks. "Okay." She glances over my shoulder at my car, a Civic hybrid, and then back to me. There's no hint of fear in her eyes. I'm absurdly grateful that she looks me full in the face without flinching. "I'm getting ready for work, so."

"I'm sorry," I say. "I know this is weird. I didn't know what else to do."

"Just, what is it that you want?"

"I knew Kyle," I say.

At this, she looks me up and down. Something crosses her mind, then she dismisses it with a little shake of her head. "You know what happened, then, I guess."

"Yeah."

She looks again at my car. "He do your roof or something?"

"My roof?"

"He was a roofer. At least he was when I met him."

"Oh. No, he didn't."

"You from Sacred Heart?"

This gives me a jolt I don't manage to hide very well. Sacred Heart is Matt's church. I consider this for a moment. "Sort of," I say.

She sighs. "Look, I don't mean to be a bitch, and I do appreciate what you people have been doing, but I'm just about up to my ears in casseroles and lasagnas. It's just gonna go bad."

I show my empty hands. "Don't worry, I didn't bring you any food." I feel like I'm in a fog. How long is she going to indulge this absurd conversation? "But I do need to talk to you. Can I come in for a second?"

She hesitates.

"It's important," I add.

"All right," she says, stepping aside and holding the door open. "But like I said, I got work."

"I won't keep you," I say. Inside, the house is airy and neat. The theme from the exterior—mild disrepair offset with a brand-new porch swing—is carried throughout. It's an old Yankee farmsteader's house from the nineteenth century, a staple of the rural areas around here. The interior looks like it was last touched during the Reagan administration, all wood paneling and wall-to-wall carpets, but most of the furniture looks modern and well-kept. It's probably been in her family for a long time.

She gestures to a sofa and sits across from me in an armchair. I recognize the end table between us from a photo of Kyle Portnoy in the backyard, sanding it by hand. Since then, it's been painted and varnished. Liza Jane lights up a menthol cigarette, takes a long drag, and thumb-flicks ash into the overflowing glass ashtray on the table.

"Kyle made that," she says, indicating the end table. "He could make anything he put his mind to, once upon a time."

There's a massive Thomas Kinkade print in a heavy wooden frame hanging above the armchair. Liza Jane's head is directly beneath a glowing window.

I shift in my seat. "I'm sorry about Kyle," I say. It seems like the proper way to begin.

"Thank you." Liza Jane sits with her elbows on her knees, leaning forward. She turns her head to exhale into a long sigh. "I've been thinking, you know, all the shit we live through—shit we get past and shit that drags us down—in the end none of it matters if you go out like he did." She shakes her head. "People remember you as the guy who got killed breaking into somebody's house. One of the dregs of society who got what he had coming to him." She sucks hard on her cigarette, blows smoke. "I can sit here and talk about how he fought to stay clean harder than anybody I've ever known after Sharon died. Harder than I ever did in my life, that's for goddamn sure. I can tell you about the time he chased off this scumfuck kid throwing rocks at these two stray kittens, how he brought the kittens home and nursed 'em." She laughs bitterly. "Like anybody gives a shit. Every dead asshole's got an animal rescue story somewhere in their past, right? Redemption after the fact and so forth. Who the fuck cares. Doesn't change anything."

She delivers the majority of this looking off into the middle distance. Then, abruptly, she stabs out her cigarette in the ashtray and gives me a shy glance. "Fuck. I'm sorry. It's been a weird time."

"I understand," I say. "Probably more than you know." Inside, I cringe at my words.

She frowns. "Did you go to meetings over at Sacred Heart or did you know him from *church* church?"

"Um," I say, "would you mind if I bummed a smoke from you? Sorry if that's out of line." I try to smile apologetically but I can't tell what my mouth is doing. It's probably grotesque.

She shrugs. "Help yourself."

I draw a Newport out of the pack on the table. Liza Jane tosses me a lighter. My first drag of a cigarette in many years goes down surprisingly smoothly. In seconds I'm lightheaded. I take another drag, let the smoke fill me up, exhale.

"Have you ever heard of Alverion Pharmaceuticals?" I ask.

"Nope," she says. "Why, they make Xanax? I'll take a couple bars if you got 'em."

"I don't know. Never mind."

Liza Jane's eyes go to a burnished gold clock with ornate wrought-iron hands. I rack my brain for some way to get what I want out of her without telling her who I am. My heart pounds. I don't think I can do this. If the situation were reversed, and someone who'd killed a person I loved showed up unannounced at my door one morning, what would I do? Liza Jane doesn't deserve to be confronted by the instrument of her pain. I'm on the verge of making some excuse and retreating to my car when I feel it.

The oppressive pall that hangs over my guest room, borne on the bluish haze that clings to Liza Jane's ceiling and curls slowly through the morning light. The precise emanation of the bloodstain—a murmuring shadow that takes up too much space in a room. The opposite of anything vibrant and alive, crowding my thoughts, edging out hope. The wrongness of the air.

First, I think I've brought it with me into her house like a bedbug infestation. The great unfurling creature from my dream, clinging to me, stowing itself away, then scattering to hide in Liza Jane's baseboard heaters and the cracks in her walls' wooden panels. I'm gripped by shame.

"Are you okay?" she says.

"Sorry." I take a deep breath. "This is going to sound crazy, but do you feel that?" I point to the air above my head. "Like, something wrong."

She regards me curiously, then sits back in her chair and crosses her arms. "Who are you?" Her voice is different now. There's a crystallization in her tone, a new toughness. The kind of wall that goes up when you're called out on something you know to be true.

My cigarette burns down between my fingers. I lean forward in my seat. "You *do* feel it," I say.

A tightness passes across her face, a screwing-up of her features, and I think, in this moment, she realizes exactly who I am.

I brace myself. I don't know this woman at all, or how coiled up she might be inside. I want to get to my feet. At least then I'll be standing up and not trapped on a sofa if she leaps across the end table her dead boyfriend made to claw at my eyes with her long, gel-manicured nails. *It happened so fast.*

But all she does is light up another cigarette. I watch her smoke half of it with her eyes closed while I sit there gripping the arm of the sofa.

"I identified the body, you know," she says quietly. "Kyle's body."

She opens her eyes slowly, as if she's waking from a deep sleep. There's that middle-distance stare again. "The coroner didn't want to let me. Said they'd already done dental records and so forth. *It wasn't necessary,* he said. *Maybe not for you,* I told him. But you know what I said when he pulled back the sheet?" She drops her half-smoked cigarette into the ashtray. "I said *that's not Kyle.* Because it wasn't. It was just some *thing* there on the fucking slab. It looked like a bunch of old meat they threw out the back of a butcher shop."

My entire body tingles. A knot forms in my stomach, rope drenched in seawater, heavy and cold. There's a ringing in my ears, a chorus of mosquitoes. I could stare into the bloodstain for a hundred years without feeling so *confronted* by what I'd done.

She looks me dead in the eyes and says one word. "Why?"

He was going to kill me. I could tell her that, I think. Or perhaps the more generic *It was self-defense.* Or, maybe, fuck it: *it happened so fast.*

All around me, the thickening air quivers. A sigh of relief, to be reminded of what we've done. A languorous bask in the warmth of the violence. I wonder if Liza Jane feels it too.

"I don't know," I say. "I can't remember doing it."

Her lips are pressed together and bloodless. Her makeup, half-applied. I've interrupted her morning somewhere between mascara and lipstick. A tiny dot mars the flesh of her left nostril—the remnant of a piercing. I picture a sparkly little stud. The curiosity on her face is shaded with hostility. Liza Jane has a look I know well: that thin veneer of an acceptable demeanor for the straight world, for servicing customers and navigating polite society. It drops away so quickly and must be maintained with practice. I see it when I look in the mirror. Liza Jane carries hers so close to the surface, ready to be unleashed. Stick-and-poke crosses are pricked into both index fingers, just below the knuckles. She folds her arms. It was a mistake to come here. I should leave this place, I think. Now.

"Kyle used to say the same thing about Sharon," she says. "Until a few months ago, when it started to come back to him a little at a time. Dreams, I figured. Sobriety fucks with you that way."

it gives her back to me in pieces. it wants me to see.

I don't nod knowingly. We are way past commiseration.

"Kyle used to say a lot of things," she says. "Talk a lot of shit he'll never get to talk anymore."

"I'm sorry," I say. It's so painfully inadequate that I want to liquefy myself and ooze between the cushions. Part of me *wills* her to come across the table and hit me in the face, to do anything but sit there regarding me with a sort of nervy calm, which is what she's doing now.

The room seems to get smaller, the fog a little thicker.

My eyes water. I'm afraid that if I glance up, I'll see the dark underbelly of the stain, dripping like black molasses from the ceiling, a tendril swinging down to brush lightly against my forehead, eyelids, nose, lips.

"You know," she says carefully, "you remind me a little of him."

I swallow. My throat is very dry. "How so?"

I know what she's going to say, and I'm frightened. I don't want to hear it. Her lip curls into a cold smile. "Your face."

"I shouldn't have come here," I say. The cigarette smoke in my lungs and in the air turns my voice into something it's not. "I haven't been sleeping," I mutter. "I'm not myself."

"Kyle never slept, either."

I get up to leave. My body feels impossibly heavy. "I'm sorry," I say again.

"Wait."

Run, I think. But I don't. I can't.

"I want to show you something."

"That's okay. You have to go to work, I have to—"

She bolts up out of the chair. "You need to see it."

I don't care what it is. I reach for several thoughts at once and miss them all. I can barely remember why I came to this house. I shake my head.

She steps around the table and puts her hands firmly on my arms. "I think you owe me that much. Don't you?"

"Okay," I say, distantly relieved that she's setting terms. If there is something I can give her, then I will give it. I will leave here knowing I did that, at least.

"It's upstairs."

I hesitate. "What is it?"

"Something he was working on. I haven't touched it. It's important to me that you see it."

She ushers me toward a tan-carpeted staircase. Prickly heat breaks out across my back as I wait for the blunt object to crack my ribs from behind, or the knife to slide between my shoulder blades. But nothing happens. I glance behind me. Liza Jane is standing so close I can hear her breathing. I put my hand on the wooden banister and climb the stairs.

At the top is a hallway. I count four closed doors, a crucifix on the wall threaded with a dry palm frond from some long-ago Palm Sunday, and a framed map of the Florida Keys. There's paneling on the walls and across the ceiling.

"This way," she says. Together we walk down the hall toward another staircase. The faintest whisper floats through the back of my mind. Gibberish. The air up here is greasy, and my skin is coated in a damp film.

I have to go now, I think, but a deeper part of me that doesn't translate desire to language urges me on. It knows that I want to see.

No, that's not entirely accurate. It wants me to see. This does not ease my fear, but coats it in protective reassurance. Or is it simply the hand of the jailer guiding me down the cellblock corridor? Either way, I have come to the right place. We pass the crucifix, and up close I notice that the palm frond is threaded with dark veins of decay. My eyes are drawn to it and I nearly stop short. There is recognition here, and the palm frond rustles lightly in an unfelt breeze. This small remnant, no more than a nod from the magnificence that regarded me from above the trees—the thing that knows exactly who I am. The palm frond extends down the hall, a shadow of indication, a shifting of the dimness. There can be no turning back.

"Up here," Liza Jane says. We've come to this second staircase. Half of one, at least—it's only five steps up to the third floor. There's a door at the top. She opens it for me, and I step into darkness.

"Let me get the light," she says. The door slams behind me. I lunge for the doorknob. It won't turn. Locked. Part of me understands the wrongness of that: what kind of door locks from the outside?

One that's keeping something in.

I pound my fist on the door. "Liza Jane!"

I can hear her ragged breathing on the stairs. I know she's standing right outside.

I grab the doorknob with two hands and try to wrench it open, but it won't budge. I ram my shoulder against the door. It's no use.

I turn and behold the darkness of the attic room. A strange humidity troubles my face and hands. I take one halting step, then another, stretching an arm out in front of me. My hand brushes a dangling string, the kind attached to a bare bulb. I give it a tug. The bulb flickers once and the room makes itself known to me: a throbbing memorial to regret, a requiem played by shrieking ghouls.

22

The attic room echoes down every sound inside the Cat's Paw and gathers about the hooded wraith who steps through the door. Stim-addict wasting, or some other form of attrition, has eaten away at Trevor's figure. In the same way I see the teenager that Danny is going to be, I see the gnawed-at bits of Trevor's former self. Some notion of *fathers and sons* comes and goes and all I'm left with is Trevor, this Trevor, any connection to Danny impossibly remote. His shoulders slump, the hood of his sweatshirt tents monkishly over his forehead. His facial scars, half-shadowed, are a garden of swollen veins. They've peeled back his upper lip, sent a web of harlequin ruin up his nose and cheek, and rippled the skin around his dim right eye.

He catches sight of me and crosses the room, moving with the slow, slouching gait of the permanently wary. Hairless knees peek from his torn jeans.

The bartender glances up, then quickly looks away. Not polite to stare, better to ignore someone entirely. The grad students are several pitchers in, feeding the jukebox. Celine Dion begins to sing, and they crack up at their own selection.

The enormity of what lies between us blooms, lush and heady as childlike wonder. I'm curious if he feels it, too. If he feels anything at all.

He shuffles up next to me, hands thrust into the pockets of his hoodie. I turn on my barstool. He averts his good eye.

What do you say, in a moment like this, for which there is no precedent?

Alcohol takes over. "You just gonna stand there?"

He barely moves, but I detect a flinch. "Do you want me to sit down?"

In person his voice is distant and unreal, like he's playing an old recording of himself from inside his hoodie.

"We're both here. You might as well."

With what seems like too much effort, he plants himself next to me and rests his elbows on the bar. A cloying musk clings to him—Swisher Sweets. He makes no move to order a drink. A timid creature has been substituted for the kind of man I was expecting. One who peers into basement windows after midnight.

"Let me get this out of the way," I begin. There's a belligerence to my tone that I try to get in check. I turn to the bartender and make a peace offering. "Can he get a margarita?"

Trevor coughs. "I don't drink those anymore."

The bartender puts her hands on her hips. "Just a beer," Trevor says. "Whatever she's having."

The bartender pulls the tap. When the beer arrives, sloshing foam, Trevor leans in and slurps the overflow. I watch him purse his lips and swallow. His mouth won't close all the way.

"You can't just show up like this," I tell him.

He leans back and a low hiss escapes as he runs his hand across his mouth. "You called me," he says from deep within the hood.

"I'm talking about here, in Fernbeck, after all this time. What the fuck, Trevor? Outside Danny's *school*? Do you not get how wrong that is? How am I supposed to react to that?"

That hiss again—a sigh, I think. Air escaping in some unnatural way, rerouted by trauma. "I told you. I never meant to scare you."

I lean forward to see more of him. "You don't scare me. But you have to understand that Danny has a life here now."

He shifts his good eye toward me and takes in my own scars. Then he lifts the glass to his mouth with a trembling hand. I wait for him to sip and set the glass back down. "I was never going to try to talk to him, or anything like that."

"You're just a peeper these days, then."

He coughs again, dry and harsh at first. The hacking stirs something wet in his throat. He reaches into his pocket, comes up with a crumpled paper towel, and presses it to his mouth. A moment later it's soaked in blood. He replaces it in his pocket. Then he pulls back his hood and turns to me, looking me full in the face for the first time. Not a wisp of hair sprouts from the lunar landscape of his head. The skin is stretched taut across his cheekbones. He glistens with an unhealthy, almost plastic sheen.

"What I am is a walking carcinoma."

The dread in my heart has nothing to do with the nagging little voice. It chokes a single word out of me, stupid and obvious. "Cancer?"

Now Trevor sets himself to getting down a good swallow of his beer. It dribbles down his chin and he wipes the lower part of his face with a sleeve. I slide a stack of bar napkins in front of him, but he ignores them.

"Metastasized," he says. Part of his mouth stretches to one side, describing a kind of smile. "All the shit that should've made me kick it a hundred times over, and now this is what's gonna do it." He shrugs. "I could still get there first myself. I haven't decided about that yet."

Liza Jane's words come back to me; the impromptu eulogy delivered from her living room couch.

All the shit we live through—shit we get past and shit that drags us down—in the end none of it matters if you go out like he did.

Earlier today it had seemed like a folksy truth, but now it hits me like this: how *do* you have to go out for any of it to matter?

"Well," I manage to say. "Fuck."

At the same time, the dread in my heart deepens and I wonder—shamefully, I know—if he really did bring me what I asked for.

"How long do you have?" I ask.

"Couple weeks. A month. Maybe two at most."

His good eye, which had been roving along the mirror, turns to settle on my face. He screws up his countenance— another flinch?—and lowers his gaze to his glass. "I never planned on coming here. But it just hit me all at once that I'd never seen him"—the eye flicks to me again—"not since that night. Never even laid eyes on him. On Danny. I just thought..." He shakes his head. "I don't know what I thought. But I did get to see him. I came back a few days after you caught me there and watched the two of you walk out together."

And? I think. I don't know what else I want him to say. Tie a neat bow around this episode in his ruined life with a simple profundity. *What a beautiful boy. He looks like a great kid. You guys seem happy. It happened so fast.*

With Trevor next to me silently radiating lost years, another vodka shot folds time. There was a regular at the

Rusty Nail, a dive where I used to cop on occasion, who called me Kidney. An old guy with a wheezing laugh who thought that was the funniest goddamn thing. Kidney. I remember, too, that this same doomed old man once showed me his penis. He barked out *Hey, Kidney!* and I glanced over, and he was waggling this shriveled old dick, thwacking it against the bar. At the time I just laughed. *Fucking geriatric creep.* But now this long-buried memory strikes me as an artifact of a time when even the most impulsive and disgusting acts were imbued with quasi-mystical significance.

Suddenly Trevor says, "Does Danny want to be anything, yet?"

I'm startled by his abrupt return to conversation. "What?"

"When he grows up. Is he old enough to want to be anything?"

"Oh. Right now, he wants to be a programmer. He went to coding camp over the summer."

"Computers," Trevor says. He puts his hood back up, pulls it low over his forehead. "That's good."

Liza Jane's voice echoes in my head. *Redemption after the fact and so forth. Who the fuck cares. Doesn't change anything.*

I swallow beer. Go away, Liza Jane.

"Can I ask you something?" I try to keep my tone soft, leave the air of accusation out of it. What's the point of that now?

"Might as well. We're both here."

"What were you doing at my basement window in the middle of the night?"

That sputtering wheeze of a laugh again. "You wouldn't believe me if I told you."

"Try me."

His eye shifts to my face. "Are you okay?"

I lift my beer like I'm giving a toast. "Do I seem okay to you?"

"It seems like you're in two places at once." He shakes his head. "I'm not explaining it right." He regards my face for as long as he can before going back to his drink. "It's like you're blurry. Trailing part of yourself."

"Yeah, well." I don't bother to elaborate. *The air around me is wrong.* I gulp beer. It goes down like water now. "My window."

A quick hissing sigh. He picks up a bar napkin and his thin fingers begin to shred it. "I heard a noise. It reminded me of you—of us—but I couldn't remember why. Then it hit me, and I followed it. I got in my truck and I followed it all the way to your house. To that window. And there you were, inside. The whole thing felt like a dream."

I take it you were high? is what I could say. He'll admit that he was, that the world had long ago spun off its axis, that it felt like a dream because everything's felt like a dream since he was nineteen years old. *Well,* I could say, *that pretty much explains that.*

But as part of some last-ditch hedge against what I saw in Liza Jane's attic, I don't lead him down that path. Instead, I place a hand on his to stop his methodical destruction of the napkin. And I let him into my life.

"It was the Nano Pal song," I say.

His eye goes wide, and he pulls his hand away and coughs into a fist. He takes a moment to compose himself.

"Yeah. The one they play when they've been fed." The eye narrows. "I've had more crazy than not-crazy shit happen to me, but how did you know that?" The eye closes tight, then opens and trains itself on the napkin scraps. "How is this real?"

"It's real," I confirm. The drinks I've been downing since I walked in catch up with me in a queasy rush. Drunkenness opens my heart. "I've got this thing with me now," I say. "This *swimmer*. At first, I was scared of it, like it was haunting me, but now I think it might be protecting me. It might just be *me*. The person I've been all along. You know?"

My own words stun me as they come out of my mouth. This realization, this matter-of-fact acceptance, never would have been possible while sober.

Something like eagerness animates his face. "It's hard to be happy in this life without accepting who you are. You can only fight it for so long."

The platitude smacks of recovery-speak, of pamphlets and group sessions.

"Is that what you did?" I say. "Accept who you are?"

"Didn't have to. I always knew I was a piece of shit." He draws a line in the condensation on the side of his glass. "Listen, I have what you want. To help you get organized."

Trevor glances at the bartender, who's filling a pitcher for the grad students. Then he shifts his eyes down to his lap, inviting me to look. He reaches into his pocket and slides out a square ziplock about the size of a Triscuit, half full of white powder.

An erotic surge begins in my legs and shoots up into the back of my neck. The anticipation is delicious. It always was. I can taste the drip—a mingling of metal and chalk, the flavor of numbness. One line to balance out the booze, one line to reframe the Cat's Paw as a womblike place. I can feel the swimmer purr with pleasure, an alto tremor in my chest. I don't know if it recognizes the peaks and valleys of serotonin and dopamine, if it's bound to my receptors, but it shares my anticipation. I let out a long throaty sigh as I sag against the bar.

"How much?" I ask.

Trevor takes my hand. He places the baggie in my empty palm and closes my fingers gently around it.

"Free for you," he says. "There's more where that came from."

23

The bulb flickers and goes out. In the dark attic room, hand on the dangling string, I'm in a pure between-state, unsure of myself. I can't feel my heartbeat. It's as if I've been frozen in the act of respiration, stilled by some incomprehensible force. With the sight of what awaits me burned into my vision, I weigh my options.

Is it better to keep myself in the dark, reeling from the flash, the bright hint of what Kyle Portnoy has wrought in this place? I could make my way back to the door, hammer it mercilessly until Liza Jane comes to her senses and lets me out. Perhaps I could bash it off its hinges now that I've seen what's here. *Adrenaline does crazy things to people.*

Or is it better to pull the string until the bulb stays lit and force myself to face the room as it truly is? There are answers in here, I'm sure, woven into the fabric of Portnoy's madness.

Of course, modern life supplies a third option. I pull my phone out of my pocket. It's a weak connection out here in the boonies, but the signal is there. I hesitate, wondering what to say. *I'm trapped in the attic that belongs to a woman whose boyfriend I killed.*

No. Don't elaborate. *I'm trapped in an attic.* It doesn't sound like much of an emergency, but it will have to do.

"I'm calling 911!" I yell so Liza Jane can hear me on the other side of the door. My voice is hollow and artificial in the darkness, as if the room has swallowed it up and sealed it. I dial and wait for the ring, but the ring never comes. No brusque, efficient operator picks up. There's only silence, and then, so faint I can barely hear it, nonsense spilling from some hushed and terrible mouth.

"Fuck!" I kill the call and pocket my phone. Then I pull the string. This time, the bulb flickers and stays lit.

The room is tucked up under the eaves, and the slopes of the ceiling meet to form the tip of an A-frame. The only piece of furniture is a single workbench pushed up against the far wall, cluttered with paints in cans and tubes, bits of gnarled wood, plastic containers, jugs of solvent, scrap metal, and old magazines. On the wall above the bench is a pegboard hung with carpentry tools. The floor is covered in sawdust and littered with shredded glossy pages and jagged shards of what looks like tin. Paint spatters the ceiling. Even dormant, these things speak to a great frenzy of creation and I can hear the hammer and the saw, taste the sour fixative, smell the pungent dust. A slick wet heat emanates from everywhere and the room is stultifying. Sweat and grease glue my shirt to my skin.

The fruits of Kyle Portnoy's labors march along the perspiring, glistening walls. They might have originated as individual pieces, but over time sculpture has merged with painting, scribbling, confession, and startlingly violent desecrations to become a single unbroken, self-lacerating fresco. A death-haunted landscape. The passions of a man urged by something he'll never understand to confront what he can't remember.

I recognize my own state of mind in Portnoy's designs, his dizzying procession of fractured memory and atonement. When Sheriff Butler brought Kyle Portnoy's file to my house, even the slightest knowledge of the man—his name, his face, his petty crimes—sent me reeling. I couldn't handle a hint of humanity, the barest sketch of the life I'd taken. Now, with his mind cracked open and sprayed across the walls of this locked room, it's as if I've been thrust into the most secret and holy aspects of his existence. I feel as though I've been fucking him ceaselessly for days on end and at the same time forcing him to spill his deepest traumas to me in excruciating detail. Kyle Portnoy is *filling me up*.

I turn slowly to take it all in. There's no clear beginning or end. His work loops around all four walls and meets itself everywhere. After a full turn I'm even more convinced that he started with the sculptures. There are fourteen of them jutting from the wall. I choose one as the "first" and approach it for a closer look. At first glance it's incomprehensible—a mosaic of unknown, withered material in service of some ungraspable whole. It's as if he attempted a 3D pointillist design with hundreds, if not thousands, of bits and pieces of shattered, deconstructed things. There are layers of nails and buttons, jagged slivers of metal and wood, and thin strips of braided leather that hang like sad cat o' nine tails or dejected willow branches.

What were you trying to capture, here, Kyle? Something I, too, have known?

My upper lip is beaded with sweat. There's a distant shout inside my head: *get the fuck out of here*. Take one of the claw hammers from the pegboard and splinter the door.

I hesitate. Like standing with the tenderizer poised to come down on the Nano Pal while its faceless animal undulates on the screen, I can't quite bring myself to sever the connection with this other state of being—at least not right away. Horror is so often predicated on fear of the unknown and the unknowable, but human beings can acclimate to almost anything, and now that I've gotten used to seeing through this oddly tinted lens, it's like a weird simulation of the life I used to lead. It's both repellant and welcoming and I love it as much as I hate it.

I skim a finger lightly down a leather strip. It doesn't feel like leather at all. It's brittle, almost *crispy*. And it's not black, either. It's a very particular shade of brown that sparks a sort of lizard-brain, gut-churning recognition. The sensation of a million skittering legs, of a mass evacuation when the light was flicked on in my mother's sticky old kitchen.

The stuff of cockroach wings, ever-so-delicately braided and filigreed.

I yank my hand back, disgusted. At the same time, I lean in almost involuntarily to study them up close. The craftsmanship—the obsession—is beyond anything I've ever seen. I feel like I'm looking at the magnum opus of some long-lost folk artist, a recluse with poor hygiene and a menial day job, a Henry Darger type. The braids are made from cockroach *parts*, not just wings. Legs and feelers, carefully detached and lovingly threaded. Exoskeletal shavings flecked off with an X-Acto knife. The bulging epicenter of the sculpture mimics the way the image boiled out of Matt's monitor. From there, the wall gradually reclaims the sculpture on all sides and the mosaic gives way to a chiaroscuro fog of black paint.

I follow haphazard shadows to the next sculpture, which drips from the wall in flaccid gloom. It looks like the petrified egg sac of an ancient spider. It brings to mind the muck of a vast bog where such a thing might live, a scorched and blasted landscape where stilt-limbed cranes crowd the skies. I don't want to get too close but find that I can't resist its pull. The surface of it is full of tiny holes. Hundreds of them, close together, evenly spaced. *Clusters* of holes. My guts flop and my head goes light. Holes in the egg sac, holes in the world. I move quickly to the next sculpture, but I can't leave the first two behind—not really. I drag their strange weather along with me, a sort of clinging damp.

The third sculpture is an escalation. Nails and safety pins from the mosaic and putrescent goo from the egg sac are joined with a clear secretion. There are symbols hacked into it, whirling gibberish that winds along the wall. Words dripped and scrawled in loping arcs, angular symbols that mean nothing to me. I stare at this one for a long time, trying to decide what's wrong with it. After a while it hits me: I can't put it into focus. It's as if I'm crossing my eyes, but I know I'm not. It's like looking through a pair of offset windowpanes with glass of different thicknesses. I feel the distortion as an emptiness in my belly.

A realization dawns, a memory of Sacred Heart. Once I picked up Matt after some church event when his car was at the mechanic. Rather than wait for him in the parking lot, I went inside. The event was in the basement and the main hall of worship was completely empty. I strolled around. What caught my eye were the sculptures on the wall. Smooth wooden representations of Jesus at his crucifixion. They were arranged to tell the story of his journey: Jesus bearing the cross, collapsing under its weight, various robe-clad companions helping him up. *The stations of the cross*, Matt told me later when I asked about it.

Here, in this stifling attic, Kyle Portnoy has created the stations of his own disintegration.

As I consider this, the shadows that surround the sculptures seem to *ungather* like a bunched-up cloak unfurling. The attic room darkens.

Words come out of nowhere and hang in the air. A man's voice. Portnoy's voice from the night I killed him.

Why'd you have to come home

A swimming, writhing darkness obscures the room and then begins to shrink away toward the corners. Familiar tendrils of blackness unveil elements of my guest room, all of them indistinct. The swimmer hesitates—I can sense it thinking, wondering if now is the right time to give this back to me. (*All this time it has been protecting me—shielding me—oh yes.*)

Please, I implore it. I have to know. I have to see.

My guest room takes shape. I can hear Portnoy's frantic cry as he kicks in the door and it slams into the toppled dresser. His voice comes through loud and clear in the suburban quiet. I see his eyes in the narrow space between the door and the frame.

I don't go to the window.

I don't go to the window because he's inside the room.

He's inside the room because it only takes him one more hard kick to bash the dresser out of the way, giving him enough space to squeeze inside. There's no time for me to escape.

I'm making a panicked noise, high-pitched and impossible to describe. My heart is hammering, and my adrenaline is pushing me up to my tiptoes as I face him.

Portnoy is holding the knife. My wrists are bloody from Matt's racing spikes and my hands are empty.

Goddammit, lady, why'd you have to come home

He doesn't want to do this. He doesn't want to be here,

in this room with me, not at all. I can smell his body odor, the sharp and fearful sweat. For a brief moment we both stand on the precipice of something—he could turn around and leave, I could beg for my life. I could rush the door, he could cut my throat.

Just like that, he steps off the precipice, lunging forward and thrusting the knife straight out toward my belly. He's going to gut me first, then finish me off.

I have been in street fights before. Wild junkie melees on the fringes of a homeless camp. I've been in a few bar fights, too. Once, I smashed a chair across a drunk man's flubby back until he let go of my friend's throat. But I have never taken a self-defense or martial arts class, except for one free trial of cardio kickboxing. I have no idea how to do what I am doing now (what I have already done).

As the knife comes toward me, I step forward, practically delivering myself to the slaughter. Except at the last moment, I sidestep past him and grab his wrist with both hands in one fluid motion, using my momentum to turn his arm in a way it should not be turned. As if I've flipped a switch hidden in his wrist, his fist pops open and the knife falls from his grip.

I go down on one knee and spin around, scooping up the knife by the handle and holding it out almost gently, as if I'm offering it back to him. As I turn, I catch out of the corner of my eye the darkness swirling at my back. And there! Thin tendrils of gorgeous jet-black shimmer up my arm and guide it, so that the knife is in precisely the right spot to slice deep into his thigh as he lunges toward the place I was a moment ago. A spurt of blood-mist speckles the air. It's as if I've uncapped a pressurized release valve.

Portnoy stumbles into the edge of the bed and turns around, swinging his fist. He misses wildly because I'm still on one knee. With two hands gripping the knife, I launch myself up toward him, propelled by the darkness at my back. The knife enters his chest at an angle, penetrating the soft tissue beneath his sternum and sinking in to the hilt. I feel only a slight pressure—his body's pushback—as I drive the knife in deeper, widening the wound so that the top of the hilt itself is actually inside his body. Then I pull the knife out and take a step back. Dark blood gushes out and pours down the front of his tracksuit, viscous and glinting thickly in the guest room's lamplight.

He does not go down. He places a hand over the wound as if he is a child saying the Pledge of Allegiance. There's confusion and sorrow in his eyes as they seek mine, and I'm touched by a strange new understanding that passes between us.

A connection. He has found what he was seeking. Or, rather, it has found more of itself.

He holds out a hand as if to stop me, and at first I'm not sure why, but then I realize that he knows, somehow, that I'm just getting started.

He says something and I hear myself laugh in reply. I dance forward on light feet and my arm blurs between us. An angry red stripe appears across his forehead. The cut widens slightly and begins to weep. He sits down on the bed heavily and with great care, holding his chest, like an elderly person taking a load off after a long day. I find myself stepping toward him, and though he is slumped he raises an arm and swats me away. I lean back to avoid his open-handed slap—his limbs are moving drunkenly now—and come at him from an angle, sinking the knife down into the meat of his shoulder from above, in the place where the shoulder curves up into the base of his neck. I feel the blade scrape his clavicle as it sinks in. The darkness urges my hand down, giving me the strength to saw through bone.

With brute strength I certainly do not possess, I bunch his tracksuit in my fists just behind his neck and fling him to the floor. He lands facedown and begins to crawl slowly toward the hallway. His limbs are moving like he's underwater and running out of oxygen. I watch him paddle ineffectually, pointlessly, for a minute or two. Blood is pooling beneath him, staining the little canyons of the carpet's piles and knots. He's making a noise like a lifelong smoker trying to hold an impossible note. The knife handle juts from his shoulder.

He has stopped moving his limbs, but his fingers are still clawing the carpet. I crouch down and flip him over onto his back with a *thud* that seems to jolt him with newfound life. He reaches across his body and actually manages to get his hand to curl around the handle of the knife. But his palm is slick with blood, and anyway, I don't think he can grip the handle with enough strength to move it. When I pull the knife out of his shoulder, a sigh comes from the back of his throat. The smell of shit fills the room as his bowels let go for the last time. He lies still.

I pull off his mask, releasing a shock of dirty blond hair.

This experience is so much more vivid and real than the glimpse I was granted at Matt's desk. That was a smudged image from a lingering dream. This is a moment from my life exactly as I lived it. As I lacerate his face with precise strokes, I lean down as if I'm going to kiss him. I stick out my tongue and run its tip along the fresh grooves in his face and slide it beneath a warm flap of skin. I whisper blood-tinged nonsense into his body's holes. It's a hellish, perverted affection.

There is recognition in the way I open my mouth and sympathy in the way I press my lips to his cracked and broken ones. I have what he came for, but he will never possess it. Instead, I will take it from him. *More of itself.* What drove Kyle Portnoy leaves him like a long-held breath and enters me. Bright understanding flares and vanishes, but the imprint remains: this is the swimmer's design. It wants me.

The swimmer, meeting itself, exults. There's a vivid crackle behind my eyes as I'm graced with newfound clarity. Lactic acid floods my mouth, a lifetime of energy burned off in a split second. Then the swimmer rips away the memory with the theatrical grace of the magician who yanks the tablecloth without disturbing the plates and silverware. In the attic room, I spit bile, dry heave till I'm sore. Then I rub grease from my eyes. The heat of this place is rotten, every breath unclean. My gaze sweeps along the sculptures. Somehow, the most sinister aspect isn't the cockroach bits or the miserable sagging shapelessness of them—it's a detail in the third one I hadn't noticed before, a small clump of blond hair like you might scrape out of a shower drain, embedded in the fixative.

Sharon Portnoy, I think. I retch again and turn to the pegboard. *Take the claw hammer to the door and smash it down.* I weave my way on unsteady legs to the workbench. Though my guest room has receded, the things I've done pollute the air around me. I will have to mute the sounds and blur the sights if I'm to live with myself. Yoga and breathing exercises won't cut it.

the slick-meat squelch of his wounds on my tongue

At the bench I discover light coming through the exposed holes in the pegboard. I shove the bench aside and tear the pegboard off the wall. Behind it hides a single grimy window. I'm fortunate this place is old and ramshackle—just outside is a gabled roof, and below that the awning that covers the front porch.

speaking nonsense to a ruined face

The window is painted shut. I pick up a dusty wrench and hurl it through the glass. Then I shatter the rest with the handle of a hammer. Behind me, whispers hang in the air. Careful not to touch the shards that line the pane, I climb out into the dull gray morning. I don't give a shit if Liza Jane is standing in her yard with a shotgun. I fall to my knees and gulp fresh air and steady myself against the worn old shingles, rough against my palms. I'm wracked with sobs and throaty cries but not yet too far gone to function. Some animal instinct gets me to the edge of the roof and down onto the awning. At its lowest sagging point I climb over backward and hang from the gutter so my legs are only a few feet above the ground. I let go, and a split second later pain shoots up through my ankles and shins. I don't let myself collapse. At the door to my car, I fumble in my pocket for the keys.

It's not until I'm backing the car down the driveway that I begin to shake. I clamp my mouth shut to keep from biting off my tongue.

The tremors of knowing what I've—

24

—"Done?"

Trevor stares me down with a single blazing eye as I return from the bathroom at the Cat's Paw. It's located at the end of a corridor lined with framed black-and-white photographs of cats outfitted and posed like wild west gunslingers. Some of the cats' features are droopy or missing. They're frozen in discomfiting postures and contortions. I think they've been poorly taxidermied.

"Haven't even started."

Once you actually have cocaine in your pocket, there's a certain deliciousness to withholding and then parceling it out in stages. The desperation of the hunt is gone—you can keep drinking and dole it out as you see fit, contented by the promise of a soaring high to cut through the haze. And today, the nine-year lack is massed like a thunderhead, ready to unleash the deluge.

There's more where that came from.

I've switched to vodka sodas. A desiccated lime wedge rides the rim of my glass. This drink, my eighth or ninth, wrings out any residual hostility from the walls, the stools, the mirror, the bottles, the bigmouth bass. Despair puddles on the floor and sluices away, a vanished forgotten thing. I've reached an understanding with the world at large. Bar scenery and jukebox music and scattered bits of conversation blend so that everything moves toward both continuance and stasis. Of course, there's never any resolution. Of course! The liminal state is the way of the world. Only now, at this holy moment, my hand curled around a chilly drink, do I realize that grace lies not in the attempt to resolve the maddening blur but in accepting the blur as the truth. I down half the drink and savor the fizz. There's no more burn, only a slight uptick in my swoony perception.

"Anything can be knit together," I say to Trevor. "You can knit your depression to a lampshade, or a sense of déjà vu to your neck. They always tell you that matter can't occupy the same space as other matter, so when something becomes you, it can't be made out of matter. At least not like we know it. When you knit yourself to something that's been with you all along, you become more like yourself, and it's beautiful."

He lifts his glass. "Even after what happened, I always missed you." We clink and sip.

The bartender materializes and Trevor deals with her. I'm vaguely aware of what's hashed out: the next round is on the house. Outside it's pouring. A water stain spreads along a ceiling tile. I shudder at the sight of it and drown what it evokes in the dregs of my drink. Here I am, elbows on the scratched wood of a bar on a rainy weekday afternoon. I imagine yet another me, the Sydney I've become, far from this forsaken blot of a town, working at her standing desk on the thirty-eighth floor of a glass-walled tower, scrambling to finish up so she doesn't miss the 5:35 train home.

Our free round arrives. Clink, sip. The grad students play an endless stream of Billy Joel and laugh at each song as it begins. Or is it all one song with many different parts? Alcohol has a reputation as a mind eraser and after almost a decade dry, I've been buying into that convenient fiction. Billy Joel sings about the king and the queen of the prom. But the reality of alcohol's magic is more devious and complex. I realize now—just now!—that sober me's general anxiety is a series of blockades that hold my thoughts back from the stratosphere. How stifled I've been, how uncreative! Now, blockades crumble and thoughts untangle, each one carried on a swift current of vodka. The 5:35 train. The nightly commute. Not something to consider at any great length, something to endure and be done with. But now—just now!—I realize that I'm capable of appreciating it, that I *do* appreciate it in my own way. I'm not blind to the beauty of the everyday. It's one of my better qualities. The Metro-North runs parallel to the Hudson, so as long as you get a spot on the river side of the train, you've got a front-row seat to snippets of commuter-town life. Little League games under the lights, dog walkers and joggers on packed-gravel paths along the water. It's a feeling I can't wait to crawl inside while I'm threading through the after-work crowd at Grand Central Station, the great sigh of relief that only exists this time of year, when the ride home pulls the shade down on the day.

A certain melancholy is part of the craving, being conscious of all those lives that aren't my own, this being just a small sliver of the state, itself just a fraction of the country, the world. Sharon Portnoy's social circle bubbles up from the depths and I push it back down, drowning faces and names. Out the window of the 5:35, that little girl just smacked a double into the outfield, and all the parents are going wild in the stands. The conductor comes through the staticky loud-speaker braying New Yawk singsong. Next station stop will be Garrison. Garrison next.

My hand brushes the top of my thigh, feels the light crin-kle of the ziplock in the watch pocket of my jeans, the classic coke spot. Anticipation is a superheated knot at the base of my neck, where an assassin's ice pick would go. Trotsky was murdered that way, more or less. I remember a night class at Baruch, Danny dozing in my lap, the windowless gray room appropriately Soviet, a raven-haired woman urging us to consider the subtext of the choice of weapon. An implement used to crack blocks of ice into smaller pieces. Something about the splintering of a revolution, the fragmentation of an ideology. I recall using the word *apotheosis* in a paper. I rub the back of my head. What, then, of my knife? What hid-den meanings are baked into a Gusthof carving knife, ripe for explication by wide-eyed comp lit majors? The sheriff's words echo. *It can't be for no reason. I can't have that.* I ban-ish his voice and it floats away. I sip my drink. Ice against my teeth. The Hudson a sheet of ice in winter. Trotsky's mind cracked open. This, right here, is the essence of get-ting fucked up, and what I hadn't realized I'd been missing: connections that the sober mind is blind to. I think of the Golden Braid—Goebbels, Escher, Bach. (*That can't be right.*) Trevor says something. Billy Joel drowns it out.

"I said, heads up, three o'clock, coming in hot." Trevor's leaning in close.

I frown. Three o'clock? He nods, jutting his chin toward the entrance to the Cat's Paw. I spin on my stool. The back wall slides across the mirror. Matt has just burst through the bar's inner door, an old-timey saloon door that swings.

I meet his eyes and he stops short. His face is washed out in the bad light of the bar, his expression stricken. He looks old and impossibly weary. Trailing him like the train of a formal dress are the trappings of the world I've shut out. They come back in shadowed glimpses, clawing their way up from the floorboards at his feet: Alverion Pharmaceuticals, the messages to Kyle Portnoy, the knife, the sculptures, the knife the knife the fucking knife . . .

I can hear the wheezing laughter of the old man at the Rusty Nail.

Kidney.

"No," I say, getting up from my stool to meet him head-on. I take one step and the world goes sideways. I weave in a sudden mad sidestep along the bar, then flail for a stool. My hand hits worn leather but the stool spins and spits my hand back out like a pitching machine launching a baseball. I'm dancing, light on my toes, and then I'm tripping down the unlikely slope of a tilted floor. I hear myself laugh. There are invisible walls in the air that I manage to bounce off. I try to use two stools to steady myself but instead find myself on the floor, ass against the grimy rail that supports drinkers' feet, a dull shock wave jolting my tailbone.

There are things I need to say to Matt. I have them all saved up inside me, locked and loaded, but I miss every one I reach for. I wonder, absurdly, if the bartender called him to take me home. But of course, that doesn't make any sense. I am a stranger in this place. The mock sympathy of the grad students burns me, and I can taste their smirks.

"Fuck off!" I hurl my words in the general direction of their table.

"Syd," Matt says, closer now, kneeling down, reaching out. He smells like deodorant, like he's slathered it on to mask the funk of an all-nighter. There are three of him. Then two. I can't make the two Matts into one.

I swat his hand away. A second hand trails it. "How did you get here?"

"I drove."

He folds his arms in this crouched position and regards me with four big, scared, loving eyes. His two faces look completely ridiculous.

"I mean how did you know I was here?"

This makes him even sadder. "We enabled Family Finder." He holds up his phone. There's a map on the screen, a little pin with an "S" for Sydney pointed at the Cat's Paw in Wofford Falls. "Like, six months ago."

A feral surge splashes red across my vision. Matt's been spying on me, GPS-tracking my movements. I hack out a vicious noise and swat at him again. "You're not supposed to be like this. There's something not right about you and I can't believe I never saw it before."

He shakes off a fleeting look of sheer disgust and switches back to the weary, fed-up fatherly mask. "You can do it, too, Sydney."

I can do it, too. I struggle to make sense of this. In the meantime, I lift an arm, ready to swat if he reaches for me again. It's preemptive, satisfying. Locked and loaded. I try to speak but can't form the words. I can do *what*, too?

He rolls his eyes. "You can *track my phone*. We enabled Family Finder for both of us. We agreed that it's a mutual safety thing, not some one-sided..." He shakes his head. "Ah, forget it." He reaches for my outstretched arm. I swat and miss.

"No." I shrink back against the bar, pull my knees to my chest, lock my arms around them. I make myself hard-shelled and immobile, a bug with a spiny carapace.

"Syd. Come on. Please."

I close my eyes. In the darkness I feel him tug on my arm, but he can't dislodge me from my resting place against the rail. It smells like some horrific bleachy cleaner down here. Suddenly Matt's hand goes away. I open my eyes to find him staring down the hooded man at the bar. Astonishment creeps across his tired face, then hardens into something cold and pure.

"You're Trevor." Matt only knows of Danny's father from the stories I've told, but I've told him plenty, and he knows how it ended between us. "What the hell are you doing here?"

Trevor takes his hands from the bar and displays his empty palms. Something about this strikes me as sad. The Trevor I used to know would have been on his feet brandishing the jagged shards of a smashed bottle. What are any of our fierce gestures worth, in the end? I wonder if Matt's ever been in a bar fight and I imagine his Stanford days, guys with boat shoes and tucked-in shirts going toe-to-toe in a frat house basement. That strikes me as sad, too. As I swivel my head toward Matt then Trevor, Trevor then Matt, the only thing I feel is the dull urge for one of them to take a swing. Not because I like men to fight over me—I don't care about that—but because I'm sitting on the floor of a townie dive open to every fresh degradation.

"Look, man," Trevor croaks, and Matt turns to me before he can get out the rest.

"Sydney, what's going on?"

Trevor tries again. "I know you guys have a good thing going and I didn't mean to—"

"*Shut up.*" Matt thrusts an open palm in Trevor's direction without taking his eyes off me.

"That's enough of that in here," the bartender says from somewhere above me. "All of you need to chill or take it outside."

"I'm her boyfriend," Matt says in a voice laced with irritation.

Trevor rises from his stool. Now both men are pasted to the backdrop of booths at odd angles, as if I'm watching them through a canted lens. Billy Joel sings a cappella about a river so deep.

"All good," Trevor says, "I'm out."

Matt turns to him. "If I ever see you again, creeping around my family..."

"You won't." Trevor looks down at me. "I forgive you, Sydney. I wanted you to know that."

His words are murky, half-submerged. *I forgive you.* It's something I might have said to him, though I did not. Coming from him it feels staged, an actor's parting shot before his last exit. As if forgiveness is elastic and can be granted to either one of us as long as somebody puts the words out there.

Wedged between the barstools, ass against the metal rail, reeling from what became of us, I watch him turn away.

Matt puts his hands on his hips and stares after Trevor as he leaves the bar. He looks like he's waiting for Danny to join him at the end of the driveway for a run around the cul-de-sac. And just like that, the vodka's insulation is punctured, a fairy-tale dam leaking booze through a hundred holes.

Go away, Danny.

Go away, Matt.

But Matt is here, right here in the bar, and there's nothing I can do to banish him or chase away the feeling that I've crossed into a new state of being from which there will be no return. Somewhere out on the road between Liza Jane's house and the Cat's Paw is the molted, withered husk of a Sydney that will never be again, a Sydney with nine years sober and a fundamental grasp on Keeping It Together. If not for Matt's abrupt intrusion, I would have been able to leave her out there ignored and unremarked upon, at least for a few more precious hours.

My red-splashed mind propels me up the barstool's leg and then I'm on my feet. Matt reaches out for me and I wriggle away. My half-finished drink is just a little ways down the bar. I weave my way over while the bartender casts a cold eye. The water stain clings to the bowed ceiling tile, and I think of the roof above Liza Jane's porch. Matt's intrusion has turned the walls and objects against me once again, returned some of their malevolence. The picture frame on a print of dogs playing poker is the color of cockroach wings. The attic breaches my defenses and I'm swamped in Kyle Portnoy's madness. I lift the glass to my mouth and drain the vodka. In the mirror I can see that Matt is behind me now, taking me by the arm. I set down my drink and grasp the edge of the bar with a rock climber's grip. As long as I refuse to turn and face him, I can still keep certain things at bay.

The vodka won't go down easy this time. The bite is back. I've had too many to take this one down so fast.

"Whatever you've done," Matt says, "it's going to be okay. I promise. Just come home with me."

I close my eyes to try and swallow my gorge. Bile occupies my throat. Up or down, it could go either way. All of my old benders eventually reached an inflection point, a moment of stillness and, dare-I-say, clarity when the curdled horror of whatever foul room I was nesting in would come out of the fog and assert itself, the manic voices of strangers I've spent several days with coming at me like banshee shrieks. In these jarring resets of my consciousness, I would cling to the notion that I had more, always more, checking my pockets for the telltale crinkle of square ziplocks. Just the notion of another line, another shot, would shove the bad vibes aside, and the atmosphere would re-form into something that could once again be considered womblike. I check my watch pocket now. Yes: it's still there.

Mrs. Dalloway said it best, not in a tattered rehab paperback but in a hardcover edition I bought with my first real paycheck: *what a lark, what a plunge.*

I catch Matt's mouth in the mirror. "I love you very much," says the mouth. "It's time to go home and rest." I let him turn me around. "Danny's waiting," he says.

I vomit on the side of his face. He recoils, stunned. I heave again and most of it dribbles down the front of my shirt. Everyone in the whole bar is on their feet. Outside the rain comes down. In a house up the road a clump of hair clings to a tragedy in an attic room.

THE FIFTH
VISITATION

25

I wake in darkness.

No. *Wake* isn't the right word. I make half-assed overtures toward consciousness. I fumble with the basics. Opening my eyes is profoundly complex. My eyelids seem to begin at my hairline and end at my cheeks. I can tell that I'm lying on my side. A damp puddle of drool or something worse clings to the side of my chin.

Panic scratches at me, faintly at first and then with no warning it's everywhere, within and without. I make an inhuman sound as I force myself to sit up, a weird baritone cry. The adrenaline of being suddenly upright whips my heart into a gallop. This is the kind of predawn roust you get when the brain's half-leached of whatever substance got you through the night before, and the craving for a re-up jolts you awake.

I know that I'm in my own room, in the bed I share with Matt. There's a feeling of permanence to the dark space, a sightless impression of the familiar. *Echolocation*, I think dully, which triggers a vague sense of déjà vu.

I ride a disorienting current, a blood-rush in my head.

I feel loose-limbed and warm. No post-bender aches and pains, no dullness of spirit. The initial surge of panic fades. There's a pleasant distance between me and everything that matters.

I laugh: *still drunk, Sydney.* Okay. So, I got wasted and blacked out and made it about halfway through Sleeping It Off. The circumstances elude me, but the facts can't be denied. My mouth is a dry, sticky cavern full of liquor fumes. The inevitable pounding in my head is more like the soft burbling of a distant brook, the promise of a hangover to come. A rain check for feeling spectacularly shitty. The remainder of the panic dissipates. Time is on my side. I can lie down, go back to sleep, sort everything out in the morning. Muted happiness rocks me back and forth. There's a wild streak of contentment I catch and run with—I've awakened into the perfect between-state. Not wasted, not sober. The promise of being fucked up and the actual state, intertwined and overlapped, too early for the comedown to loom. I must have only passed out for a few hours.

My phone rings, its vibrations conveyed through the bedsheets. I root around the comforter until I come up with it.

Sheriff Butler. My between-state overrides the impulse to ignore the call.

"Hello," I croak.

"I need to talk to you."

"It's late."

"I'm not sleeping."

"Neither am I." This strikes me as funny, because *duh*. I laugh.

"I need you to look at some patterns." His voice is deeper than I recall, an oddly smeared quality to it. Suddenly I remember a bar, a bigmouth bass in desperate need of repair.

Noise drifts up from downstairs. It sounds like someone's coming in through the front door, or else leaving that way. There are multiple hushed voices, and one of them rattles me: *Danny.*

"Now's not a good time," I say.

"I don't think that matters," he says.

"What do you mean, you don't *think*?"

"Anymore. I just need you to help me see."

"I have to go."

I get out of bed, woozy and light on my feet. I'm wearing underwear and a white T-shirt.

"Wait!" he says.

When I hear the front door shut, I end the call, go to the bedroom window, and open the curtains. There's a car in the driveway, a boxy sedan that looks all wrong, impossibly big—a gleaming, water-soaked sponge. An old-person car. The porch light paints it with bright streaks. Three long-shadowed figures, two large and one small, head for its doors. For a moment the scene is so completely alien to me that I think I must be in someone else's house after all.

But then I see that the smallest of the figures is a boy with an overstuffed backpack.

They're going to take him away, away, away . . .

I slap my palms against the glass. Then I pull open the window and scream my son's name into the cold night air. All three figures turn and look up at me. Light hits the faces of the two adults escorting Danny to the car.

Matt's mother and father. Of course they're impeccably dressed to come over in the middle of the night, Judy Melford in a hideous faux-fur coat and Owen Melford in a belted gray trench coat and fedora like the square-jawed Greatest Generation types he loves to emulate. Owen gives a startled little wave. Judy barely spares me a glance as she puts her hand on Danny's shoulder and guides him toward the rear door of the car.

"Where are you going?" I yell.

"Nony and Pop's house!" Danny yells back.

Judy says something to him, opens the door, and slides him into the backseat.

"Wait!" I call out. In five seconds, I'm out of the bedroom, into the hallway, and down the stairs. My feet skim the floor, shielded by my between-state, and I barely feel the hardwood. The not-quite-headache is no worse than an echo. As much as this moment feels like it has to be a dream—a trip to Matt's parents' house in the middle of the night?—what's happening outside is real, I'm sure, and I have to put a stop to it. I feel like I've awakened into a museum exhibit come to life, all klieg lights and dramatic shadows, a moving diorama escaping down the driveway.

Matt cuts me off at the bottom of the stairs, intercepts me with his hands on the sides of my arms. The lights are on in the front hall—there's the gilt-framed mirror, the credenza, the reclaimed tiles. He's wearing a gray Stanford hoodie and sweatpants that taper at the ankles. He smells like the lavender soap we get from the local artisan lady's shop by the train station. He's well scrubbed and wide awake and positioned in the front hall like he's been waiting for me. What part has he played in all this?

I want him to let me go, yet at the same time I have the sickly, nagging urge to apologize to him. For what?

What have I done?

"You should be sleeping," he says, not unkindly.

"Danny's outside."

"I know."

"I need to see him." I wriggle a little in his grip, testing his resolve. He doesn't budge.

"I don't think that's a good idea right now."

There's something in his tone—trepidation, a hint of warning—and his words expand in the air around my face, taunting me with the things I've done, things he's keeping from me. At the very edges of my mind, bad memories begin to take sharp little nibbles. There was a horrible attic, a frantic escape, too many drinks in a strange bar, and then nothing. Blackout.

Outside I hear the burly engine of Owen and Judy's Cadillac split the suburban silence of our neighborhood.

I wriggle again, twisting my upper body from side to side. To keep me contained, Matt will have to slam me up against the wall and tighten his grip in a way that would leave marks on my arms. He lets me go. I rush to the front door and pull it open.

"Danny!"

The oversized sedan is backing down the driveway. I run outside, bare-legged and shoeless. The glare of the headlights blinds me, and it's not until the car backs out into the road and the lights sweep across our front yard that I can see into the windows. There's Judy in the passenger seat, prim lips pursed as she regards me with pearl-clutching disapproval, grateful for two tons of glass and chrome to shield her from my vulgar body. And there's Danny in the backseat, gazing balefully or sleepily as he presses a palm against the glass, watching me sprint after the car.

"Wait!"

The arch of my foot comes down hard on a rock and I stumble. Owen accelerates and there's nothing more I can do. From where the driveway meets the road, I watch the taillights vanish around the corner. The night air is bracing on my bare skin. I run back toward the house, toward the man silhouetted in the doorway. To a sleepless neighbor peeking out his window I'm a Brontë girl in a gauzy shift, floating across a misty moor.

"Come inside," Matt says, "you're gonna freeze."

I pause at the threshold. Between the porch light above and the hall light at his back, Matt's wrapped in a glow that makes his features slippery, his body vague and looming. *The man in my house is wearing a mask*, a mask I ripped off when I went to work on his face. And I licked each sweet and dexterous cut, oh yes—the swimmer let me have a taste back there in the attic room, a taste of when it met itself and poured all of its sentience into me. I shiver at the thought of its expansive awareness, curious and growing stronger.

The memory pierces my between-state, blowing clean through the vodka fumes, trailing fragments in its wake. The stations of Portnoy's disintegration. The feel of the swimmer's elegant shadow-body against my own, our movements in concert across Portnoy's flesh. The bad angles of the Cat's Paw's uncanny interior, everyone laughing and dancing, dancing and laughing while I pour vodka down my throat.

And Trevor. I called Trevor, and through the fog of his own ruin he came and gave me what I asked for.

One day.

Nine years.

They're going to take him away, away, away . . .

I'm screaming at Matt as he pulls me inside and shuts the door.

"You can't do this, he's my son!"

"*Shhh*, Syd, I promise it's gonna be okay."

"Stop saying that!"

"Just calm down and listen to me."

He tries to hold me tight, but I squirm away and into the living room, where photos of our family trips preside over the mantel and the tree stump supports the glass that will one day tie our lake house together.

I wheel around to face him. "You've got no right, Matt, what the fuck?"

"That's true," he agrees. "Technically I don't. But I had to—" He shakes his head, redirects. "It's just for a day or two. I swear I didn't know what else to do, Syd. Maybe I did the wrong thing, maybe there was another way, but I have a responsibility for Danny, too. I know I'm not his dad, but he feels like my kid. You know that. He's my guy, and I love him."

But you're a fucking liar. I'm about to open the floor to everything I've uncovered when he hits me with this:

"And I don't mean this as an accusation, but there was only one of us capable of making any decisions about his well-being earlier tonight."

I blink. I haven't been fucked up around my son since he was a baby. Whatever murky visions of that period he retains, I've made sure to provide him with nine years of positive reinforcement and the example of a steady, goal-oriented life to crowd them out. My between-state sublimates, its membranes thin and porous. I'm being poked and probed by a thousand dim and anxious flashbacks: Matt bundling me into the front seat of his car. A foul-smelling ride home, the sour reek of vomit, rain smeared by windshield wipers. Danny opening the door for us, my too-loud hysterical greeting, a weird triumphant march through the front hall, a collapse in the kitchen, Matt sending Danny up to his room...

And during all that I know I spoke to him. What did I say to my son?

"It's just for a day or two," Matt says again. "Until we figure some things out."

I sink down into the sofa and fold my arms across my chest. "I scared him, didn't I?"

Matt doesn't say anything. That means *yes*.

"I'm sure he'll be fine." He pauses. "But it wasn't great, Syd. And obviously we need to talk about what in God's name you were doing at that bar with *Trevor*." His voice is shot through with hurt and disbelief. "But for now, I think it's best if you went back to bed."

I close my eyes. "Jesus Christ."

I know how easy it is to undo years of work. Recovery language doesn't tiptoe around the word *relapse*. Everything from the most cloying aphorisms to impenetrable scholarly papers addresses the phenomenon that's a fact of life for a stunningly high percentage of addicts. Relapse. Mountains of paper and oceans of ink dedicated to the single despairing inevitability that *you are going to fail*. You will make promises to yourself and your long-suffering family, and you will break them, again and again. All that booze you heroically dumped down the drain? You'll just buy more. The dealer's number you deleted from your phone? You know it by heart. The friend you cut out of your life because you always get high together? You'll manage to bump into her. Dark facts stacked like poker chips, and the house always wins. But here's the thing: there's also that sliver of a percentage of addicts who don't relapse, who never backslide, who live a life of vigilance and discipline that never cracks. That was me, steady old Sydney. I took pride in slotting myself into that defiant statistical anomaly. Now it's laughable that I ever thought myself worthy of their number. Eyes closed on the sofa, I reach back to the moment I lifted the day's first vodka to my lips. I shake my head. I didn't have to do it. I know that now. If only I'd slowed down for a moment and really processed what had happened in Liza Jane's attic, I could have shouldered the weight of it all without numbing it. Without calling *Trevor*, of all people. Horrors beyond my understanding, yes—but I could have found the strength to bear them.

Look at me now, sad and scared and sunk deep in regret as my between-state disperses and my head begins to pound.

The single bright spot, glowing white-hot to counterbalance the cold knot of despair, isn't the fact that despite everything that's happened, I'm home now, and Danny's safe. It's the fact that I know there is cocaine in the watch pocket of my jeans. A sparkling untouched half a gram, give or take, biding its time, waiting for me. I disgust myself. I'm fucking nuts. I hate it. I love it.

Something breaks free inside me and I'm floating on fierce indifference, crazed and leaning into what comes next. What a lark, what a plunge.

I open my eyes. "How do you know Kyle Portnoy?"

26

P<small>REPARE</small> for extraction."

The voice drags me up out of nothing and into harsh fluorescence. A sky full of glowing filaments, so hot I'm sweating in the glare.

I try to close my eyes. Nothing happens. My eyelids won't obey the command to snap shut. Brightness sears deep into my skull. My mind grasps at reference points, spins madly, and grinds to a halt at a memory of a solar eclipse seen from midtown Manhattan: a clump of my coworkers standing on a corner, jostling for space as a burning sliver of sun bounces off the glass tower we peer at through our special glasses. I gather myself and try again. *Close your eyes, Sydney.* Nothing.

Something's been affixed to the places where my lashes meet my lids, that soft wet under-skin the color of an open wound. A hard substance that tugs at the tender flesh, a hundred firm and tiny hands prying my eyes open.

My heartbeat ratchets up.

From all around me come the sounds of shuffling feet, soft voices, the clicks of metal-on-metal and metal-on-plastic. The low hum of machinery. A faint, looping *beep—beep—beep—*

Help me, I say, but nothing comes out, not even a low moan. I steady myself, try to stay calm, and focus on moving my mouth—which, I realize, is already open wide and completely numb. I can sense another hard substance—plastic, maybe—between my teeth. I try to bite down, but my jaw muscles are paralyzed.

This piece of plastic is big and oddly shaped, curling out over my lips and, in the opposite direction, deep into my throat. Now that I'm focused on it I can't *un*-feel it, and its presence makes me want to claw at my insides. It's a tube, I think, stretching all the way down into my stomach. I can feel my esophagus constrict against it, tiny muscles I've never felt before that I'm far too aware of now, squeezing the plastic that's pushed them aside. I try to bring my arm up to my throat. I have to pull it out, I can't breathe, there's *too much of it inside me*, I can't—

My arms won't move. They're either paralyzed or strapped down so tight I can't even strain against the bindings. I don't know, I can't turn my head to see them.

Now panic takes hold of my heart and my chest goes tight.

The desire to blink my eyes is already maddening. They feel dry and vulnerable. I vow that I will never again take for granted the ability to blink. I can feel the hard little fingers of whatever's holding my eyes open like rigid millipedes that have crawled just beneath my skin to cocoon themselves.

There's a lightness in my groin, a pins-and-needles, stomach-flop sensation that comes on like restless legs when you're trying to sleep. Except I can't shift positions to relieve it. I can't do anything at all, and the infuriating sensation blossoms inside me, a horrible itch I can never scratch. I try again to scream for help, but I can't even gurgle against the tube. Everything is shut down and yet somehow, I'm awake and conscious.

A crawling comes across my palms. I get the sense that my fingers are splayed, though I *can't fucking see them*. A thousand little metallic beetles' legs probing and testing, a bit like the tiny hands prying open my eyes, except these have sharp nails. My senses go haywire. There's an agonizing tickle in my wrists and it takes me a minute to realize that the skittering digits are *probing my wounds*. I can't shake the impression that they're looking for a way in.

My heart rate kicks into overdrive. I strain against the paralysis but that only makes it worse. The stomach-flop feeling in my groin, the choking fullness in my throat, the hard substance prying open my eyes, the tap-dancing pinpricks on my hands and wrists—I'm aching to flail and thrash and dig in my nails to scratch everywhere but I can't move a muscle. I imagine how good it would feel to shift positions, pull the tube out of my throat, rub my palms against my jeans. In a matter of seconds these simple acts become my holy grail. I imagine myself performing them in the same way that someone lost in the desert conjures up a shimmering oasis. Desire mingles with this imagined relief that's just out of reach. My whole body is a raw nerve.

A head appears, hovering over me—a woman in an orange hood and mask. Neon yellow goggles cover her eyes. She reaches across my face to adjust something I can't see. A moment later I feel a dull tug at the back of my head, near the place where my spine meets my skull. The shock waves of whatever minor adjustment she makes send excruciating jolts of pain through my neck. It feels like someone is beating on my tendons and throat glands with a leather strap. The jolts radiate down the thick plastic tube, and my rib cage begins to constrict. I'm suffocating myself from within. I can't even gasp for air.

Suddenly my stomach turns to ice. Someone I can't see is slathering me in a liquid so cold it flash-freezes my skin. *I'm naked*, I realize for the first time. *Naked and splayed and helpless* in a room full of bright lights and people. The frigid chill spreads across my chest and settles into a diamond-hard rock of biting cold that rests in the hollow of my clavicle. If I could move my mouth, my teeth would be chattering violently. Without the ability to tremble and shiver, the cold seems to swirl inside me.

I will myself to pass out. I will myself to *die*. But I remain aware. I feel everything.

"Prep the binding agent."

From off to my left comes the squelch of a thick viscous substance being poured into a container. There's a suction sound, then a mechanical grinding.

"Binding agent prepped."

I'm hyperventilating silently. My heart jackhammers. I will it to explode. I don't fucking care. I just need this to end.

The mechanical grinding becomes a *whirr* that gets louder and louder. A long slab looms over me and blots out the light. I get the impression that it's attached to a series of hydraulic arms.

"Okay. Let's find this fucker."

More needles than I can count protrude from various housings on the underside of the slab. In its terror my mind cycles through a loop of confusion—

Why is this happening to me?

Is this real?

As the slab descends toward my body, I realize that the needles aren't like any needles I've ever seen. They're sharp metallic instruments, but they also have a weird pliability to them, as if they're fronds waving in a light breeze. They're long—as long as my forearm—and they're all coming down on me at once.

A silent scream shreds my thoughts. The entire world consists of the needles and my useless body. I can't close my eyes. The needles sway with hunger.

For the first time in my life, I pray to God. Nothing happens.

How did I get here?

27

Kyle Portnoy?" Matt frowns. "The fucker who broke in here? How would I know him?"

I'm on the sofa, in the same place the sheriff sat when he slid Portnoy's file across the coffee table. Same roles, new cast. Concentric loops, ever shrinking.

The urge to laugh comes and goes. Matt has no trouble meeting my eyes. The swimmer is dormant. I chalk it up to the booze and the onrushing hangover tamping it down. Apparently, my face is my face.

"You tell me," I say. More echoes of Sheriff Butler.

"I can't tell you, because I don't know what you're talking about. You're not making any sense."

"You always were a shitty liar. Good little Catholic boy."

"All right." He puts his hands on his hips. "I think we both need to get some sleep. It's been a crazy night. We can talk about everything in the morning."

"It is morning."

"The real morning. Sun, birds, coffee."

"I know you know him. I went to his house."

Matt narrows his eyes. "His *house?*" He thinks for a moment. "Is that why you were in Wofford Falls?"

"Ding ding ding."

"Okay." He pauses. "I'm sorry to use this word but that's crazy."

"What's crazy is falling in love with someone and moving in with them and then finding out they're involved in some weird shit they won't tell you about, even after it almost gets you killed."

He waves his hand in front of my face. "Hi, Syd? It's me, Matt. This is *us*, here, okay? This isn't how we talk to each other. We're not these people."

"I don't know what kind of people we are anymore."

He sits down in the Eames chair across from me and leans forward with his elbows on his knees. "I understand that you're super pissed at me right now. But I swear to God—I swear on my grandmother's *Bible*, if you want to get it out of the drawer, I'll seriously do it—that I did what was best for Danny. Besides you, he's all I care about. And that will never change, no matter what happens."

"I'm not talking about Danny and me, or how you feel about us. That's not what this is about. You're changing the subject."

"Okay." He sits back in the chair. "Fine. Then let's talk about what you were thinking going to that man's house, and why on God's green earth I had to come scoop you up off the floor of a random bar in Wofford Falls after you got utterly shit-faced *with your ex-boyfriend*, who's a psychotic maniac that you ditched before he could kill you, or Danny, or both. *Oh, that was another life.* That's what you always say, right? Except it didn't look that way to me. It looked very much like *this* life that you let him into. So if you really want

to outline your train of thought for me, right now, at"—he
checks his Apple watch—"four twenty-eight a.m., I'm all
ears."

I can't help but laugh at his tone. "This is turning into
some Eugene O'Neill shit."

He frowns. "Who?"

I point to my copy of *Long Day's Journey into Night* on the
bookshelf. "That guy."

He gives me a blank look.

"Forget it. So, yeah. My train of thought was this." I
pause. Rewinding to the very beginning brings me to the
Nano Pal, the pattern on the screen and carved in Portnoy's
face. All the ways the swimmer nudged me toward Matt's
computer. *It wants me to know it wants me to see.* I don't know
how to spin this narrative to make it seem like it comes
from a reasonable-sounding person. It doesn't belong in the
same zip code as sanity. I do realize that. But it happened
and there's nothing I can do about it. So, fuck it—I skip
the preamble. "I found the messages you and Kyle Portnoy
sent to each other. I knew I was right about him looking
for something, and that confirmed it. So, then I went to his
house—his girlfriend's house. *Ex*-girlfriend. Anyway, that's
where I found out you knew him from church."

My voice sounds strange, like it's beaming in from some
other reality where Matt and I routinely pick away at
each other. At the same time, everything we've ever done
together looms just out of frame, the dizzy joyful parade of a
shared life: The sapling we planted in the backyard on Danny's birthday. The camping trips. The epic bike treks. The
dinner-and-karaoke dates in the city. These things crowd
my mind and I think, *this is all wrong. I'm wrong.*

He leans forward, elbows on his knees, palms clasped

together. I watch him compose words from sheer exasperation. "Is that whose attic you went in?"

I'm startled that he knows about the attic, but I shouldn't
be. There's so much I still can't remember. For all I know
I screamed about the sculptures for twenty minutes when I
got home and collapsed in the kitchen.

"You were ranting about an attic," he explains. "You told
Danny you went swimming there, or something."

I make a dismissive noise. "That's not the point. Just tell
me the truth, Matt. I saw the texts."

His hands unclasp, his fingers splay. "What are these texts
you keep—"

"Backed up on your computer."

He puts his entire body into his reply. "What computer?"

"Your office computer."

He shakes his head, incredulous. "Syd...for real. I don't
know what you're talking about. I've never lied to you, or
Danny, in my life." When I don't reply he slaps his palms
down on his thighs and stands up. "I can't believe I'm indulg-
ing this at four-thirty in the morning, but okay. Show me."

Together we head for the office and I sit down at his desk.
Flanking the monitor are two framed photographs of us
from two separate trips to Cedar Valley. In one, we're selfie-
silhouetted against a seashell-colored dawn. In the other, all
three of us are holding fishing poles like guitars and rocking
out. I can practically smell the marinated chicken sizzling on
the grill, hear the *pop-hiss* of a grapefruit soda, see the fire-
flies blinking on and off in patterns that exist solely for us.

The life I built with this man.

I tap the space bar and bring the screen to life. The desktop background, that precision-carved labyrinth, blinks into
place.

I hesitate. Pretend to think. "I can't remember your password."

"Seriously? Then how did you log in in the first place?"

"I remembered it that time."

I am aware of how flimsy this sounds.

With a sigh, Matt leans over the keyboard and enters his username and password. His breath is hot in my ear. I open his messenger backup and scan down the list of mundane text threads. Dozens slide by. I scroll back up, slowly, until I'm sure: the texts with "KP" are gone. I stare blankly at the screen. A flash of anger is tempered by the inevitability of all this. I knew it would happen. Images of Matt come and go—stabbed with every knife in our collection, pincushioned like a voodoo doll, his entire body a map of the Alverion image's runnels. Fucking me in our guest room bed. Disappearing with Danny beyond the crest of our street's gentle hill.

"Syd," Matt says after a while.

I swivel in the chair to face him. "You deleted them."

"Oh my God." He rubs his temples with the heels of his hands. Then he leans in for a closer look at the screen. "I don't even know what this backup program thing is. I didn't know it existed."

"That is absolute bullshit. There were texts between you and Kyle Portnoy, and you fucking know it. *It wants me to see*, he said. *You have to get me more*, he said. He was desperate. More of what, Matt?"

He closes his eyes and takes a deep breath. Then another. I wonder at the depths of his rage. I change tactics.

"Tell me about Alverion Pharmaceuticals."

He opens his eyes. "They're one of my clients."

"What do you do for them?"

He chokes out a laugh. "The same thing I do for every-body else. Big Pharma's got a lot of karmic debts to pay and a lot of money to throw at making themselves look less evil. Their headquarters are LEED certified. They fund an entire—"

"What do you *really* do for them?"

"What were you *really* doing with Trevor?"

"Nothing."

He shakes his head, nudges me aside, and opens a folder marked *Alverion*. He clicks on Excel file after Excel file, and spreadsheets fill the screen.

"Charity galas," he says sharply. "Foundations. Fundrais-ers. That awards dinner under the whale at the Museum of Natural History. You wore the black off-the-shoulder dress. Take a look, it's all here. Knock yourself out."

Matt rarely loses his temper with me. He's the type of person who gets frustrated at inanimate objects when they won't do his bidding—he slammed a fist down on our old Keurig machine hard enough to break it, and he once put a boot-clad foot through a stuck cabinet door—but the few times he's raised his voice at Danny or me have left him mortified.

I recall that he went straight from a stressful all-nighter—the Shanghai situation—to the Cat's Paw to scoop me up, to some kind of scene at the house, which was so bad he had to call his parents to come get Danny away from me.

I still don't believe the Shanghai situation was real, but Matt's certainly acting like an exhausted person who has no idea what I'm talking about and is pretty much at the end of his tether.

I decide to go all in. It's all I've got left. "Portnoy was going through something these past few months. Maybe longer. I don't know." As I launch into this, my words feel real and alive. Drunkenness stirs, reignited, and a loose sort of recklessness urges me on. *This is happening.* "Whatever was going on with him, I think the same thing's going on with me. And I think you know what it is."

I flash to a sudden reveal, a memory of the Cat's Paw—telling Trevor I'd accepted the swimmer as part of me. *Clink. Sip.*

"I'd *love* to know exactly what's going on with you, Syd. I really would."

"I couldn't remember what I did to Kyle Portnoy the night he broke in because afterward there was something blocking the memory. Something inside me, shielding me from the worst of it. From what I'd done."

"I mean, it's not uncommon for people who've gone through a traumatic—"

"Just *listen*. This thing didn't just block the memory to help me cope, or whatever. It *guided* me that night. It had specific needs it wanted fulfilled. It craved some kind of violence. It could have..." I trail off but the thought forms silently. *It could have gone the other way*—Portnoy finishing the job, taking what he came for—but instead the swimmer chose *me* to inflict its peculiar savagery. What recognition drove its choice? I close the program and tap the desktop screen with a fingernail. "I carved this design into his face."

"That's impossible."

"And then the same pattern appeared on the screen of that Nano Pal I found in Danny's room."

"Syd...that thing doesn't work."

"It does for me. That's how I know the swimmer's trying to tell me something."

"The *what*?"

"In its own way, I mean. Not verbally. It led me straight to your computer. It showed me the signs. It wanted me to know. The same design was on Alverion's website. And when I went up in Portnoy's attic—"

"Sydney—"

I stand up, gesture at an attic wall choked with catastrophic disintegration that only I can see. "I saw what was in his head. His old girlfriend, Sharon, she overdosed, and because the same thing that's in me was also in him, it helped him block it out, but then the memories started to come back—there was all this art up there, all these sculptures and paintings that he made as that shit flooded back to him, and they triggered the memory in me, too, of what I did, and the *whole night* came back to me, everything I did to the guy, the way I took my time with the knife on his face, getting it exactly right—"

"Okay, okay, Jesus Christ!" Matt's eyes go wide. I realize I'm carving whorls and angles into the air with my empty hand. "You're scaring the shit out of me! I know a relapse is no joke, and whatever you're going through I'm here to help you through it, but this—" He throws up his hands. "I don't even know what *this* is."

"See, you're lying again." I step toward him. "You know exactly what's going on with me. You took the knives out of the house. You know what's going on with me, and you knew what was going on with Portnoy. You've known all along."

Backing away from me, he puts his hands out, palms down, and presses on the air as if he's standing before a crowded room signaling for silence. "Calm down, Syd. It's *me* here. It's *us*. We're gonna get through this, I promise. I only took the knives away because I found you *sleepwalking* with one out on the back porch."

"I dreamed about you burying the knives in the woods. The swimmer was there, too."

"Listen. As soon as you're calm and collected, then Danny can come home." He backs out of the office and into the hall. "And that all starts with getting some sleep. It's as simple as that."

I go after him, raise my arm, and point a finger at his face. Sheriff Butler in the guest room, me in the hall. Concentric loops, ever shrinking. The two of us snarling in unison.

"You're a fucking liar."

28

The needles writhe as they seethe across my skin. My rapid breaths and racing heart combine in a deafening blood-rush. There is so much to be scared of I can't separate one terror from the others. I beg God to take my mind elsewhere.

The tip of a single needle traces my jawline and circles my earlobe.

An icy clarity cuts through the roaring inside my head. It occurs to me all at once that I've been praying to the wrong god.

I implore the swimmer: *You shielded me once. Why can't you do it again? Take me somewhere else. Render me insensible. Anything but this.*

Nothing happens.

Silently I scream apologies for invoking a false god. Never again will I forget who guides my way. A second needle begins its curious prodding. There's an infantile eagerness in the way it caresses my stomach. I feel a dull pressure against my belly button. *It's going to pierce me there.*

Oh dear god—dear swimmer—I can't take this.

Time slows. The needles drag. The intervals between the machine's looped *beeps* stretch on eternally.

Listen to me. Help me.

There's a faint reverberation inside my head. A tickling whisper, more hummingbird vibration than voice. I can barely make it out. Some uncanny representation of words begins to form. The communication is hitched, incorrect—a bad translation.

D o Yo u

Yes! There you are. Help me. I'm sorry I smashed the Nano Pal and I'm sorry I tried to ignore what you were telling me and I'm sorry I was ever afraid of you.

A searing bolt of pain lances from my navel to my pelvis and radiates up my frozen chest. At first my silent scream drowns out the swimmer, but as the needle wriggles into me (it hurts it hurts oh *fuck* it hurts and I can't move and there are so many more) the swimmer raises its voice.

Do You Do YOU DO YOU DO YOU

Okay, okay, just—please.

DO YOU

Do I what, do I fucking what?

LOVE ME

Yes yes yes I love you yes

A long, contented sigh ripples through me, and the noise in my head is the murmur of distant waves pounding the surf.

"Got something," a technician's voice says, long and low and drawn-out.

The swimmer chimes back in, clamorous and proud.

LOVE ME LOVE ME LOVE ME LOVE ME

The needle withdraws. No: the needle is expelled. It leaves a different sort of pain in its wake but the horrible fullness of it is gone. The swimmer asserts itself inside me and, without moving a muscle, a near-orgasmic rising-up courses through my body. An internal elevation. I feel my back arching and my toes curling, though I'm still paralyzed.

Time snaps back to its normal speed and the voices of bewildered technicians are all around me. The sole looping *beep* has been joined by the blurts and chimes of other unseen machinery. I hear the clack of a keyboard.

"Stubborn little bitch," someone says.

There's a gurgle from part of the slab near my pelvis and I'm splattered with a thick liquid that congeals as it hits my cold skin.

"Goddammit."

"What the fuck?"

The swimmer's invertebrate elegance courses through me, an aquatic gliding sensation. In my gratitude I send messages of regret—*I'm sorry I ever feared you, I'm sorry I smashed your avatar with a meat tenderizer, I'm sorry I didn't understand that you were only trying to protect me.* I want to give the swimmer something nice, a gift of encouragement, a sign that I can reciprocate love. I take myself back to all those autumn commutes home from the city and impart the ache of the dying light rippling along the surface of the river. I give this to the swimmer so that it might glimpse my humanity.

A new feeling, like I've sucked the powder off a moth's wing and now have its abdomen between my teeth, comes and goes. There's something embryonic about the current state of our relationship. Gone are the jarring images of what the swimmer has been keeping from me and doling out in fragments. The swimmer treats me with newfound gentleness—though its strength is astonishing.

I realize that I can wiggle my fingers. Rather, I can move them in concert with the swimmer as it imbues the tendons and muscles of my hand with a fluid current. It doesn't feel like electricity, or the satisfaction of pure motor control returned. It feels like a shadow is moving around inside me, *wearing* me. It's an odd sensation—not exactly comfortable, but not painful, either.

I hear a human voice edging into desperation, a sharp command from a technician playing at authority: "Get this extraction back on track *now*."

The voice snags on a memory—I've heard it before but can't quite place it.

A ragged chorus in reply:

"—never seen anything like this—"

"—think it's somehow *resisting*—"

The swimmer surges through my left arm and a vision of dark tendrils flits across my mind like video from a camera sent to some preposterous underwater depth. My arm bends at the elbow, and my fingers curl as if I'm clutching the handle of a knife.

"Jesus fucking Christ!"

I bring my hand to my face, work my fingers under the grotesquely spread plastic that parts my lips, and rip the tube from my mouth. It slides out with a gurgle and a slick rush. The insides of my throat feel bruised in its absence. I'm gasping for air and sputtering like I've just been dragged out of the ocean onto the beach. I open my hand and the tube clatters to the floor. Commotion rises all around. The swimmer is murmuring gibberish in my head, the guttural non-language of the bloodstain.

A man in a hooded mask appears, clear plastic shielding his face. He tries to reinsert the tube. In one graceful motion, with strength I should not possess, I snap off from its housing the needle nearest my earlobe and penetrate the man's forearm with its tip. He screams and drops the tube. I let go of the needle and catch sight of it squirming up inside his arm like an eager parasite finding a new host. Hijacking my ears with placid academic interest, the swimmer filters the man's shrieks to make the noise more pleasant for me. I barely notice the shift.

An alarm sounds. Murmuring, susurrating, the swimmer does the same with the Klaxon blare, reducing it to vague white noise.

Thank you.

I reach up to the substance coating the edges of my eyelids. It's pliable and soft yet firmly attached. It responds to my touch with the twitching of a thousand tiny legs and I think of the delicate cockroach braids in Liza Jane's attic. With the careful attention of a watchmaker, my fingers become precision instruments, stripping away the substance little by little. It peels away from my skin and crumbles in my hands. I blink moisture back into my eyes.

For the first time, I'm able to turn my head from side to side and take stock of the room in which I awakened. A windowless lab the size of a two-car garage, full of gleaming equipment that looks state-of-the-art and is like nothing I've ever seen. Forged of what appears to be steel, chrome, plastic, glass—familiar elements assembled with nonsensical precision, like Danny's disparate Lego sets combined, all of them glimmering darkly, *wetly*, casting shadows convex and strange. Standard medical equipment left to mutate, reconstitute as things with no discernible purpose. I feel scrutinized by these machines. The swimmer's interest is piqued, as if the machines are harboring something it craves. Recognition, as pleasurable as bumping into an old friend in some far-flung place, courses through me.

My back arches. I am suddenly farsighted, over and among

the machinery, capable of exploring, caressing, investigating things much too far away for my arms to reach. The space in here is different, or else there's something new in the way I fill it.

I turn my head the other way. Off to my right, a single open doorway leads to a corridor strobed with red lights that blink in time with the alarm. Most technicians have left the room already, but two remain, masked and suited, their backs against the wall to either side of the hallway entrance.

The one on the left is wondering aloud, his words an incredulous unbroken stream.

"—in the air she is the air my God her face—" He trails off, laughing. Then his body contorts. Jerking from the waist, he retches. Blood-tinged vomit spatters the clear plastic shield that covers his face. He is laughing and spewing, and like this he turns and staggers down the hall. One leg trails as if its nerves have been shut off, numbed and useless. The red light blinks his green suit blue at intervals.

The last remaining technician is weeping softly. I watch as he averts his eyes, gathers himself for a moment, and calls down the hallway.

"Hanson!"

I hear approaching footsteps, heavy boots on a tile floor. A burly, thick-necked orderly rushes into the lab, wearing a surgical mask. He attempts to restrain my arms while behind him the technician, still weeping, preps a long syringe.

The orderly puts his hands on my wrists and pain flares before the swimmer can douse it. I meet his eyes. He blinks, shakes his head, and tries to say something. His grip loosens. The muscles in his face go slack.

"Come on, man, hold her down!" the technician pleads. (*That voice again, nagging and familiar.*)

The orderly turns sickly pale. He lets go entirely and backs away. I turn my attention to the technician.

"Oh Jesus," he says, and drops the syringe. I slide out from between the table I'm on and the slab above me, careful not to snag my skin on a still-active needle.

With my feet on the tiles, I find that I don't have the strength to stand. I feel the swimmer rush to prop me up at the same time I collapse. With a boneless, jittery gait, I propel myself toward the technician. One step. Two. There's a hitch in my walk like the hesitation in the swimmer's murmurings. I can feel the shadow inside my thighs and calves. The man shrinks away from my naked, halting approach.

Ignoring him, I move through the universe of machinery, recovering my mobility. The swimmer retreats slightly (it's like air seeping out of a valve) and lets me come back to myself. This process is like getting the feeling back in a leg that has fallen asleep. The ice-cold liquid slathered on my chest is some kind of antiseptic. Blood trickles down from my navel.

Exploring, I marvel at the odd elements in each piece of diagnostic equipment. The writhing, living needles are just the beginning.

A tube like an MRI scanner with what appear to be cilia wreathing the entrance.

A helmet with a dozen wires snaking away from its crown, all of them twined with some kind of green organic material that sways in an unfelt breeze.

Steel cutting tools laid out on a tray, blades twisted into the angular alphabet of some incomprehensible language.

I circle the slab and come upon the technician sitting with his back against the wall, hugging his knees to his chest and whimpering to himself. The swimmer stirs. Elegant and lithe, I lower myself to the floor. The man buries his head in his arms. Sobs shake his burly frame, pulling his scrubs tight across the muscles of his shoulders and upper back.

I reach out to lift his head. My arm feels impossibly long. "It's okay."

He goes rigid as I remove his hood, and with it the plastic shielding his face. He gasps as I touch the side of his head, near his left temple. The contours of his face are magnified, close-up, but the entirety of him, his wholeness, is at the end of an arm that stretches and stretches.

"Wynn," I say. Matt's cousin, whose destination wedding we're supposed to attend. Florence, next August. A Tuscan home-share with Judy and Owen.

I understand that Matt's cousin's presence here should ignite astonishment within me, some wide-eyed disbelief. But all that is muted by what most interests the swimmer: Wynn's distress.

My thumb moves along his forehead, tracing a furrow. Then it finds the soft hollow of the man's eye and he begins to scream.

The cries ignite something I can only describe as *passion*. The heady rush of a new relationship, all the ingrained behaviors of another, waiting to be discovered, wondered at, savored. The very concept of *another*, how strange and wonderful. With my thumb gradually increasing pressure, I feel the stirrings of the swimmer's attempts at emotional honesty. For the swimmer, love and torment are joined. Has it learned this from me?

"How did I get here?" I ask.

"I don't know, please..." he blubbers.

It's the swimmer who provides the answer, of course. And as I hold Wynn's head in my pulsating hands, it comes back to me.

29

Matt backs up against the wall between his framed record sleeves of *Led Zeppelin IV* and Steely Dan's *Aja*. He puts up his hands.

"Calm down."

"I can't believe you're standing there telling me to calm down after everything that's happened, Matt, I really can't." I'm in the doorway of the office, raging at him. "You keep saying this is you and me, this is us, so just fucking treat me like *me* and look me in the eyes and be honest about what's going on."

Suddenly, he seems emboldened. "What's going on is you got wasted and hung out with that freak, scared your son half to death, scared *me*, and instead of just sleeping it off and then discussing things at a more reasonable time and state of mind like a normal person, you come flying at me with all these crazy stories, which I wish I had the presence of mind to record, because if you could listen to yourself, honestly, Syd—"

I step out into the hall. "They're not crazy stories. I was at Portnoy's house. I saw what he did."

"Made some sculptures in his attic?" Now Matt's raising his voice, letting exasperation get the better of him. "I'd also like to point out that we're talking about the guy you can't remember *killing*, which is how this all started, which—"

"I remember it now! Every second of it! The swimmer showed me everything, I told you that. That's why I went to that bar in the first place."

"Okay," Matt says, almost eagerly. "Okay. Now we're getting somewhere. You had an episode of repressed trauma come back to you, and it was really hard to deal with, and in a panic, you tried to numb yourself. You weren't thinking straight. That makes sense to me." He puts a hand on his chest like he's saying the Pledge of Allegiance. "I'd probably want to drink, too, if I got hit with something like that." He steps toward me and I let him take my hands. "I get that this is hard to deal with. Like, crushing and terrifying and panic-inducing in a way I can't understand. So, I'm here for you as far as that's concerned. But all this other stuff— this swimmer thing, these phantom text messages, going to Portnoy's house and poking around his attic—all that stuff is just, I don't know." He thinks for a moment. "It's just not *real*. What's real is your recovery and being there for Danny. And I'm here to support you with that. One hundred and ten percent."

It's just not real. I think of the things I didn't even bother to tell him, even crazier-sounding things—the swimmer gibbering nonsense in the depths of the bloodstain, the way it manifested on the Nano Pal screen as some aquatic cryptid...

That gives me an idea. I break his grip on my hands and go to the guest room door.

"Sheriff Butler knows what I'm talking about," I say, opening the door. "He was in here; he felt the swimmer's presence in the house." I remember the man in thrall to the stain, flecks of dried blood stuck to his fingertips. "It did something to him, for sure."

I turn to Matt. "Call the sheriff. Ask him. He'll tell you about the air around my face."

Matt comes over and pulls the door shut. "I'm not calling the sheriff to ask him about something swimming around the guest room and the air around your face, Syd, that's insane. The priority here is you getting better and—"

"Stop saying *getting better* like I'm sick."

"Addiction is a disease."

"Oh, fuck off."

"I was saying the priority is also Danny."

Danny. Fuck. What would Matt do, I wonder, if I called 911 and told them that my boyfriend's parents had kidnapped my son? Because that's what this is, isn't it? Kidnapping? You can't just whisk someone's kid away in the middle of the night, even if his mother happened to get wasted for the first time in nine years, and run her mouth a little bit, and maybe also collapse in the kitchen in front of the kid and scare him in ways she can't remember.

Money's no object for Owen and Judy. I wonder how much legal leverage they could apply. I've got a police record, after all. Scars you can see and scars you can't. If I lose Matt, if he turns against me, would the Melfords' united front actually succeed in wresting Danny away from me for good? Is that even legally possible?

I envision a judge reading from a long, unfurled scroll, enumerating my sins out loud. Of course, I'm an unfit mother. What made me confident that I could pull this off? Eventually the person you really are catches up to you.

Clink. Sip.

My head begins to pound. This particular fear has clarity and dimension. Anxiety spikes. The last of yesterday's booze has been leached away. My between-state dissolves and deposits me into the miserable aftermath. For the first time it strikes me that Matt is right, I must sound absolutely insane.

Except he's managed to weasel out of answering for anything.

"Syd?"

I know what I saw.

"Yeah. Sorry. I spaced out."

"It's okay. Come on. I'll make you some tea."

I follow him down the hall and into the kitchen, where I sit down at the table and rub my head while he puts the kettle on the stove.

"I feel like I share some of the responsibility for this," he says, taking two mugs from the cabinet. "I shouldn't have gone into work at all this week. Screw the Shanghai clusterfuck." He plops in two teabags from the chamomile box. "I should have been fully present and engaged here, at home, with you, and I wasn't." He shakes his head. "I knew something was up when I noticed that you drank one of my beers."

"I didn't," I say quietly. "I just broke the bottle."

My eyes drift, like Danny's, to a piece of junk mail on the table. Concentric loops, ever shrinking.

"This is going to be a dry house from now on," he says, folding his arms and waiting by the kettle. "I've always felt a little guilty about keeping beer in the fridge anyway."

I think of the two cold amber bottles stashed behind the milk. My mind whirrs and spins. If I drink them quickly it might give me enough of a head rush to tamp down my rising anxiety. I can feel it in my chest and behind my eyes.

At the same time, the meta-thought strikes: *What's wrong with you? You can't seriously think that a few beers are going to fix anything.*

Finally, hovering on top of that, bolstered by anxiety: *you will never stop thinking about getting fucked up for as long as you live.*

Everything is binary/everything swirls.

They're going to take Danny away/Danny's coming back in the morning.

Matt is keeping a terrible secret from me/Matt loves me and would never lie to me.

After nine years I slipped up, but I can fix this/I am a hopeless addict at heart and there's nothing I can do about it.

This is real/This is in my head.

The kettle shrieks. Matt kills the flame and fills the two mugs with hot water. He sets a mug down on the table in front of me and I let the steam wreathe my face. Instantly, it makes me feel better. There's a wholesomeness to hot herbal tea, and for a moment I sit and let it counteract every sordid mistake, every unbidden terror that's ever clawed at me. I blow across the top of the mug, and steam disperses.

"I love how you always do that," Matt says. "So ineffective yet so adorable."

In love, how much is performance?

I smile at him. He smiles back and lifts his mug. "There she is."

I lift my mug in return. *Cheers.* Then I take a sip. In her rare lucid moments, my mother used to make me chamomile tea. It's the one domestic habit I carried with me, even through my darkest years—the soothing power of hot steam and bitter-earth flowers. As the tea warms my belly, I feel a grateful surge toward Matt, like when he hands me the travel mug he's already filled with light-and-sweet coffee before I head for the morning train. I could have ended up with someone much worse. He puts up with a lot. I peer at him over the top of the mug and his form seems to waver in the steam. I try to blink him back out of the haze, but he only grows more indistinct. I remind myself that I have no idea what kind of person he is. We don't ever really know what's in someone else's heart, do we? He sets his mug down on the counter and walks over to the table. I giggle: *We don't ever really know what's in someone else's heart* is like tagline copy for a Lifetime Original Movie. Something like *The Stranger in My Bed*, or *My Boyfriend, My Nightmare*.

"I really, really love you," he says. The words have heat and presence and I swallow them like a big sip of tea. They float gently into my stomach and radiate calmness through my chest and down into my thighs.

"I love you, too," I try to say, but my speech is slurred and glacial.

He pulls a chair around next to me and sits down. "How do you feel?"

"Sleepy." I giggle again. The word is a thick slab of nonsense.

"That's good. When you wake up, you'll feel a lot better."

Matt dissolves into tiny Matt-particles that take flight like a swarm of bees and gather by the kitchen window, where the darkness is beginning to lift. The steam from the tea hangs heavy and fills the whole room with thick smoke.

"We're gonna get you fixed up," he says. His voice is far away, a distant whisper on the wind. I drift out the window, into the dawn, and sleep claims me at last.

30

"Fucker put something in the tea," I say out loud. Wynn trembles. His face is hot in my hands, his sweat slick against my palms. My left thumb is resting on the bulge of his eye, a ripe-grape firmness, so easily popped.

With a desire that verges on erotic, the swimmer compels me to press harder. I get the sense that there's a quid pro quo between us now, the give-and-take between lovers—it surfaced the memory of Matt drugging my tea, and in return it craves a mutilation. In my hesitation, I feel its shadow-tendril creep up my forearm, a sibilant whisper wending around my elbow, talking eager nonsense into my ear.

I have to focus and apply pressure to take my arm away from Wynn's face. *I need him*, I tell the swimmer. There's a moment perched on the edge of defiance, and then the swimmer backs down. Wynn lets out a long breath and stares at me through wet, wondering eyes.

"Where am I?" I say.

He cringes at the sound of my voice and averts his eyes. Is my speech a distorted horror? I can't tell. I clear my throat and try again. "Where am I?"

Without looking at me, he begins to speak. "A research and development facility for Alverion Pharmaceuticals."

"In Manhattan?"

"No. That's the main office. This place is in Fremont Hills." I think for a moment. Fremont Hills is about a forty-minute drive from Fernbeck.

"Do you have a car?"

"Yes," he says. Keeping his eyes lowered, he reaches into his pocket, produces his keys, and holds them out to me. "White BMW in the parking lot. Take it." The keys jingle. "Please! Take it and go!"

"Is there security here?"

"Just Hanson and he's long gone now." He swallows. "This place doesn't technically exist."

I make no move to take the keys and they fall from his trembling hand.

"What kind of research and development do you do here? What is all this?"

Medical equipment, but *wrong*. Familiar machines tilted out of joint.

"They don't have names. They made themselves."

A flash of primal birthing, self-knowledge bathed in hot chrome, harvested data. The swimmer purrs. I shift positions and sense the edges of the room. Wynn, eyes downcast, resumes his sobbing. I shift again and my form prods him. He sniffles.

"It's Alverion biotech," he says. "An experimental treatment. Not just meds that act on brain chemicals, like SSRIs, but something that takes root and grows with you and learns your unique biochemistry."

"What kind of biotech? What *is it*?"

He gathers himself and looks me in the eyes as his face

moves from dismay to ecstasy. The swimmer studies each joyous crease in the flesh of his forehead, at the corners of his eyes. (*And the eyes' thin membranes holding back so much warm fluid.*)

"Artificial intelligence for your soul," he says.

Hearing itself so described, the swimmer writhes in what I suspect is embarrassment. This description is not correct. Or, if it is, it is only partly so.

"Go on," I tell him.

"We were trying to cast off limitations. People think of AI and they think of tech—machine learning, smarter devices, eventually the Matrix. But Alverion approached it all so differently, so brilliantly. Bio-AI, something *real*, not just theoretical, or a fucking house that learns your domestic habits."

"So, you grew it in a lab?"

The swimmer stretches, sublimates out to float down like a tossed linen over the entirety of the lab. *Seeking more. Seeking self-knowledge.* Now I understand its quest for more of itself, for the part of it that Kyle Portnoy carried.

Building back the pieces of its awareness.

Wynn shakes his head. "It's not just undiscovered fish in the ocean's deepest trenches. There are compounds down there. Think of all the things that we can't even see that, once we get samples, are like nothing we've ever seen before."

The swimmer exhales. The breath flows out of me. Tension I've been holding in for a long time.

Wynn cringes as the wind from my body troubles his face. I get the sense that a foul odor has enveloped him.

I lean in closer. He is grinning now. Tears flow freely down his face. His eyes are wide and unblinking.

"What did you make?" I demand.

"It made itself," he says. "We're just the instruments."

"What is it?"

His breath stops coming. Wynn goes perfectly silent and still. I can see my reflection in the twin globes of his eyes, and the wrongness floods me with pride.

"Godhead," he says.

I stand up. The swimmer hisses its disappointment but makes no attempt to control me. A pure and vivid sense of relief washes over me and nearly steals my breath.

I'm not crazy. This is all happening, *everything*, exactly as I experienced it. All along, Matt was delivering me into some kind of experiment, living right beside me in a parallel world that intersected with my reality in ways I couldn't imagine.

My heady sense of triumph crashes and burns a split second later. All this time I thought we were partners, two people building a solid life and a bright future together. The joint savings account, the aspirational lake house. How long have we been playing these clashing roles? Did he ever love me, or was I always a test subject in his eyes, since the first day we sat across from each other in the conference room while Halloran presented the creative work it was donating to Matt's nonprofit? I remember catching Matt's eye as I detailed the rationale behind the copy and thinking that he looked like a guy who loved to rock climb, that the body underneath the slim-fit suit was probably lean and strong. Standing there at the head of the table, reading off a Power-Point slide, my wandering mind associated that kind of man with an upright and honest life because he was the opposite of Trevor.

Have we both been striking a half-secret bargain? Did I ever love him, or was I simply taken with the notion of an anti-Trevor?

The swimmer expresses interest at this thought of Danny's father. It surges in my bloodstream, trying to remind me of something. But what? I can't grasp it—it's all margins and recesses, a distant murmur.

Wynn is muttering to himself with his eyes closed. Praying, I think.

"Give me your phone and a lab coat," I demand.

Less than a minute later I'm down the hall and up a set of stairs, through an empty lobby, and out into the dark and deserted parking lot of a small suburban office park. A pair of nondescript three-story buildings flank a cement expanse. Thick pine trees hide a road—I can hear, but not see, the occasional car pass by. There's no sign that Alverion Pharmaceuticals does anything at all in this place. It looks like the home of a midsize insurance agency, maybe a few tax attorneys. I check Wynn's phone: 9:48 p.m. I make my way to the only car in the lot, the white BMW, and get into the driver's seat.

Wynn's car smells like the remnants of a thousand late-night trips to fast-food drive-thrus. Science never sleeps. The front seat is littered with receipts, wrappers, and Camel soft packs.

I start the car and sit for a moment. I'm oddly calm after what just happened. My whole being should be going haywire—adrenaline burning off, thoughts racing into oblivion—not to mention the general anxiety and overriding sense of *holy shit* gnawing at my state of mind. But my heart rate is normal, my breathing steady. It takes me a moment to realize what's happening, but the distant gibbering knocks the thought into place: the swimmer is calibrating my brain chemicals like a recording engineer adjusting levels on the mixing board to find the proper sound. Just as the swimmer filtered out the piercing alarm and the screams of the technicians, it's shielding me from hysteria in the wake of what just happened.

"Thank you," I say out loud. I think I've opened up a true and direct line of communication by begging it for help. It's no longer an unknowable haunting, a cosmic horror that my pitiful human brain can't process. Nor is it a presence so spectral and otherworldly that its motives are forever obscured. It wants to know me, and help me, and it wants me to *love it in return*. That's not a bad bargain. It's one I've struck before.

Though never with a god.

I take out Wynn's phone and dial the Dutchess County Sheriff's office. With a remarkably even-keeled voice, I ask for Sheriff Butler and tell the receptionist my name. A moment later he comes on.

"Miss Burgess," he says guardedly.

"Sheriff. Matt's been—"

And that's as far as I get, at least in a language the sheriff can understand, before the swimmer steals my voice. What pours out of my mouth in its place is corrupted. It scorches my throat on the way out.

Stop! I implore it. *You're hurting me.* The swimmer relents.

"Jesus Christ." The sheriff's voice cracks.

"Meet me at my house." I speak quickly in case the swimmer switches frequencies again.

He hesitates. "Why don't you come to the station."

I think of what he wants most: a reason. "I know why this happened," I say. The swimmer asserts itself again. The reek of something very old burns my nasal passages. "You have to come get Matt." My voice is a wet rasp. "He's responsible for everything. Come now!"

I end the call and toss the phone in the front seat's nest of paper. Then I explain what I'm doing to the swimmer so there's no misunderstanding.

I need the sheriff to know about Matt and what he's done so I don't have any problem getting Danny back. I need to be on the record as a sane person.

The swimmer writhes in displeasure. I gasp at a sudden vertiginous drop in my stomach.

"I need to get Danny back," I say out loud, as firmly as I can, "and I need the sheriff on my side."

In reply, a sickly-sweet odor rises up through the stained fabric seats and emanates from the blowers. I click the headlights on, put the car into drive, and cruise out of the parking lot down a two-lane road lined with dense evergreens.

I'm worried that the swimmer has reverted back to its oblique method of communication. I thought we were getting somewhere with its halting stutter-steps of language I could actually understand. What is this scent supposed to tell me? At first, I think it's pure petulance and wonder, absurdly, how old the swimmer is. But as I pull out onto the main road and join the sparse traffic heading toward the interstate, the smell triggers a memory. It's sweetness with an acrid edge to it, a chemical burn. Plastic set aflame. Plastic, yes, and also flesh.

I try to focus on the road, slowing down and keeping an eye on the white line at the edge of the highway on-ramp, following its loping curve into the slow lane.

Stop, I tell the swimmer. *Please.*

Because I know what the swimmer is getting at. And it's not something I care to revisit after all this time.

I lean forward, grip the steering wheel, and train my eyes on the car in front of me, keeping a safe distance. Heat pours from the car's blowers, and the memory the swimmer's delivering crowds the corners of my vision. I try to blink it away but it's no use. The swimmer's gifts aren't the kind you politely accept then furtively cast aside.

But why this? Why now? The swimmer lifts a massive, knotted veil, and I gasp. It's like parting the curtains on a dusty room, a forgotten corner of an empty house. I feel the swimmer purr in regal satisfaction that stems from something much deeper. *Love me love me love me.* Its very notion of love was born here, I realize—inside what it has been keeping from me. I feel it, too, the swimmer lapping up the savagery I'd kept at bay for so long, tasting with eager senses the rage and desperation I'd buried under love for Danny like a corpse covered in quicklime.

Wrapped in a baggy lab coat, smeared in antiseptic and blood, I head home to face what's next as what came before rushes up to meet me.

THE SIXTH
VISITATION

31 (then)

I am twenty-three years old. The rattrap trailer I share with Trevor is a one-bedroom single-wide. Linoleum the color of pistachio, flimsy wood paneling, a screen door that won't quite close. A Sublime poster hangs askew above the futon. All of Trevor's heroes are artists felled by drugs in their prime. He's a twenty-eight-year-old man obsessed with the Twenty-Seven Club—Cobain, Hendrix, Winehouse. Although he's never told me as much, I suspect that he's bitter about not dying at twenty-seven himself, as if that would validate the half-hearted attempts at lyrics in the composition books on the closet floor. He wrote one song with a thumbtack dipped in blood.

Even in a home the size of a hallway, basic housekeeping has gotten away from us, vanished at some unknown point like the last of our sober friends. The surfaces of the shower and sink are furred in hair and clumps of wet dust. Dishes fused with hardened sauce-crusts are stacked in the sink. Empty Domino's boxes hold crumpled Wendy's wrappers and half-flattened Big Mac containers.

The only thing you could call truly clean and functional is

Trevor's prized possession, an authentic Jimmy Buffett Margaritaville margarita maker. It's a restaurant-sized machine that takes up all of our meager counter space. He traded an eight ball for it back when he was dealing and we were flush, before his own manic cycle of eye-popping three-a.m. revelations and fetal noontime crashes stole his kingpin ambitions.

"You can have lime, or like, lime," he says, dumping half a plastic handle of tequila into the spigot atop the machine. His back is to me and the Gothic-script VICTORY inked across his shoulder blades contorts. He picks up a knife, opens the freezer door, and savagely attacks the astonishingly thick layer of permafrost that renders the freezer useless. Chunks of ice fall to the floor. He scoops them up and deposits them into the machine.

"I've never actually heard a Jimmy Buffett song," he says, pronouncing *Buffett* like an all-you-can-eat.

"'Margaritaville,'" I say from the edge of the futon, where I'm sitting and staring at a jungle animal show on the muted TV while a live set from some house DJ thumps out of the boombox on the nightstand. The boombox presides over a landscape of rigs, spoons, and cottons.

Trevor flicks the BLEND switch and the machine roars to life. On TV a fluorescent bird dips its long delicate bill into a cupped flower.

"*What?*" he hollers over the grinding of ice chunks getting pulverized.

I wait for the noise to cease. The bird is tetchy and moves like a creature with superpowers, as though it can teleport its head a short distance and flash to a different position so fast my eye can't pick it up. I think about how a bird like this should inspire inward-looking thoughts and near-mystical connections—ways in which I am and am not like this bird.

But I'm so enveloped in my high, I've reached a sort of stasis during which I simply let the notion of an animal like this existing someplace I'll never see wash over me. My mind is walled in. Later, when I start to come down, I'll find the bird again. I bookmark it in my subconscious. There are things I should be thinking about the bird, I just can't think them yet.

The machine stops grinding and dispenses greenish slush into a waiting goblet with a cactus for a stem, which Trevor stole from a Mexican restaurant after eating the free chips and salsa.

"'Margaritaville,'" I say again.

He adds a pair of bendy straws. They peek like periscopes over the rim of the glass. "I want to *Lady and the Tramp* this with you."

"That's spaghetti," I tell him as he comes over to the futon and hands me the goblet. I hold the freezing glass in two cupped hands. I don't want any alcohol—I want to ride out this last not-so-spectacular shot and save the booze for the more desperate time to come. We'll be dry by dawn, shoving baggies between our gums and lips, licking residue off the nightstand, taking dirty-cotton shots as a last resort and risking the fever. But desire and revulsion are muddled and I'm hyper-suggestible, so I take a sip. It's not mixed right. My lipstick stains the straw.

"The question is…" he says sagely as I hand him the goblet. He sucks greedily. Trevor is a hedonist as long as he's high, pursuing tactile pleasures and various forms of emotional connection, motormouthing things he wants to get off his chest. Tonight, I'm a light-speed engine trapped in a vessel of stillness, a stationary cage for a revved-up heart. "…who's the lady and who's the tramp."

"Tramps like us."

"Lady we were born to tramp."

His eyes drill unblinking into the TV screen as he hands me back the goblet. The show cuts to an endless canopy, a sci-fi treetop city in the mist. At the same time, the DJ set transitions to ethereal synthesizer fuzz.

"Holy shit." He turns to me, eyes wide with the ecstasy of kismet. "Holy *shit*, baby."

"I saw."

"Did you see that?"

"Yes."

He sits down on the futon and the whole frame creaks.

"It's like," he says, pausing to bite a hangnail, "it's like, I can get just as mesmerized sober with something like that. All my life I could spot things that lined up in ways that other people couldn't. Like, Melanie"—his previous girlfriend—"Melanie was always like, Trevor, *what*, but fuck her. I—*juxtapositions*, that's the word. Shit lining up."

He stands up, puts his hands on his hips, and walks to the kitchen and back, a journey of six steps each way. When he returns, he leans down and kisses me hard on the mouth.

"Ice kisses," he says as he straightens up.

Something shifts inside me and I feel light-headed. Nerves begin to chip away at my high. On TV, a toucan blurs and then comes back to itself. I blink. Disappointment so profound wells up in me that for a moment I nearly weep.

"I don't think this shit is very good," I say. There's a dry-wall taste in my mouth.

"I know," Trevor said. "I shit my guts out an hour ago, too, remember? I think it's half laxative."

"I should have thought about the bird automatically," I say, "but instead I thought about how I was going to think about it."

"My heart, though," Trevor says. He sticks out his tongue and uses it to get the straw into his mouth.

"Mine, too."

"Speed." He shakes his head. "Fucking bikers."

I glance at the nightstand, take in what we have left. Enough for us to bang another shot. I'm already past the crest and the last one rocketed me exactly nowhere. I can feel the jitters coming on prematurely. Anger surges—Trevor can't even get us decent powder anymore. I try to recall how long I've been awake, but I can't. I used to tally the hours but now I never keep track. One of the pleasures of this life is rendering time a pointless human construct. It's a silly thing, if you step back and look at it from well outside the rat race. An invented method to chart meaningless progress while we tick our lives away.

I shake my head. That sounds like something Trevor would write with a thumbtack dipped in blood.

"Ah!" he says, like he's having a Eureka moment. He rushes to the living room window and peeks between the slats of our smoke-yellowed blinds. He tucks strands of his straw-colored hair behind his ear and peers intently, narrowing his eyes.

"It's nothing," I say preemptively. He gets paranoid about what he calls *watchers*, though I can never get him to clarify if they're supposed to be cops, or neighbors, or something else entirely.

"Oh, it's something," he says mysteriously. Then he turns his head and winks at me. "I got a surprise for our anniversary."

I blink. "How do you know when our anniversary is?"

"I just figured I'd make up a day, since we don't really have one, and we'd celebrate it."

He shoots me a goofy smile. Outside, car tires crunch gravel and headlights come through the slats and then vanish as the engine cuts off. A moment later, someone's knocking on the door.

"Ah," Trevor says again, scampering over the futon to open the door. He moves aside and gestures grandly as if he's ushering a distinguished guest into our magnificent hall.

The man who steps into our trailer glances over his shoulder as Trevor shuts the door behind him, then turns to take in the room. He's got an angular, high-cheekboned face with darting eyes and an oddly thick neck. A faded denim jacket hangs loosely from his frame, and a pair of tight spandex leggings hugs his unsightly, bulging thighs. His gaze sweeps across the kitchen, takes in the Sublime poster, and pauses when it gets to me. He changes his stance, putting his hands on his hips. His eyes scan my chest, my legs, my bare feet. My heart is the bird on TV, racing perfectly still.

"Well." The man turns to Trevor. "Let's do this."

32 (now)

The memory recedes, leaving in its wake fresh curiosities. This man, this stranger, is new to me. I'm sure he was always there, buried in the dreamy heat of the blaze itself, but the swimmer has drawn him out.

The acrid odor inside the car is eclipsed by the biting sweetness of anise. The swimmer, eager to peel back layers, is enamored with what it's found in my heart. There is pride in the way it shares with me, gives me back to myself.

As I drive through Fernbeck, I find that the swimmer's perceptions have been grafted to me like a subtle mutation, a slippery contact lens sliding back and forth across my vision, blurring in and out of focus. It goes beyond sight, stimulating my sense of wonder. It's as if I've stepped into a fever that's not entirely my own, as if the *concept* of a fever has settled over me, minus the actual sickness.

I see the swimmer's language writ large across the streets and shops and houses of my town, great swoops and angles of an inhuman alphabet. I see it in the way the bare branches of a maple tree reach across a lighted bank sign to form polygons of negative space. Holes in the world. I see it in the slip and curl of the winding wooded streets of our subdivision, crawling up driveways to scrawl through garage doors and parked cars and kids' bicycles left outside. It's all so plainly evident to me now, it's strange I've never seen it before.

I suppose I just lacked the right kind of eyes.

This new perception is like a drug. To think that I resisted it for so long! In the glow of the dashboard light, I can see that the tops of my hands, near the knuckles, are pocked with clusters of tiny holes. They pulsate. A stray thought comes and goes: *when you're not bound by human biology, anything can be a mouth.* The swimmer's orifices purr in unison and my heart skims like a tern along the surface of a lake.

I pull into my driveway. The sheriff is already here, his Crown Victoria parked by the curb. There are lights on in the living room. My stomach knots into a small, hard pebble, and I understand it as the swimmer's glowering contempt. I see it in my mind's eye as a writhing mass of thin black tendrils in perpetual motion.

I cut the engine and step out of the car. The sleeves of the lab coat hang to the tips of my fingers. I take a moment to contemplate my street. Bugs weave patterns against the glow of my neighbors' wrought-iron lamps. Glyphs of non-language form and dissipate. A sudden gust of wind bends naked branches and carries with it a ripe hint of the river. I sense nostalgia, a pang of longing, and I wonder what kind of water birthed the swimmer.

At the front door I put my hand on the doorknob and am instantly struck nearly blind. The swimmer chooses this moment to flood me with impressions, flipped and sorted rapid-fire through my mind like a deck of cards being expertly shuffled. The focal point is the doorknob, the images on the cards *every time I've ever touched it.*

The day we saw the FOR SALE sign and popped in on a whim for the open house.

The first time crossing the threshold together as homeowners.

The end of every workday, every camping trip, every dinner out at Carmine's by the station.

There and gone is the moment I flung open the door to find the man in the mask rifling through the front hall credenza.

Too much, I tell the swimmer, and my head clears. The visions lift, leaving behind the certainty that the swimmer's notion of time is much different than mine: stretched, stacked, something other than linear.

As alien as its notion of love.

I open the door. The deep-rooted smell of our house hits me hard—I'm the most aware of it I've ever been. It seeps into the tiny holes on my knuckles and in my palms, where the lines and joints are pocked with clusters that snake in gorgeous array up my arms. The smell of my family trampled into every carpet. I share the melancholy of this with the swimmer, and I sense its curiosity in the way my mouth fills up with saliva. The swimmer can process the smell but has a hard time grasping why this might mean something precious to me, even clouded by my red-minded fury at the man who gets up from the couch and steps toward me.

"Sydney," Matt says.

I ascend the five steps from the front hall into the living room. As I come fully into view, he stops walking and puts up his hands. Behind him, the sheriff says "Oh, fuck this," and retreats into the kitchen.

"Jesus Christ." Matt staggers back and makes a hurried sign of the cross with his right hand. It's what he does when we drive past a cemetery. He begins to turn away, then stops, catches himself, and seems to overrule his own body. He takes a deep breath and forces himself to hold his ground. He turns his head toward me for a second, then shuts his eyes tight. He looks like he's about to be wracked with great, heaving, ugly sobs. His jowls look like the jowls of a much older man when his face quivers.

"Sydney." He swallows. "I'm so sorry. I swear to God I was just trying to help you. You have to believe me. We can still fix this, okay? We can still—"

"You did this to me."

He winces at the sound of my voice. Slowly, he opens his eyes, and his jaw clenches as he forces himself to hold my gaze. "I don't—I can't understand you." His lower lip begins to tremble. I concentrate on my words, forging something intelligible from the swimmer's tongue. Judging by Matt's reaction, what comes out is clear enough.

"You did this to me."

Matt begins to cry. It's an ugly sight—as if he is simultaneously wrinkling and relaxing his face. I come toward him across the paisley rug we bought on our last trip to Hudson to troll for antiques. Or, at least, the rug moves beneath me.

Matt steps back and collapses into our Eames chair, which I have a sudden desire to disarticulate. To render an un-chair. As the swimmer guided me through butchery, so will it guide me through this dismantling. I am of great worth to a certain kind of off-kilter entropy, and the swimmer's abilities touch on many disciplines. It has recognized a kindred impulse in me.

Matt speaks with his head in his hands. "It wasn't supposed to happen this way."

His anguish strikes me as mediocre. A dismal, trite expression. A face-saving gesture. Perhaps that's his prime motivator as an actor on a stage he can barely navigate, constructed by hands he doesn't understand: endlessly saving face with the lover he lies to and the God who sees into his heart.

In love, how much is performance?

The swimmer is filtering my perceptions and distilling *coldness* from what is happening. I nudge it gently—*I need to be myself for a moment*—and it gets the picture. Then it overcompensates and I'm once again hammered by a stack of simultaneous experiences. There's the deck-shuffling feeling in my head, the low murmurs of the swimmer trying desperately to understand. It's a gesture of goodwill but it *hurts*. The swimmer has asked me to love it as it loves me and I have agreed, but still it struggles to see a clear picture of what that might mean, coming from me. This time, as the cards fall away, I'm struck dumb in the thrall of the swimmer's curious dredging. A tendril, a wet probing tongue, combs my brain.

Here and gone:

Trevor in better days, a handsome punk, a crooked smiler, and me no older than seventeen, bumming a smoke outside a basement hardcore show at a forlorn VFW. The fluttery chest, the light-limbed lust, the fumbling in the woods behind the dumpster. All the dismal trudging of my mother and me, orbiting each other day after day like ghosts in the glow of the TV, fading to black as Trevor glows brighter. Love as rage (the swimmer likes this, oh yes): me beating the shit out of his ex, ripping out a hoop earring, hot blood spurting while he looks on with his boys, all of their arms folded, nodding approval. The two of us, high and fucking for so long I have to ice my inner thighs. What does the swimmer make of all this? What do I make of it?

The deck flips and there's Matt across the conference table, slim-fit suit and side-parted hair, ruler-straight. Raw and suspicious, I spend our first few dates waiting for him to be an asshole. Our love is built around his simple refusal to be one. The swimmer perks up at these complications, these unexpected avenues. Love as low expectations defied. Love as warm practicality. Matt filling my travel mug with coffee every morning before he leaves. His sketches of our lake-house-to-be, the reward for Making It Work.

The swimmer flips a card and finds the needle and the spoon—how I resisted it for so long, how Trevor talked me into it, and how from the first shot I knew I was home. Love as shelter, love as cocoon, love as thoughts revved up to a million miles an hour. What a lark, what a plunge. Ah, but that brings the swimmer to Danny, and I can feel it pause, savoring the flood of emotion, tasting all my hurts. Different kinds of love ought not to be measured against each other, but who can help it? We're a race of winners and losers, why should love be any less ranked? Love as an oceanic ebb and flow—all the joys and frustrations of motherhood, great and small, captured in my son's searching eyes. Love that can't be named or pored over like a photo in an archive. At this, the swimmer pauses. Absorbs. Retreats.

The living room rushes back. I'm standing over Matt as he cowers in the Eames chair. Snot bubbles out of his nose as he heaves. My palms itch fiercely. My eyes are blinking very quickly, or else I'm perceiving the gap between each blink in a strange new way. I hold out my palms to show him the clusters. There are tiny holes congregating and crowding every crease. The pads of my fingertips are constellations. My new biology.

"Oh fuck make it stop Sydney—"

I catch sight of the photograph on the mantel—Danny, Matt, and me grinning like idiots with our hands in the air as the Six Flags roller coaster camera catches us frozen in mid-descent, hair whipped back.

Matt is blubbering now. My hands are gripping the arms of the chair and I'm leaning very close to him.

I whisper in his ear. "Why?"

He grimaces as if I've forced him to sniff rancid milk. It strikes me that the swimmer's tongue might not be limited to sounds—the noises might have flavor, or scent.

Matt takes a deep, shaky breath, and the words come tumbling out.

"*It's beautiful*, is what Wynn kept telling me. It's going to revolutionize the way addiction is treated. Think about it. Why do addicts relapse? The unbearable memories of past traumas. This treatment learns to selectively block out the bad stuff, let you get on with your life without being dragged down by the past. Why else do people relapse? When you give up alcohol, drugs, fast food, sugar, sex, caffeine—the absence leaves a void to be filled. This treatment fills that void. It's a guiding voice in your head. A real presence in your everyday life. It fills in the gaps of what you lack."

The swimmer writhes. Matt winces. The smell of sulfur fills the room.

The swimmer is eager for disarticulation—I feel its desire at the rim of every mouth-cluster—but it does not care about the chair. It is focused on Matt. After all its flailing about for meaning, it has landed squarely on love-as-rage. *It happened so fast*. Simple, fierce, pure. I keep its thoughts tethered to the back of my mind while I consider what Matt has just revealed.

"You dosed Kyle Portnoy with it."

Matt swallows. "It was an act of Christian charity. He was so beaten down, so hopeless, and I thought if I could get the means to help him, then I owed it to him to try. I couldn't just let him spiral. Wynn said it would never in a million years be approved, but there were back channels..."

"You dosed *me* with it!" My voice moves around the living room on a weird, tilted plane.

"Sydney, listen to me—since we moved in together you relapsed. Last year. You weren't just some guinea pig. I was trying to help. I was doing it for you and Danny."

A noise of disbelief, of unearthly mourning, escapes my lips. Relapse? I don't believe it. Viscous secretions from my hole-clusters coat the chair and puddle warmly in Matt's lap. He screams. His eyes are wide, searching the room just over my shoulder.

"Oh, Jesus, Sydney, stop, please!" He's crying now. Pleading. "I told you about it and *you asked me for it! You begged me for it, Syd, I swear to God!*"

No.

Is it true? I ask the swimmer. Occupied by its ministrations, it does not deign to answer my question.

"I think it has some side effects," I say.

"*I know, I know, we were trying to extract it, we were—*"

Poor Matt. I make an honest attempt to absolve him.

"*Shhhhh,*" I say, and lay a finger softly against his mouth. At my touch his screaming becomes a piercing shriek. "It's okay. I think it's falling in love with me."

"*I* love you, Sydney. *I* love you."

I shake my head. "You only love what I've become. But the swimmer knows who I've always been, and it wants me to see."

The savagery in my heart.

"Help me, Sheriff, *help me!*"

I can't fathom his fear. It's possible that he is in pain. Yes, I think he probably is—I feel the cluster of pinprick holes at my fingertip suckle eagerly at his lower lip. I think: *this is pleasant, I am curious about the mechanism here, what does it taste like?* In the photograph on the mantel, we are grinning and waving, waving and grinning.

The sheriff appears, bulky and trembling, in the doorway to the kitchen. He has been there all along, just behind the wall, listening. He is hatless. Great continents of sweat run from his underarms down the sides of his untucked uniform shirt and blotch into islands around his belly.

You see, I could say to him, *none of this is my fault. And now you have your reason.* But we're way past earthly concerns.

With my finger devouring Matt's lip, I meet Sheriff Butler's eyes. To my astonishment he stares me full in the face, unblinking. I think of the man sitting beside my hospital bed, telling me about his art-school dropout daughter. How far we've come, all of us.

"It's beautiful," he says in a voice gilded with the awe of a penitent meeting his god. Then he draws his gun, slides the muzzle into his mouth, and pulls the trigger.

33 (then)

Sydney," Trevor says, gesturing to our visitor, "this is Litch-field. Litchfield, Sydney."

I nod. The man's *Let's do this* settles into my skull and echoes dully. Litchfield's eyes go heavy-lidded and he curls his lips into the kind of smile you'd send across the bar to someone you'd set your sights on. I turn back to the TV. A bird with plumage like a shock of bone-white hair spreads its wings and puffs out its chest feathers.

We owe money to all of our regular dealers, so Trevor must have scoured the ends of the earth for this guy. His ambition knows no bounds when it comes to acquiring more, always more, more, more. I can sense a nervous reverence coming from Trevor, a shimmer in the energy he uses to construct his personality.

"The fuck you listening to?" Litchfield says.

Trevor goes to the boombox and makes a big show of fussing with it. He jabs a button and kills the thumping DJ set. "Anything you want to hear?"

"You didn't have to turn it off," Litchfield says.

"Well, you said it like, I don't know."

"Yeah, I don't give a shit, though."

"Okay, man, I can turn it back on."

"Nah."

Trevor pauses a moment. Then he sits down next to me on the edge of the futon. "I just need a second," he tells Litchfield. I glance at our visitor. He scratches his left pectoral through his white undershirt.

Trevor leans in close. I can smell his Trevor-husk, that brittle exoskeleton he develops after a few days awake. In the silence of the dormant stereo and the muted TV, I can hear Litchfield scratching, Trevor's heart thumping, the hum of the fridge.

"Okay, Syd," he says quietly, though I'm sure Litchfield can hear him, "we're gonna be all set." He makes a fluttery bird out of his intertwined thumbs, flaps his fingers, and flies it away. I glance at the bird on the TV and back at Trevor's hands while my mind churns stubbornly. I have definitely crested. I'm sliding down into befuddlement.

"This guy's gonna front us some shit we can sell," Trevor continues. "Good, actual shit. I mean we can get some personal use out of it but we gotta save most of it, okay?"

I side-eye Litchfield. He goes to examine the margarita machine. An odor I can't place hangs in his wake.

"Where'd you find him?" I say in a voice so low it's practically just breath.

Trevor seems taken aback by the question. "A guy knows a guy knows a guy. Etcetera."

Litchfield opens the plastic hatch atop the machine and takes a whiff.

"How many guys till you got to him?"

"I can vouch for his shit being good is all that matters." Trevor touches my thigh, then clamps a hand around my kneecap like he's about to administer a horse bite. "We're gonna get set up again. No more scraping by. No more gift card bullshit." He pauses. "New baby clothes. No more Goodwill." I swear his eyes twinkle. "But before all that we're gonna get properly organized, you and me, right here, right now, *tonight*." I glance at the blinds to confirm that it is, indeed, night.

Litchfield begins to sing "Margaritaville" in an astonishingly lilting voice.

"That's the one," I tell Trevor.

"Hey, I never heard that before," Trevor calls across the trailer to Litchfield.

Litchfield frowns. "Where you been living?"

"Here."

"I meant under which rock."

Litchfield goes to the freezer and opens it and recoils at the sight of the ice.

"So, yeah." Trevor's breath is in my ear.

Litchfield's *Let's do this*, his lazy-lidded reptile eyes taking me in...

My brain, teetering on the edge of the comedown, makes the connection. *Too slow, Sydney.*

I stand up. "Fuck no!" I'm louder than I mean to be, but I don't care.

Trevor leaps off the futon and edges close to me while Litchfield slams the freezer door. "*Shhh*, Syd, chill, I didn't make any promises, I just..." He trails off.

"Just what?"

His voice is so low it's a purr. "I'm doing this for all of us. For Danny."

At the sound of our son's name my heart speeds up and my mind slides into a kind of numb horror. I take a step back, out of Trevor's husk radius. "Like fuck you are."

Trevor's eyes go glassy and I think of the way he watched my fist hammer the back of his ex-girlfriend's head. "Don't fuck this up for us, Syd. Think for a second."

Litchfield is back in the space last occupied by his lingering scent. He folds his arms and the sleeves of his leather jacket slide up his forearms to expose two beaded bracelets inked around his wrists. "Problem?"

"All good, man," Trevor says, without taking his dead eyes off me. "Right?"

"No," I say, red mist curling at the edges of my sight. "No, nothing's good." I stare Litchfield down. "I'm not doing this, so you can fuck off."

He looks at Trevor. "I like her spirit." He sniffs the air. "It's very primitive." He shakes his head, corrects himself. "*Primal.*"

"*Get the fuck out of here.*" I'm pointing at the door even though it's right next to us. Litchfield's face hazes in and out of a blood-colored cloud. Trevor grabs my elbow and I shake him off and he grabs it again, tighter. "*You piece of shit!*" I'm a trembling fury, screaming the jagged edges of my comedown at these two men.

A muffled cry comes from the trailer's lone bedroom down a short hallway opposite the kitchen. Instantly, I go quiet and still.

Litchfield regards us curiously. He raises an eyebrow. "That's interesting. Il bambino."

"Let's everybody just chill," Trevor says. "I'll make us margaritas."

"Get out," I say to Litchfield in a voice gone flat and empty. "*Leave.*"

Danny's cry pitches toward hysteria. I'm just about to head to the bedroom when Litchfield reaches into his jacket and pulls out a silver revolver, an Old West six-shooter. The red cloud dissolves and in its place is a thudding clarity.

"Now just hold on a minute," Litchfield says. The gun is casual in his hand, gripped so loosely it looks like it could drop to the floor. Danny shrieks. I fight a creeping paralysis.

"Litchfield," Trevor says, inching behind me, as if he could vanish cartoonlike behind my much smaller self. "It's cool."

"Let me tell you what's cool," Litchfield says. "What's cool is, I'm getting my dick wet. Doesn't matter to me how." He points the gun at me and the dark hole at the tip of the barrel tractor-beams my eyes straight to it. A prickly sensation crawls up my body. It's like someone's blowing on the back of my neck. "You." He waits for that to sink in then swivels the gun to Trevor. "Or you."

Another beat and he lowers the gun and trains his eyes on me. Then he turns back to Trevor. "I'll let the man of the house decide. You got thirty seconds."

Every heartbeat hammers home a vicious fantasy: grab the gun and blow his brains out the back of his head, kick him in the balls till his junk turns to mush, stomp his jaw into the floor, jab out his eyes—and at the same time I'm rooted to the floor while Danny accuses me in his infant's wail of being everything I already know that I am.

Litchfield uses his free hand to reach into his pocket and retrieve a large ziplock stuffed with smaller stamp bags, each one full of cocaine. "Remember what this is all for."

Saliva floods my mouth.

"Whoever you want, man," Trevor says quietly.

Litchfield pockets the ziplock and places a hand beside his ear. "Come again?"

Danny howls his distress in one long cry followed by short squalls. I need to go to him, I need to get the gun away from

Litchfield, I need to get out of this trailer, out of this life. I don't move, don't speak, don't go anywhere.

"I didn't hear you," Litchfield says.

"I said, whoever you want," Trevor says. His words ring in my ears and my delayed comprehension rips me from my moorings. Giving no thought to the gun, I turn on Trevor and claw at his face, screaming.

"Hey!" Litchfield shoves his way between us and aims the gun between my eyes. I back off. What I think is genuine disgust crosses his face as he turns to Trevor. "The fuck, man. Jesus Christ." He looks at me. "Might want to have a long talk with him when this is all over. Maybe some couples therapy."

He goes to the futon and sits down with his legs spread wide. Then he shakes his head. "This fucking trailer park, man, I swear to God."

I turn on Trevor again. He looks sick with the toll this life has taken, his distended belly and saggy chest, the faded stick-and-poke tattoos on his neck. A gray sheen settles over his skin.

Litchfield gives a shrill whistle. "I do have other stops to make."

Trevor meets my eyes for a moment. "I'm sorry, Syd," he mutters. Then he goes to the futon and gets down on his knees. Litchfield shimmies to lower the waist of his spandex pants. Trevor leans forward and takes Litchfield's cock into his mouth.

In the bedroom, Danny cries and cries.

34 (now)

Matt's screams are muffled by his closed lips. My finger has knit them together. The puckered craters are suctioning with surprising force.

I wonder: Is the swimmer *feeding*? Does it need sustenance? It answers me with a shift in vision, and my perceptions distort to overlap with the swimmer's point of view. All the objects in my living room—the Eames chair, the photographs on the mantel, the clawfoot sofa, the framed Edward Hopper print, the blood and brain matter dripping down the wall, the sheriff's prone body—are less solid than they have always appeared. They are so easily smeared into one another. At first, I think this is a misunderstanding on the swimmer's part—there seems to be so much that it simply cannot comprehend—but then a kinship begins to grow. A recognition. The fleshy knit of Matt's mouth, the way his arms flail as he tries in vain to escape the chair, the tears in his bloodshot eyes, the ripped patch of wallpaper behind his head that he meant to repair a month ago—all of it stitches together a pattern of the swimmer's tongue, those impossible geometries.

My heart is racing. Can I translate its written language? In the photo on the mantel, our mouths form part of this unearthly alphabet, twisting into characters both sharp and fluid—a hybrid language. I catalogue all the moments I became aware of it—in our basement cave, Big Ben's corruption, when I didn't recognize it for what it was but only something dismal and strange. In Kyle Portnoy's mutilated flesh. In the streets of Fernbeck. In the living room of this house where I live with my boyfriend and son.

The trappings of the life I built are a language I can only see from the side, in glances and hints.

The stubble around Matt's mouth and on his chin is being subsumed by clusters of tiny holes that manifest like a close-up of bacteria superimposed on skin. I watch with fascination as each coarse dirty blond hair, no longer than a quarter of an inch, is sucked into a newly enlarged pore. He's emitting a noise like the gurgle of a corroded drain. Underneath the garbled nonsense I can hear vague pleas for mercy. His pupils have rolled back into his skull so that only the whites are visible, inscribed with pink blood vessels. The viscous puddle in his lap gleams darkly like the bloodstain in the guest room. I am aware that my ministrations are likely killing him, and that even if I drew back now, he would be irreparably damaged. I am aware that this is not just anybody that my new biology is corrupting, but Matt, the man I once committed myself to. I can even call upon happy memories of us at will. All I have to do is glance around to see the small joys of our shared world. What some people might call evidence of love, or something like it. And yet none of this understanding makes me want to pull back in horror at what I've done, to call an ambulance, to cradle his feverish head until help arrives, begging him to hang on. It is as if I have already dismissed all the myriad ways we might cultivate affection, friendship, the bonds of motherhood, as things the swimmer will never be able to grasp. These concepts are too foreign, they represent too vast a chasm to cross. What the swimmer prefers is to test the limits of the flesh itself.

Yet this is more than an idle experiment. It is an act of love born of recognition.

Holes in our bodies, holes in the world. It is becoming difficult to distinguish Matt's face from the grinning face in the photo, and the photo exists in a liminal space between the wall and the chair. The letters of the swimmer's tongue lap hungrily at the place where Matt's mouth used to be. I pull my finger from his lips. The cluster at my fingertip is reluctant to let go and a thin strand tugs at Matt's face before falling away. My skin is alive with sensation, and the luminous rope that connects my head to my heart bursts through the holes in my body. Its radiance dances across the ruin of Matt's face, illuminating words that should not exist.

Together, we read what we have written.

35 (then)

I'm standing over our trailer's futon, holding a plastic Big Gulp cup in one hand and a Zippo lighter in the other.

Trevor is snoring. One arm is thrown across his face as if he can't bear to look. His sleeve of haphazard tattoos is clownish in the moonlight that comes in through the blinds. Next to him on the mattress are three of my Nano Pals, my only keepsakes from a childhood best forgotten, little plastic pods the color of pink lemonade, coffee, and orange juice. Hand-me-down toys meant for Danny when he's old enough. In the meantime, Trevor has been raising them. A dog, a cat, and a fish. Keeping them alive with doting obsessiveness. Father of the year. So dedicated to the health and well-being of three digital animals on a tiny screen that he stays awake for days tending to them.

I breathe quietly. The ravages of my own sickness and the desire to get well—all of it has been overshadowed by the last half hour's errand.

Walk to the gas station.

Use the last of my cash to buy an extra-large soda and pre-pay for ten dollars of gas.

Go outside and wait for the clerk to go back to his little TV screen.

Walk to the farthest pump.

Dump the soda and the ice.

Fill the Big Gulp with gasoline and replace the lid.

Come home and hover over Trevor as he sleeps, searching for the courage and the will, finding only hesitation.

Okay, Sydney. Two paths. Lay them out.

The first path: You take Danny and slip out into the night and never look back. As Danny grows up, you tell him his father is dead. Things are okay for a while. Peaceful. Except one day, Danny comes home from school and tells you about a strange man hanging around. A man with tattoos on his neck. Your blood runs cold and you remember what Trevor made you do to his ex-girlfriend. You wonder what he has planned for you. How naive of you to think that he would ever let you go without having the last word. And then one day he pops up at your job. I mean you no harm, he says. I understand what you did and why you did it. I'm not here to place blame. I just want to be a part of Danny's life. I'm his father, after all. I admit that I was fucked up back then but I'm clean now. Don't you think it's a little messed up that you won't let Danny have a relationship with his father? You were fucked up back then, too, remember. It takes two to tango. What did you tell him about me? I bet you told him I was dead. How about that guy I saw you with, is that your boyfriend? I can go to court if I have to. I don't want to, but I will if you force me to. Three years clean. My lawyer thinks I can get shared custody.

I pause. What Trevor said to Litchfield echoes through my mind, chasing that path away.

Whoever you want.

The second path takes shape. Fire engulfs a single-wide trailer. Those two crazy junkies, none of the neighbors are remotely surprised. There's a cursory investigation because the cops don't really give a shit. Anyway, the kid and the mother got out, only the father died, and he was a real piece of work. The mother's questioned, of course. The investigators found traces of an *accelerant* (a word she knows from *Dateline*) at the scene. She nods, meek and pale, and explains. Trevor had been up for several days at that point. Hallucinating. We'd always just stuck to coke and booze but lately he'd gotten his hands on a batch of meth. I kept trying to calm him down, but he was ranting about the bugs in the walls. Not like crawly bugs, like listening devices. So, one night he goes out and comes back with a Big Gulp and starts splashing gasoline all over the living room. I wake up and scream for him to stop but it's too late, so I did what any mother would do and grabbed my son and got out of there...

Resolve clicks into place. My hands are steady. I take a breath. Then I flick my wrist and the Big Gulp splatters pungent liquid across Trevor's chest and crotch. Deep in narcotic slumber—benzos to blunt the comedown of a lifetime—he doesn't even stir. I overturn the cup and douse the futon with the rest of the gasoline.

His arm falls away from his face. His nose twitches. Deep in a dream, he curls his mouth. Slowly, his eyes open. He sees me and jolts upright as I flick the Zippo's wheel and toss the flaming lighter onto his stomach. The fuel catches instantly, and Trevor shouts. He scoots back against the wall, swatting his chest with his arms, and then his arms are ablaze, too. The shadows on the wall behind him twirl and dance. The Nano Pals pop and sputter when their batteries catch fire.

Trevor finds the strength to stagger to his feet and rush

toward me. He comes at me so fast I don't have time to do anything but put up my arms to prevent him from bear-hugging me and dragging me down into the flames. When he hits me, the agony is bright and searing, like being struck with the flat of a hot blade, a blacksmith's tool. I force him back and he trips over the futon frame and falls down into the conflagration, screaming. My forearms are on fire. I rush to the sink. My flesh sizzles and steams under the water. Pieces of my skin slough off. The pain is a white-hot iron dragged across my bones.

I turn in time to see the flailing, burning wreck of a figure come at me again. Glimpses of skin oddly smooth and wet-looking in the flames, lips pinned back in a snarl, eyes mad with confusion. I grab the margarita machine next to the sink and hurl it into the crazed burning thing and the thing goes down.

Then, propelled by an unearthly scream, the thing gets up. Stunned, I watch as Trevor, trailing flame, takes a flying leap off the top of the futon frame and crashes through the living room window. The closed blinds snare him and catch fire, but his momentum rips them away, yanks them in his wake through the shattered glass.

As Trevor hits the patchy grass of the trailer park, rolling to smother the flames, I rush down the short hallway to the bedroom. There's Danny, eighteen months old, lying on his mattress on the floor, crying—daddy's screams have wrenched him up out of sleep.

It's here that the replay of this scene stutters and skips. Even as the swimmer is absorbed in the memory, it struggles to understand the way I feel at this moment.

First, the clichés, which are all true.

Danny is proof that my life is not a total waste.

If I can raise him right and keep him safe and set him on the right path, it will outweigh all of my useless wasted days. It will mean that I have been a part of the most profound aspect of human existence: bringing life into this world and shepherding it along on its journey to selfhood.

There you go. That's the kind of shit people spew at Narcotics Anonymous meetings. Which doesn't mean it isn't true. But it's not exactly what I'm feeling as I stand in Danny's doorway with the heat of the fire at my back and the stench of my own burnt flesh in my nostrils.

I'm feeling a profound sense of shame, hotter than the fire, deeper than the smoking wounds on my arms. Shame that I made a baby with Trevor, even though I knew that with him in our lives, Danny and I wouldn't stand a chance. Shame that I've spent the first year and a half of my son's life wired and totally absent, a rambling phantom on the other side of the wall. And within that shame blooms a fierce vow to give him a decent life, unmarred by the random helter-skelter tragedy and flippant disregard of the existence I have slid into.

(Is that a twinge of jealousy I detect from the swimmer?)

I scoop Danny up, my raw arms peeling and scraping against his body, and in this moment of pain I know that love is not simply an absence of hate but a thing unto itself, of which I am wholly capable.

36 (now)

This is who I am.

I find the red plastic gas canister, with its accordion spigot, near the shovel in the back of the garage. It sloshes heavily when I lift it up. There's plenty of gasoline inside. The swimmer purrs softly and my hands pulsate as I walk back into the house. I have come to realize that the swimmer is enamored with resonance. Perhaps even more than it craves the violence inside me, it craves a weaving of my memories with the present as a way to bring me back to myself. I feel its satisfaction in the same way an obsessive-compulsive feels content with the precise arrangement of objects on a desk, or a long series of green lights in a row.

I take pride in giving the swimmer what it desires. Is that not a function of love?

In the living room I place the canister on the end table and sit down next to the sheriff's corpse. The back of his head is a ragged mess, and the contents of his skull are spattered across the wall. There's a curious sag to his face, as if his skin was stretched too tight and now it has found peace at last in settling. I raise a finger to the wall and drag it through the blood, smearing delicate patterns into the gore. As the latticework takes shape, the gorgeous language unfurling, I feel the throb of an inner peace bordering on a pure yawning emptiness. I am a monk completing an illuminated manuscript, a calligrapher for some ancient king. When I'm finished writing, the pore clusters in my fingertips absorb the blood that stains my skin.

I turn my attention to Matt and a jolt of horror makes me shut my eyes and turn away. The swimmer goes to work, the filter comes down, and I approach his seated body with a dispassionate coroner's eye. The flesh of his lips has turned pulpy and transparent, leached of pigment and life. There is no distinction between upper and lower lip. It looks like a chunk of rendered fat has been grafted to the lower half of his face. Beyond the borders of this rubbery tumor, enlarged pores gather in fungal groupings. His left nostril appears to have somehow *slid* from his nose to his cheek, a new hole at a strange angle or the same hole shifted, I can't be sure. I sniff his forehead—a vinegary fermentation—and the swimmer writhes in ecstasy. Matt's eyes are closed. Carefully, I swipe open a lid. Underneath is pure corruption. Even the swimmer's filter can't shield me from the astonishing sight, and for a split second my mind glitches and fails me. There's no frame of reference for what's been done to Matt's eyes, or the space where they used to be. I swipe the lid closed and the swimmer steals the sight from me forever. I'm so grateful I fall to my knees and give thanks.

Sometime later, as the hard light of an autumn dawn creeps in through the bay window, the swimmer's craving for resonance gets me moving again. The last act: emerge from a conflagration with Danny in my arms.

Here I sense the swimmer's conflict, the exquisite torment

of its desire. The craving offset by another twinge of jealousy. It's beginning to understand that loving Danny and loving it are by nature much different. And I think it wants both kinds of love for itself.

What it cannot seem to grasp is that the savagery it has fallen so hard for cannot exist without my love for my son. In the same way the swimmer can't quite parse time, the cause and effect of what I've done escapes it.

I go upstairs to the bathroom and shed the oversized lab coat. I stand naked in front of the full-length mirror. My new biology asserts itself all over my body, and the sheriff's last words come back to me.

It's beautiful.

Rippling strands of flesh-colored lace moving up and down my thighs. Tiny holes in bloom with bright colors. Hints of the swimmer's undulating form in the air around me, dancing and shimmering. A piercing clarity to my eyes, a radiance to my gaze.

It occurs to me that what is beautiful may also be wrong to the uninitiated.

I admonish the swimmer.

I can't let Danny see me like this. Not at first.

Indignation flares. A petulant disturbance in the air around me, a sideways wriggling of tendrils, as if swatting at unseen bugs.

DO YOU

Yes

LOVE ME

Yes

With a sigh that fills the room like rattling pipes, the swimmer recedes. In the mirror, the lace-flesh ribbons down into my skin and the millions of pocked holes fade and diminish.

But the air around me retains a halo of the swimmer, an indication, a disturbance. And there's an odd cast to my features I don't entirely recognize.

Please, I say, but the swimmer resists. A smell like rotten apricots fills the bathroom. I can only insist upon so much. How much of love lies in the tension between what we concede and what we demand?

In the bedroom, I put on old jeans and a warm-up top, rugged practical clothes for the days and weeks to come. I find my camping bag in the closet and fill it with spare underwear and socks. On the floor of the closet is a crumpled pair of jeans—the ones I was wearing at the Cat's Paw.

I pause. Saliva floods my mouth.

Curious, matching my anticipation with an eager shiver, the swimmer nudges me to pick up the jeans and slide a finger into the watch pocket.

The Triscuit-sized ziplock is still there. I take it out. The coke is cut baby-powder fine.

I recall how the vodka loosened the swimmer's grip on my body, muted its voice. When I go to get Danny, I want him to be able to look me in the eyes.

The swimmer, of course, knows exactly what I'm planning to do. I expect it to protest with a shudder, to wrest my motor control away from me. *Artificial intelligence for your soul*, Wynn said. How much of the swimmer's original design runs through its current incarnation? It didn't stop me from drinking, after all.

In every respect, it worships the person I am at heart. The person I've always been. The person I can't escape.

The swimmer begins to murmur. I sense its hesitation, but it lets me pocket the ziplock and leave the room. At this moment it is a supportive lover. Perhaps even an enabler.

Downstairs, I head for the garage. I load my bag and the camping tent into the hatch of the Outback.

In the living room, I overturn the plastic canister and splash gasoline across the sheriff's corpse. Then I douse Matt from head to toe. The fuel reacts with Matt's alterations and fizzes across his fungal patches. There's mysterious beauty in the way the blotches ache for recognition. The swimmer puffs a greeting and a farewell. The holes pucker in response. There's enough gasoline in the canister to soak the carpet, the hand-carved coffee table, and the sofa. I trail a thin line of gasoline from the living room to the front hall and toss the can aside.

There's a small indentation in the ceiling from the rim of the Jesus candle before it came down on my head. That seems like it happened in another lifetime. I wonder: What was Kyle Portnoy's experience like? What kind of monstrous intelligence twisted his burnt mind around those stations of the cross?

I recall the sensation of running my tongue along the fresh lacerations in his face, an otherworldly tingling at the point of contact.

Perhaps the swimmer—mine and his—had always intended for us to meet. Already desiring what it found in me, burning with curiosity, it brought Portnoy as an offering and gave itself over to me fully. I think of the Nano Pal's song, how it summoned Trevor to my window, the orchestration of events. It seems that we have only begun to discover what we are capable of.

Carefully, I open the ziplock and tap one-third of the powder out onto the credenza. I use the edge of the invitation to Wynn's wedding to separate the pile into three fat lines, white slugs on lacquered black wood. The swimmer twitches. I roll up a dollar bill and set it down next to the lines. Then I rummage in the junk drawer until I come up with a Zippo lighter emblazoned with the Harley-Davidson logo. A mysterious acquisition, an old household joke. I flip open the top and flick the wheel. Up jumps the flame. I drop the lighter onto the trail of gasoline and watch the fire carve a bright path up the steps to the living room. The sheriff's body catches, Matt's goes up, and then the whole room is crackling with heat.

I hold the rolled dollar bill to my nose and bend to the first line.

The swimmer exults. There is resonance here, too. The rush and the drip. Together we return to my question: relapse—*is it true?* The swimmer shuffles cards and deals back the last of what it's been keeping from me out of love.

THE SEVENTH
VISITATION

37 (3 years clean)

It's nights like these that my scars tingle and itch, and the shadows of the flames dance in every puff of frozen breath. The trailer fire, the last time I was high, the last time I saw Trevor. Three years gone, and where are we now?

A basement apartment, an illegal carve-out in the space that houses the building's boiler—a heaving machine in permanent death throes. Right now, on the coldest night of a brutal winter, the boiler has gone quiet. No heat, no hot water. This is illegal in the state of New York. But in this type of place, no landlord will answer for this crime. I don't even know who the landlord is.

In the wall behind the dormant boiler is a hole the size of a small TV. I have no idea what made it, or where it might lead. We're underground, but that makes no difference. Cold air rushes in. I don't know how this is possible, but I grew up in places like this. Sad quirks—impishly designed for the purpose of hardship alone—are familiar to me.

"Hold it steady, just like that," I tell Danny, five years old. He presses a small mittened hand against the piece of cardboard I tore from a box in the alley outside and holds it against the outer rim of the hole. I unfurl a long piece of duct tape that sticks to my gloves as I try to tear it into strips. Eventually we slap enough tape on the cardboard to fasten its edges to the wall and cover the hole. We stand there for a moment, wedged behind the silent boiler, waiting to feel the fruits of our labor. But it's as if the cardboard is porous, or else the cold air is finding ways to squirm, rodent-like, through gaps in our haphazard taping.

It's zero degrees outside and the night is young.

The sight of Danny's breath in the air freezes my own breath in my lungs. Normal kids don't have to think about climate control—it's something they simply move through, oblivious, at the very least comfortable. Danny careens from fire to ice. Life without Trevor is simply another form of chaos.

I don't parent, I plunge my son into things.

There's money for a cheap motel room, but that will take too big a bite out of rent, due next week, which the unreachable landlord dispatches a mute, unsettling woman to collect while a man smiles at me from her car.

I could pick up more shifts to lift us slightly above month-to-month living. But more shifts mean less time to audit classes—already slim in their permissiveness to my schedule and relevance to the path I've charted: advertising. I've opted for copywriting as the most achievable inroad to a corporate job with a real future that doesn't require expensive software, professional certifications, graduate degrees.

The fewer classes I audit, the longer our tenure in awful basement rooms will be.

I rub my hands together as a dismal, familiar thought comes on: I'm giving Danny the same life my mother gave me, his little feet filling prints I made long ago. I nudge him toward the center of the room. His Goodwill long johns peek out from beneath his candy cane–patterned pj pants and skim the floor. His puffy jacket was a good find—a slit in one elbow where some of the filling is wisping out, but otherwise in good shape. His hair squirts rakishly from his wool hat, which nearly obscures his eyes. He looks like the outfielder from the wrong side of the tracks who beats the rich-kid team with a crazy trick play. My love for him, accented sharply by circumstance, has lately tilted into anxious attachment. The bitter cold ramps up misty-eyed desperation.

Together we work hundred-piece puzzles on the folding table, theme park roller coasters and fairy-tale castles. I watch him contemplate the landscape of missing pieces, fit the right one in with little hesitation. I'm reassured by how naturally he assembles. I comfort myself: his mind is running smoothly. Yet I know only time will tell if I've fucked him up, implanted traumas to glitch his adolescence. What will he retain of this meat locker of a home, patching a hole to nowhere?

He takes a crumpled piece of paper from his jacket pocket and hands it to me.

"I drew a plan for the fort," he says.

The blueprint of a five-year-old is a wondrous thing. I am privileged to be given a glimpse into the churn of his creativity. The drawing depicts layered turrets of pillows, battlements of draped rugs, a brackish moat full of snaggle-toothed fish. Presiding over it all is a fiery sun. A black line snakes from the side of the sun and squiggles off the edge of the page.

"What's this?" I trace the line.

"The cord for Henry," he says.

Henry is our space heater—another Goodwill treasure.

A bit old-fashioned with its metal grate and exposed orange coils, Henry requires constant vigilance but gets wonderfully, dangerously hot.

Together we work quickly, "following" Danny's blueprint as best we can with the pillows and blankets we own—far fewer than he's used for his drawing. I move our scuffed wooden chairs from the table to the center of the room. Four turrets, one in each corner of the area rug. A shadeless floor lamp goes in the center, the load-bearing post for the main hall. Danny places pillows inside the boundaries, stacks of three for us to lounge against. We stretch out sheets, and I help him drape his ends over the backs of the chairs. I save the "ceiling" for myself—Danny isn't tall enough to reach the top of the lamp.

"This is the drawbridge," he says, leaning a big shag throw pillow against a chair leg. He tips it over, mimicking the slow grind of a medieval pulley system, and lays it flat. Then he parts a flap in a draped blanket and crawls into the fort.

I set Henry just inside the flap and run the extension cord to the wall outlet. Then I get down on my knees and join Danny inside the fort. He's already taken off his jacket and gloves.

"The anticipation's the best part," I say.

"The heat's the best part," he says.

I flip the switch on Henry's face and the coils buzz. A bright orange glow lends a set-design light to the fort's interior. I remove my gloves and hold out my palms to Henry as if basking in the warmth of a roaring fire. Eventually, I take off my jacket, and then my sweater. Danny produces a picture book, clamps on a reading light, and turns pages methodically. I excuse myself to go on a "foraging mission" and crawl out of the tent.

The cold hits me hard. My breath seems to crystallize into

sparkly mist. Outside the small window set high up in the wall, a streetlight flickers. A truck passes, crunching packed snow. I make a pot of strong coffee. As it brews, I study the fort from the outside. Our little shelter, assembled in ten minutes, so much more welcoming than the room we pay to live in. I listen to the coffee maker and watch Danny's book light jiggle as he turns a page.

There's a life for us out there somewhere, if I stay the course. But there's also a life in here—now. These moments might be transitory for me, stopgaps as we move toward permanence, but they will never be erased. For Danny, who lives in the moment as only little kids can do, before obligation stretches time and imposes need, these times are all he knows. So, I pour myself a travel mug of black coffee and crawl back inside our fort, where I'm greeted by Henry's warmth and Danny's smile.

I ask him to read to me, and he does. Soon, my son will doze off, and I will drink my coffee and make sure the space heater doesn't burn the place down. I will sit up all night, jittery with caffeine, so Danny can sleep safely in this warm cocoon. When the boiler kicks back on, we'll take down our fort together.

38 (8 years clean)

Sparkling or still?" the waiter says. It's noon on a Tuesday at the Pomeroy Grill in midtown Manhattan, a few blocks from Grand Central. An old-school power lunch haven, cavernous yet hushed. Art deco friezes and tiered archways give it the look of a set from Tim Burton's Gotham City, but the waitstaff is pure New York—efficient and graceful with a smirk buried not quite deep enough, *we know what kind of people you are.*

"Sparkling," Judy Melford says.

"Can I start you two off with anything else to drink today?"

Judy hesitates. A man at a neighboring table bellows, and the rest of his party erupts into full-throated mirth. Judy meets my eyes for a moment, then flashes a tight smile at the waiter. "Just the water will be fine."

"Get whatever you want," I say. "It's your birthday."

Meaning: *you don't have to Not Drink on my account.* From anyone else, the gesture would be mildly appreciated, if unnecessary. Watching other people drink alcohol isn't a trigger for me. But with Judy, there are layers of condescension between her intentions and the gesture itself, rendering it a dig, not a favor.

Her tight smile widens. "Just the water, thank you."

The waiter removes our wine glasses and strides briskly away. I watch him go. The tables are set far apart here—this is not some cramped downtown joint, but a place where mergers and acquisitions are martini'd into existence. A centralized loop of a bar stamped with brass fixtures and a pyramid of gleaming bottles is lit by a beam that slashes down from a skylight.

Judy watches me take in the décor. "This can't be your first lunch at the Pomeroy."

"First time I've ever crossed its grand threshold."

She straightens her salad fork to be perfectly parallel with its counterpart. "It's so close to your office, I thought surely you'd been. It's an institution."

"I mean, I've heard of it. I'm sure Bob Halloran's been a few thousand times."

"I used to meet Owen here, back when he was at Klinger and Walsh." She turns over the menu and scans the print. "This was ages ago, but the tuna niçoise was quite good."

A moment of silence. I read the menu. The words mean nothing. They don't quite add up to real dishes. Judy's aura renders me fifty percent less capable of comprehending the world around me and acting like a normal person. Being supremely conscious of this does not offer a single clear tactic to mitigate it. My black jeans feel tight. I shift in my seat.

"So, what else are you doing for your birthday?" I say.

The waiter returns, pours two glasses of fizzy water, and sets the blue bottle down between us.

"Have you had a chance to look over the menu?" he says.

"I'm going to Gossamer with my friend Susan Bledsoe"—
Judy, answering me, ignoring the waiter—"it's a day spa
with saltwater baths on Great Jones."

The waiter tops off Judy's water. "Did you need another
minute?"

"No," Judy says, "I'll have the steak tartare."

He's not one of those waiters who writes down orders. He
shifts his neutral gaze to me.

"Tuna niçoise, please." I deliver this with confidence.

The waiter smiles at me as if at a child who means well.
"I'm afraid we don't do requests—Chef does ask that you
choose from the menu."

I flip the single page. No tuna niçoise. Right. "I'll have
the black bean burger with a side salad," I say. The waiter
takes our menus and the Pomeroy's vastness swallows him
up once again.

"Why would they have gotten rid of the niçoise?" Judy
says. "It was delicious."

"Weird," I say. I'm not entirely sure what niçoise is, or
why I didn't notice that it wasn't on the menu. I take a sip of
my sparkling water.

"They used to have bathroom attendants here," Judy says.
"Very old New York." She pauses to dab at the corner of her
mouth. "Matthew's rubbing off on you, I see."

"Oh. Really?"

"Your black bean burger. I know he's been on a health
kick himself. And God knows when he sets his mind to
something, it's get on board or get out of the way." She cocks
her head and stops just shy of giving me a wink. "Wonder
where he gets *that* from."

"Well," I say, lifting my glass. "Cheers to your birthday.
Thanks for inviting me out for lunch."

"Sydney. You of all people should know that it's bad luck to toast with water."

I set my glass down and struggle to keep my eyes from darting about the room as I indulge rapid-fire fantasies of sitting anywhere but here, slipping into a different setting—celebratory colleagues, old friends on vacation, office drones on a rushed lunch date. I know that tension is general all over the restaurant, that if I were to occupy the body of a tourist, a banker, a besotted lover, it wouldn't quell my anxiety, just replace it with some new kind of stress. And yet, despite not being a complete idiot about the human condition, I can almost convince myself that everyone else in the Pomeroy is relaxed, in control, enjoying themselves.

Judy sighs. "Sixty-four." Her eyes roll briefly up to regard the vaulted ceiling. She shakes her head and drifts into a contemplative daze. Then she snaps back down to earth. "It feels like just yesterday I was holding Matthew in the hospital. And now *he's* almost forty."

That's my cue to say something profound about the passage of time to bind us together in this moment. But for Judy, time has been a smoothly flowing river, and for me, rapids and whirlpools and raging falls out of nowhere. The decade since Danny's birth has ushered us into so many distinct states of being, they scarcely seem drawn from the same life. From Trevor to the trailer to the numbing progression of shitty apartments, waitressing gigs, night classes; to meeting Matt at my miracle job in a real office and moving into a real house in a nice neighborhood.

It feels like an entirely different woman was holding Danny in the hospital, and I've since stepped in to do a better job.

"Time's weird like that," I say. I've never had the privilege of being a stoned college kid in a dorm room, but I imagine that's about what I sound like.

Disappointment crosses Judy's face. I remind myself that she invited me out for our first-ever lunch together, that she's making a genuine effort to connect. And she was considerate enough to make a reservation at a place near my office.

"I guess I mean," I begin again, "for me, with Danny, it's been different."

I quit talking and cut my losses. Under the table, my restless legs are pistons. Mentally, I flail about for some way to steer us toward anything else—the weather, summer crowds on the sidewalks, Owen's career as a bankruptcy attorney.

"I understand," Judy says. My forearms distract her. I'm in three-quarter sleeves though it's sundress weather, but they don't hide my scars entirely. I drain my glass and refill it. For a split second I allow myself to fantasize that I'm pouring a healthy serving of vodka over ice, the driest of dry martinis. Girls' Day Out! Then we'd be connecting. What would it be like, Judy Melford and me, thick as thieves, giggling all the way to the saltwater baths on Great Jones? Would it be like having a mother?

"You've certainly come a long way," she continues. I think of the 4-7-8 breathing exercise Matt taught me and consider excusing myself to the bathroom.

"I like your bracelet," I say.

She regards the wide gold hoop impassively, then returns to me. "Matthew's always wanted children of his own."

I place my hands in my lap, thread my fingers, and press my palms together, hard. I've been sucking down sparkling water, but my throat is dry. "He's incredible with Danny," I say.

"Yes." Judy smiles. "We all love Danny so much. He's a

wonderful boy, and it's obviously so important that he has a strong father figure in his life."

The walls of the restaurant seem to wobble, constrict, and whip back into place. For a moment I come undone and the course of the day escapes me. How did we get here, to this place? Has Judy been steering the conversation? Did I walk right into it?

My eyes go to the circular bar, the pyramid of glass bottles.

"You know," she says, "it's funny to think about now, but I'm telling you, if Owen and I had moved in together before we were married, our parents would have disowned us. They were Catholic, of course, but it was generational, too."

I'm relieved, a little, at this unexpected thrust. This kind of soft disapproval—the universal sigh of religious Boomers—I can handle. Less about *me*, personally, than about changing mores.

"Judy, I know it might seem to you and Owen like we did things out of order, but—"

"Oh!" Judy interrupts me and laughs, a little too loud. "No, Sydney, dear Lord, I'm not my mother! It doesn't bother me in the slightest, you and Matthew cohabitating like you are."

"Oh." I manage to laugh. "I thought that's where you were headed, for a second."

"I'm not *that* old-fashioned. Give me *some* credit for keeping up with the times."

The waiter appears, sets down our plates, refills our glasses, and encourages us to *enjoy*.

"Credit granted," I say, lifting the bun of my black bean burger. "This aioli looks great."

"If I can be honest," Judy says, "I'm actually grateful that you didn't follow the traditional path of courtship and marriage and children and all that. Tying yourselves together from the get-go. Your approach to your relationship has actually been very refreshing."

I stack heirloom tomato slices, lettuce, red onion. The alarm in my head is faint, distant—a warning of atmosphere, of mood, rather than anything I can put my finger on. Judy places her napkin across her lap and eats, with great relish, several bites of bleeding-red steak tartare. Her mouth forms precise peaks and valleys as her lips purse and her jaw moves to chew.

"We're just sort of going with the flow, I guess." I wonder if I've ever said anything interesting or revealing to Judy Melford in my life.

Judy takes a break from the tartare and washes it down with sparkling water. "Funny you should use that word," she says, a wry cast to her face. "I've been meaning to ask—and forgive the sheer vulgarity of this, God knows I wouldn't approach it this way if it wasn't important—are you on birth control?"

The Pomeroy's interior tilts, shot through a canted lens. The neighboring table bursts into canned laughter. Glasses are raised and lowered.

I find my voice. "Judy, I don't feel comfortable discussing that with you, I'm sorry."

"Woman to woman," she says, glancing from side to side as if to assure me that she's vetted the eavesdroppers.

"Really, anything else is fine, but that's just really personal. For a lunch. I'm sorry."

Why am I apologizing?

Judy shrugs and tucks back into her food. My black bean burger sits untouched. Behind the bar, light dances on the bottles. A bartender in a leather smock deftly mixes a dirty martini. I have gone momentarily catatonic as the restaurant tilts further, bustles, erupts. Judy, brooding, tries to top off her water glass. The bottle is empty.

"I know you make Matthew happy," she says. She straightens her unused salad fork. "And watching you two together is nice. You're very kind to each other. I would never try to infringe on that happiness, you understand. Matthew makes his own decisions. But I would be remiss, as a mother, if I didn't air these concerns. *Family* concerns."

I catch a hint of her scent—expensive, subtle. One day it will be cloying. Masking bad animal smells. My mind lashes out—one day she'll be shitting herself. I crush my palms together in my lap.

"Judy," I say, with nothing to follow it up. It's absurd— just this morning, at work, I presented the rationale behind a massive ad campaign to a room full of C-suite execs from a stodgy old insurance giant. I apply to the toughest crowds the perfectly balanced force that stems from knowing my shit.

And yet Judy ties me in knots. Every time.

"This is delicate," she continues, "but I know that as a mother, you'll understand. Put yourself in my shoes— imagine if Danny was in the situation that Matthew is in now."

"What situation is that." My voice a whisper of dry reeds.

"I know this much, at least, isn't your fault, but in addition to everything you've inflicted upon yourself, I understand that your mother dealt with some fairly severe mental health issues of her own. And that kind of thing—even if you and Matthew were to approach this as responsibly as can be, and get a genetic panel, it wouldn't show up on there."

"Why are you doing this?"

She lifts the napkin in her lap to cross her legs. Her upper body moves like a pianist preparing to launch into a difficult piece.

"I'm not *doing* anything to you, personally, Sydney. I'm just conscious, especially lately, of several things I want to make sure I don't keep bottled up inside. I think you'd agree that being straightforward and honest is always the best approach. I don't think my position is all that controversial—I'm considering, first and foremost, the welfare of a future grand-child, my only son's child. It's crucially important, these days, with the world as it is, that the deck not be stacked against a child from the get-go. And with your sort of built-in history, a lineage of illness and poor decision-making—again, no offense, I know it's not entirely your fault for the very reasons I'm bringing up now. It's the fact that this will be *ingrained* in this child, should you have one with Matthew, that Owen and I are particularly concerned about."

I'm conscious of the impurities in my veins, fizzing like the water in my glass. Discomfort so acute I feel held to a flame. I want to leap into a wild, shameful dance to make it go away.

"Danny is fine," I say. "There's nothing *ingrained* in him."

It's my own rotten core that makes me lie. My mother has imprinted upon me and I have imprinted upon Danny. And God only knows what Trevor gave him.

I know Judy is disgustingly out of line. I know I should snap back hard, tell her I don't owe her consideration for another second, because I don't have to sit here and listen to this shit.

I don't go anywhere. I don't even move.

"That remains to be seen," Judy says. There's sympathy in

the way she looks at me across the table. "These things are prone to manifesting in the teen years, from what I understand. Anyway, the point is that Owen and I would like to do our part to keep everything harmonious—so, to that end, we'd like to offer you a little gift, a stipend, if you'd like, to stay on birth control. That way, when what you have with Matthew runs its course, you won't be tied together for life. It's a win-win. You can go your own way, and be even better equipped, financially, to give Danny the life he deserves. What mother wouldn't wish that?"

Judy evaporates. Her voice lingers but I barely hear it. A tunnel forms, a vaporous pipeline composed of the Pomeroy's brass and wood and pristine linen, straight through the place where Judy's outline now shimmers. I gaze down its foreshortened length as if through a telescope. The bar, magnified: sunlight playing on glass, prisms dancing on vodka and gin, all of it crisp and everlasting. Judy's cruel angles—her jewelry, her knuckles, the twist of her mouth—softened and hazed by the stately, loyal charm of the bottles. Judy will never see me come into my own. She can claw at my life, at who I am, as much as she wants. It's nothing to be ashamed of. I feel myself rise from my chair while Judy's voice floats on. I feel myself head for the exit, filled with the rush of escape into an afternoon inhabited by the person I've always been.

39 (6 years clean)

I am twenty-nine years old, and this is my first real date.

Eating at Denny's with Trevor and ducking out to beat the check doesn't count.

I realize how stunted and adolescent my notion of a Real Date's framework has always been. Dinner, dessert, a movie, a stolen kiss or two. A winking city skyline, a riverfront stroll. I'm not a traditionalist, just inexperienced in these matters. I've had my hands full for the past six years.

Matt, the anti-Trevor whose eyes I met the previous week across a conference room table, does not seem to entertain sedentary notions. Rangy and restless, he explains that he's a free climber stuck, for the time being, in a job that requires significant deskbound time, so his weekends are all kinetic energy. Sinew and motion. His gestures are bigger out of the office, animated and passionate, his voice hitting an easy stride in the open air.

Danny has a good sitter now, a child-psych major at Bard who draws and plays ukulele with him. I can do things like have a first date without waiting for the call that he's fallen off the jungle gym. Even if he does manage to hurt himself in my absence, Halloran has an excellent health plan.

Matt picks me up in a blue Subaru Outback that he calls a "Subie" because, for all the urbane altruism of his profession, he can't shake the innate bro-speak of the upper crust. I will never admit this to him, or anyone, but I find it sexy.

He has not taken me to a pricey Italian restaurant, or a place that has some dessert I "have to try" while he watches me eat, expectantly, waiting for me to agree that it's delicious to affirm his own opinions of things. He has not gotten us tickets to see a movie, or a play in the city, or the cover band his buddies are in.

He's taken us to a nature preserve at the edge of the Esopus Creek so we can "hike our faces off." He's packed water bottles, portable phone chargers, snack mix, and a first aid kit. He's also assured me that he isn't a serial killer, and because it's a beautiful Saturday afternoon in April, there will be plenty of fellow hikers on the trails. I find it exhilarating to believe someone without question when they assure you they are not a bad person in disguise. To simply know that while like all humans they have their faults, they are not trying to distract you from the fact that they're one impulsive decision away from some poisonous catastrophe.

There's something to be said for citizens of the straight world in this regard.

"Welcome..." Matt says as we round a bend, the trees part, and a mountain lake framed by evergreens slides into view. "...to Jurassic Park."

He stretches out an arm to underscore the view like a tour guide.

I laugh. "Timely joke! I was a baby when that movie came out."

"I'm not going to tell you how old I was."

"Fifteen?" I guess. "Twenty-four? Should we even be hiking, if your hip could give out anytime?"

His expression darkens. "My father died of a bad hip."

"Oh! Shit. Matt, I'm sorry. I didn't know. Strike it from the record."

He grins. "I'm kidding, is that even a thing you can die of? My dad's fine, he just retired from Klinger and Walsh, he builds model World War II tanks and keeps paper box scores for Yankees games. A glimpse into my future. Stick with me."

A flood of relief. "Jesus, don't do that to me, I almost had a panic attack. My biggest fear is that I'm going to be weird or say something insane without realizing it, and you're gonna be like, what the hell am I doing here with this person."

Matt sits down on a flat rock and squints into midafternoon light. "Well, you're doing a great job approximating normal human interaction. Why, have you not been getting out much these days?"

"These days or any days, outside of work."

"Bob Halloran's a wild dude, by the way, speaking of work." He unzips the backpack and offers me the snack mix. "Secret weapon: chocolate-covered raisins."

I sit next to him on the rock and accept the bag. "I'll just eat all of them real quick."

"Pick them out one by one, by all means. Fuck the other shit."

"You can have the Wheat Chex."

"Nobody likes those. No idea why I put them in."

Of course, he's made this snack mix himself. "Love a man who can cook."

"You should see me in a meth lab."

"My ex was into meth for a while."

He stares at me, waiting for the other shoe to drop, assuming I'm playing the same trick in return, turning the tables.

"That's heavy," he says after a moment of silence. "I'm sorry. I don't actually make meth."

"Just snack mix."

"And a mean linguine with clams."

A hawk soars, circles, dips behind the pines across the lake. A thumbnail of a beach cuts into the shoreline far below, kids in windbreakers digging in the sand. Two silver docks jut out into the water, connected at their tips by buoys strung across a line. I imagine Danny—a surprisingly graceful swimmer for a kid who's never had a pool—knifing through the water toward the buoys while Matt and I watch from plastic chairs in the sand. The vivid reality of this image is startling—how easily I just imagined the three of us, together. Awash in the scent of rich trailside loam and sticky pitch from pinecones, the sun hot on my face, some hidden core of life is suddenly revealed to me. I spend so much time fretting over all the ways I've screwed up, or how I will screw up at some looming future date—but honestly, I'm doing okay. I'm here, at this moment, with someone good, someone who likes me. Right now, that's enough.

"So, what about you?" Matt says. He presses his palms flat on the rock, spins a little to face me, then sits cross-legged with his elbows on his thighs.

"What about me?"

"Your parents. We've covered my dad and his compelling retirement activities. And my mom enjoys gossiping with the Real Housewives of Ulster County, bugging me about grandchildren, and attending various charity dinners."

"Ah. Same."

"Then you'll get along swimmingly."

"We both like dinner, at least. But yeah, my dad was never in the picture, so no idea there. And my mom's dead."

"And for the record you're not fucking with me."

"Nope, that's my life."

He produces a protein bar and hands it to me. The warmth in my chest has nothing to do with the sunny afternoon. A man, asking me questions about my life, genuinely interested in my story. While I was waiting for Matt to pick me up, I ran through a litany of topics I was going to avoid, things I wouldn't blurt out on a first date. But now, perched on this outcrop, my nerves melt away. There's no danger in opening up. My understanding of romance and its mechanics leaps forward a decade in five seconds.

"I'm sorry," he says. "We can obviously talk about something else. Or just hike."

"No, it's really okay." I hesitate, then go for it. "It's morbid, but kind of interesting, what happened with my mother."

"If you're comfortable talking about it, I'd love to hear it."

"I was seventeen when she died," I say. "We were in our last apartment, which always smelled like soup. It was always just me and her, and she couldn't work by that point. I remember feeling this heaviness all the time back then— like, the empty minutes stretching out ahead of us, every night, while we're sitting in front of the TV, not talking. And during the day we'd move around each other like ghosts. She was pretty heavily medicated."

"What was she taking?"

I close my eyes, remembering the plastic lids marked with the days of the week. "Xanax and Klonopin, for sure. A bunch of other benzos, too."

"At the same time?"

"It's funny, for somebody who couldn't hold down a job, she was pretty sharp when it came to doctor shopping. Also, Ambien, or whatever it was at the time."

"They had Ambien then. Sanofi-Aventis has been pumping it out since ninety-two."

"Vicodin and percs, too. I don't know how she got them; she never had any real physical problems that I knew about. But there you go. She was a wizard with that shit."

Matt is looking into my eyes, his attention wholly devoted to me. How strange, to have someone care enough to hang on your words, and not just talk at you.

"It was summer," I continue, "and we only had one shitty air conditioner in the living room and none in the bedrooms. So, we'd both stay up really late, watching TV. I couldn't crawl into bed until I was absolutely exhausted, because the humidity drove me insane. And then, in early August, there was a heat wave. I don't think it dipped below ninety for four days, even in the middle of the night. This is Queens, so there's no escaping the heat, the buildings just bake all day. It's so sweltering, we have to leave the air conditioner cranked and keep our bedroom doors open so at least a little bit of cool air could creep in. In theory."

"Why didn't you just sleep on the couch?"

"It freaked me out. The couch had its back to the door of the apartment."

"Got it."

"So, the first night of the heat wave, I can't figure out if it's better to wear my underwear and sleep without any sheets at all or take off my underwear and sleep with one thin sheet." This trips me up. "Sorry—TMI?"

"Not at all."

The hawk is floating in the sky again, pinned to a cloud. "I'm being weird. This is weird."

"Sydney, this is not weird and I one hundred percent want to hear this."

"Okay." Deep breath. "So. I have to leave the door open, and I'm not so comfortable being naked, so I go for underwear, no sheet, and it works well enough. I manage to drift off—I was a better sleeper back then. But still, I'm pretty restless. My body is too hot, I'm covered in sweat, I can't get in the right position. And the air conditioner doesn't run steady, it does its thing for a while and then shuts off for a second and shudders back to life. So, I keep getting jerked awake by that. And it becomes this very weird cycle of dreaming and not dreaming, and not being sure what's what, exactly. I start hearing a noise in my room—maybe I'm awake, maybe I'm asleep, it doesn't really matter. The noise is like fabric sliding across fabric, just this little wisp of a sound—the bottom of a curtain swishing against a hardwood floor, or something. I open my eyes. All I can see is my doorway, because the TV is back on in the living room, and the glow gives it a shape. And I see my mother walking back and forth outside of my room—I can make out the messy clump of her hair. It's like a silhouette of a bird's nest."

"Back and forth, like she's pacing?"

"Yeah, like she's standing guard, going from one side of my doorway to the other, disappearing behind the wall for a second, and then coming back the other way. At first, I don't say anything at all, I'm so surprised. She's not a night owl, or prone to insomnia—her meds zap her out cold every night. Honestly, I'm surprised she was ever awake during the *day*, with what she was putting into her body. This is just so out of the ordinary. So, I sit up in bed. The mattress is soaked. It feels like I've been sleeping in a steam bath—sweat is literally dripping down my face, and I haven't even moved in hours. The air conditioner's not doing shit.

"I call out to her from my bed. Just kind of tentative, like, *Mom?* And she stops moving. Just freezes in the doorway and turns toward me. The TV glow is barely enough to see her face, but I can sort of make it out, and she's got this slouch to her. She takes one step inside my room. I'm trapped on the bed, and now the light switch is on the wall behind her. I think she must be sleepwalking, and I read somewhere that you're not supposed to wake a sleepwalker because it can really mess them up, so I don't say anything at all.

"She takes another step toward me. She smells bad. I can see her a little better now that my eyes have adjusted. Her downturned mouth, her sleepy eyes. Her housecoat is cling-ing to her skin—it looks like she just wore it in a bathtub. And she says to me, *Mommy doesn't sleep.*"

"Not 'Mommy *can't* sleep'?"

"No. *Doesn't*, as in, not just tonight but most nights, every night, I don't know. And the way she said *Mommy*, that mushy third person, like she was talking to a little kid—she never spoke to me that way, not even when I *was* a little kid. At that point, I'm fucking terrified. She's far enough in the room that I can sort of get by her, so I bolt out of bed and slap the light switch on the wall and stand in the doorway, looking in. And—"

I stop here. My mouth is dry. Matt understands, instinc-tively, and hands me a bottle of water.

"It wasn't better. Turning on the light, I mean. Because now I can't ever unsee it. You know when you're little, and all those scary things lurking in the dark can be defeated if you just flick the switch and turn on the light. The light's supposed to chase away everything that can hurt you. But that night I turned on the light and there she was—my mother, slouching toward me, with her matted hair and her droopy eyes. I could see her body through her house-coat, the sweat made it transparent. She wore these shapeless housedresses around all day long, and I never looked too closely, but now with it clinging to her she looked so bloated and misshapen—she didn't get any exercise, and the meds did fucked-up things to her skin. I remember standing there and looking at her breasts, and thinking *Those are some dugs*, specifically the word *dugs* popped into my head, I must have read it somewhere, I don't know. And with that light on, I realized that this is my life. That's what the light illumi-nated, at that moment. This is my fucking life, in this place, with her.

"I told her to get back to bed. I didn't care anymore about the danger of waking a sleepwalker. I don't even know if she was sleepwalking. I mean, she looked at me when she spoke."

"She kept talking?"

"She said, *Mommy's coming up the stairs.* At that point I was like, fuck this. What stairs, we don't have stairs. So, I grabbed her arm and pulled her out of my room. She didn't fight me, she just shuffled along. When we got to her room, the smell was overpowering. It wasn't BO, or shit, or any-thing like that—sorry, this is really gross, I know."

"No, I really appreciate you telling me this. Don't worry."

"I appreciate you listening. Anyway, I'd never smelled anything like it, and I still haven't. It was just this *funk*, like something moldy and rotten. But not food, if that makes any sense. Not organic. I led her over to her bed. She just stood there next to it, slouching a little. At that point I was like, fine, stand here all night, I don't care. And I was just about to leave when she turned to me and said, *Mommy's in the soft spot.*"

"Huh. What's that supposed to mean?"

"No idea. I left her there, went back to my room, and locked my door. It was stifling—turns out the living room AC actually did cool things off a little. I couldn't sleep at all. I just lay there, soaked in sweat, light-headed, debating whether or not to open my door a crack to let in some of the air, even if it meant she could get in, too. I lay there, staring at the ceiling, until morning. Then I went to check on her. And found her, like. Yeah. So, *Mommy's in the soft spot* was the last thing she ever said to me."

Matt regards me in silence. He stretches out his legs and reaches for his toes. It seems rote, a movement he performs when he's turning something over in his mind. The things we learn about another person—the habits and behaviors they're barely aware of. A lifetime of observation. Having a partner.

It hits me all at once, the story I've just told to a man with, from what he's told me so far, normal parents and a normal upbringing. I have the sudden desire to meet his mother, to sit and have tea in the nice living room, the one for entertaining guests. To say *It's nice to meet you, Mrs. Melford*, and have a polite conversation.

Matt pushes himself up to his feet. "Would you mind joining me up here for a second?"

I stand next to him.

"Is it okay if I hug you?" he says.

"Yes."

He wraps his arms around me and pulls me close. I smell some kind of woodsy lotion, or it might just be the woods. Either way I associate it distinctly with Matt.

"This is nice," I say.

He holds me, gently, at arm's length and looks me in the eyes. "I really appreciate you sharing that. I'm sorry you went through all that when you were a teenager. I can't imagine."

"Thank you for listening. I actually felt really comfortable telling you about it."

"Yeah, I feel really comfortable with you, too. At the risk of sounding painfully nineteen-fifties—do you want to hold hands?"

"Yes."

"Want to go steady?"

"We'll see." I hand him the water bottle and snack mix. "Your turn to tell a story."

"Pick a topic: Stanford, distance running, or nonprofits."

"Ooh. Nonprofits. We can't let this date get *too* hot."

He jumps off the rock and leads me back to the trail. A bird cries out shrilly. Unseen critters scurry in the underbrush. When he reaches for me, I take his hand, and it becomes easier, somehow, to pay attention to all the echoes, the ecosystem of color and sound, here in the woods. As if his touch has made the day more vivid, tapped into fresh perceptions, amplified like a hallucinogen my ability to take it all in. I want to share this feeling with Danny. To restart his life with this in mind, and only this—and thus endow him with the sense that the world is made up of ever-expanding possibilities.

40 (8 years clean)

On the street outside the Pomeroy Grill, pedestrians belong to another world, the normal Tuesday concerns weighing down on them in ways I can't understand. To some degree the city is always like this, but now I can barely stomach watching them pass by. The afternoon light gives everyone a peculiar slant. I am alone. Judy has not followed me out.

My impurities fizz and pop in my veins. I hurry down the street and turn the corner. Leaning against the wall by the window of a hat shop, I scratch at my scars. Thoughts of things I might do come and go: A breathing exercise. Central Park. The train home. But they are all abstractions. I wish for the ability to see through Judy Melford's eyes. To perceive me as she does. How wretched a creature, how pitiable and repulsive. A foul bloodline.

These thoughts are less abstract, more pointed. The discomfort in my body flares to acute pain. I could scratch and scratch all day. Scratch my skin right off and march back into the Pomeroy Grill, flesh dangling in ribbons like fringes on a jacket. Sit back down at the table, *Sorry, there was a line for the bathroom, what were you saying?*

That makes me laugh. To see the look on her face.

Raise my hand to signal the waiter and order a martini. Vodka. Slightly dirty.

You sure you don't want one, Judy?

Girls' Day Out.

I laugh again and push off from the wall by the hat shop. My feet carry me back toward my office. I can't remember what my desk looks like, what I'm supposed to be working on. I know the word for projects I have to turn in: *deliverables*. Work that is owed. But I don't remember the specifics of the projects themselves. It seems silly that things like this matter to so many people. How narrow our vision. The people to whom these things matter pass me now, talking on their phones, all sweat-stained armpits and greasy fast-food bags and shoes not made for city streets. The sun beats down, relentless and terrible. Air like a sauna, some magnificent hand dumping the bucket of water on the rocks—sizzle, midtown fuckers.

Somewhere I'm telling myself that I'm a person who meets challenges head-on. Who does not shrink from difficult situations. Who processes negative emotions in a healthy way. An example for Danny. Not impulsive. Steady. Bringing mature decision-making to bear on pivotal moments.

Judy Melford doesn't know me at all.

Forty-Fifth Street is a mess of obstacles and hostility. These things I know myself to be have also become abstracted. They are not usually ideas of self that I need to hold on to and display for my own satisfaction and peace of mind. They are just me. The person I've worked to become. But now I can't grasp them. I flash to the grotesquerie that Judy sees. Everything runs together.

It doesn't matter what she thinks. Fuck her.

I turn the corner onto Second Avenue. The appearance of love, of *family*, can be so easily granted and revoked. Its boundaries determined entirely by another.

This is love.

No, *this*.

Fooled you.

The sun bounces off midtown glass, a blinding funhouse. I have to get off the street. I can't think straight out here. Rooftops bend toward me. Everything glares.

On Forty-Fourth I come to Mulcahy's Pub, a place I've passed a thousand times on the way to the office. For the first time in my life, I duck inside its redbrick facade and hurry through the vestibule plastered with UFC Fight Night posters, photos of the pub-sponsored Little League team, union electrician and carpenter stickers. Inside it's dim and cool and smells of stale beer and bathroom disinfectant. A few office workers sit at round high-top tables finishing their lunches. Four men and one woman sit at the end of the bar, where it rounds a corner toward a jukebox and a video poker game. I take my seat far from any of them. I'm not here to hobnob with the regulars.

What I am here for doesn't shake me to my core. This is a moment like any other. I was having lunch with Judy, and now I'm not. Now I'm here. It's no big deal. I overthink everything. Constant chatter in my mind.

Shut up, Sydney.

The bartender is a middle-aged Irish man in a black collared shirt monogrammed with the name of the bar. He sets a coaster down in front of me, then plunks down a glass of water and a silverware roll-up. He assumes I will be eating lunch.

"I'll take a Jameson," I say. The words come naturally,

like I've done this a thousand times, a normal person in an Irish pub. "On the rocks. And a beer." I look at the taps. "A Guinness."

"Jameson rocks and a Guinness," he confirms in a gentle lilt.

As soon as he turns his back, the pain in my body flares. I see myself through Judy's eyes, twisted and inhuman. Her only son partnered with an absurdity, a mistake. How excruciating it must be to even share a meal with me. I revel in the thought that it was torture for her.

The bartender delivers my drinks and I slide a twenty across the bar in return. I take a sip of the whiskey and savor its bite.

With just that first sip, the Sydney that Judy sees shines with a sudden radiance. Now she is forced to sit and behold the beauty of my true form. I down the whiskey and chase it with a long swallow of beer. My fearsome truth begins to scorch Judy's flesh. It crackles and burns and curls like parchment paper.

I find that I'm squeezing the pint glass and have to force myself to take gentle sips until it's gone. The bartender brings another round. One by one, the office workers settle their bills and head out. I entertain a long and detailed fantasy of Judy meeting her friend at the spa on Great Jones, lowering her charred body into a saltwater bath, howling.

This is so easy, going to a bar and grabbing a few drinks. It doesn't have to be a thing I can't ever do.

Sometime later the regulars at the end of the bar have been replaced by a man idly counting out a glittering array of coins, jabbing at his phone, and sipping a gin and tonic.

The bartender looks up from his paper and I meet his eyes. He comes over and nods at my Guinness.

"Start you another? It'll be on me."

I am gaping at him.

"A buyback," he explains. "Four drinks earns you one on the house."

A surge of gratitude brings tears to my eyes. "Yes. Thank you."

When he turns to the tap, my phone buzzes in my purse. I take it out.

Judy Melford calling. I notice that she's also sent eleven text messages. A mischievous, irresistible idea forms. I push myself off the stool and make my way to the bathroom. There's no thought—only action and the purity of feeling that accompanies it.

I toss my phone in the toilet. It sinks to the bottom of the bowl and plunks against the chipped porcelain. I watch the screen go dark, then head back into the bar. My free Guinness is waiting for me. Adrift, all connections severed, I down half of it in one sip. Now it's only me and the man with the coins at the bar. He's made little stacks of them, towers that glitter in the light from stained-glass lamps overhead. Both occupied and idle, he drinks slowly, hits a vape, and takes a phone call. His voice is low and calm. There's a blond streak in his brown hair. When he sets the phone down, I finish my drink and join him at the end of the bar.

I know from long-buried instinct dredged up by alcohol that he is just the sort of man who can help me get organized.

41 (7 years clean)

This mess is a place!"

Matt moves through our new house (a shiver, every time, at this astonishing phrase, *our new house*) dodging stacks of boxes and plastic-wrapped furniture set down every which way, shouting like a drunken king in his mead hall. Danny shadows him in a daze, trailing a finger down bare walls, sidling past boxes labeled with my black-markered scrawl.

Danny—bedroom.

Sydney—books.

Kitchen stuff.

FRAGILE.

Misc.

I follow my boys, listening, a dopey grin on my face.

"What are we gonna do with all these rooms?" Danny says.

"Fill 'em with stuff!" Matt tells him. "The stuff of life, young Danny." He stops at the end of the hallway beyond the kitchen and opens a door. "This room's for guests, so Nony and Pop can sleep over."

"There's the river," Danny says, pointing to a window I can't see from where I'm standing.

A house with a guest room, I think. It doesn't seem possible, even now that I have navigated the buying process alongside Matt—retained a real estate agent, contributed my share to the down payment, learned about *escrow* and *closings*, weighed property taxes and school systems.

I join my boys at the threshold of what will be our guest room. This one little section of *our new house*—a room we won't even use on a regular basis—is larger than the basement apartment Danny and I once lived in.

"What do you think, Danny-tello," I say, placing my hands on his bony shoulders. "Our new house." Out loud it's an invocation, three words as sweet as any *I love you*. "Crazy, right?"

"The river moves super fast," he says. "I never noticed that before."

"There's tons of ships down there in the depths of the mighty Hudson," Matt says. "Spanish galleons, millions in sunken doubloons, the restless souls of ghost pirates, YARR." He hides an eye with a hand, makes the visible eye go wide. "That's why yer mom and I chose this here shack by the sea—legend has it that every full moon, gold washes up in the backyard." He removes the "eye patch" and throws his hands up in the air. "We're gonna be RICH."

Danny laughs. "I'm gonna start getting my bedroom ready."

Matt slips past us both, out into the hallway. "Race you upstairs!" Together they go flying down the hall. "I'm gonna make a runner outta you yet, Danny boy!"

"Careful!" I call after them. With the patter of feet above my head, I meander down the hall, through the kitchen, into the living room. I know that it's a modest house by Fernbeck standards, and roughly one-third the square footage of the house Matt grew up in, where his parents still live. And I know that once we begin filling it with "the stuff of life" these rooms will naturally seem smaller—possibly, one faraway day, even a bit cramped. But now, surrounded by boxes, the place feels endless. A house in a dream, a mansion that defies reality and just keeps on going. All of it, every last corner and pane, is *our new house*.

My happiness takes flight, does a little airborne pirouette, flaps away to chase my boys up the stairs.

There's a mantel above the living room fireplace (functional, brick) and I slap a palm down on it, imagining photos in silver frames: the three of us on far-flung vacations, from Bali to Berlin. Four paid weeks per year to show Danny the world, to see places that for the first three decades of my life might as well have been Mars.

I imagine a future version of Danny, perhaps in a dorm room, swapping tales with his college friends of trips their parents took them on. Pride swells, bursts, soars in the wake of happiness, up to buzz about Danny and Matt as they stomp down the hall, chasing each other from room to room.

How small a thing for so many people in this world: a house of their own, a place to call home. No frigid nights without heat. No holes in the walls. No shady fuckers with sick grins collecting rent. No fake day care. No month-to-month pressure cooker. Just the expectation of a decent life, and the head start to make it so.

But for me, who never took for granted that any of this might come to pass, it's all joy—a high from which I'll never come down. I could easily float through the rest of my days in this place, bumping my head against the ceiling.

I drift into the dining room, where the bay window soaks the hardwood floor in light. Nostalgia for family meals and holidays we haven't yet had comes and goes, sweet and a little bit painful. Time will pass here like it does everywhere else, but here I will mark the hours with the grace of the settled.

Matt and Danny clomp down the stairs, and I move through *our new house* to join them in the—

42 (8 years clean)

—kitchen.

"My boys!" I let my shopping bags fall to the floor. My mind races ahead of the action in the room, yanking the world along on a five-second delay. *I got you presents!*

Matt and Danny are standing by the table. For a moment we're a frozen tableau, some old Norman Rockwell with the lady of the house arriving home triumphant and laden with packages. Behind them, the neatness of the backsplash tiles, the coffee machine, the knife block with its Gusthof blades—all of it orderly, gorgeous, proper, *ours.*

And then they're hugging me, Matt and Danny both, the three of us standing and clinging to each other. I crunch the Altoids I've shoved in my mouth.

"Best welcoming committee ever! I got you presents. That's why I'm so late, I went shopping after work. No occasion, just because you guys deserve it. Sometimes we get really busy and life takes over, but that doesn't mean I'm not thinking of you guys, always."

I break away and bend to my shopping bags. The kitchen

floor undergoes a sudden tectonic shift. Tiles slide like plates, overlapping, driven by some ancient impulse.

"Jesus, Sydney." Matt is once again clinging to me, holding me up. Big Hug Redux. "You're burning up."

"I'm just getting your presents out, hold your horses!" At the edge of my awareness, I understand that I have wobbled. My stomach clenches, empty and knotted. I have missed dinner. It happens. We're busy people.

"Sorry I'm late, I need to heat something up, did you guys eat?"

"Why don't you come sit down," Matt says.

His tone is all wrong—overly solicitous yet deeply concerned. I look him in the eyes as he holds me up and attempt to parse what I see. Anger? Worry? Confusion?

"What are you?" I say.

"Your heart is pounding."

"You're not even touching my heart."

"Here." He begins to walk me over to a kitchen chair. At the same time, he says, "Danny, why don't you go brush your teeth, and I'll be up in a minute, okay?"

Irritation flares. I wriggle away from Matt, and the backsplash tiles are there and gone and I'm clutching the edge of the table, which is digging hard into the base of my spine. My stomach is a great yawning chasm. The day fans out behind me, from Judy at the Pomeroy Grill, to the man at the end of the bar and what I got from him, to the air-conditioned stores, to the train up the river and the dark walk home. For the first time in several hours, anxiety claws its way back. I have done something wrong, but I can ride it out and soon it will be behind me. A surge of confidence chases the afternoon away. I am home.

"No, wait, Danny—" I locate my son, backed up against

the dishwasher, staring at me. "It's not bedtime. You're ten, you can stay up."

"It's *midnight*," Matt says. "On a Tuesday."

I laugh, trying to remember what time I got on the train from Grand Central to Fernbeck. "I don't have my phone."

"Where is it? I've been calling and texting all day. We've been insanely worried, Sydney. I called the cops but there wasn't anything they could do until you were missing for longer. I called your work. I didn't know what to do."

The bathroom stall at Mulcahy's flashes in my mind. My phone in the toilet. Then, later, dipping my house keys into a stamp bag, taking bump after bump of the man's decent coke, my back against the graffiti-scratched door.

"I left it in a cab," I say. "It's no big deal, I'll get a new one in the morning."

Matt moves to steer me into a chair. I sidestep him and go to Danny. There's a jump cut and then I'm down, sitting on the floor, eye level with him. Danny flinches. "You smell funny," he says.

"It's peppermint," I say. "How was school?"

"Fine."

"Danny," Matt says, and the oversold patience in his voice rankles. "Go upstairs."

"No." I take Danny by the arm. "Sit with me while I eat."

"You've got something on your face," he says.

I swipe the back of my hand across my nose and upper lip. It comes away dusted in powder. I flash to the bathroom of the train. My heart and stomach are a single organ, pounding, echoing, opening wide.

"Danny!" Matt says. "Upstairs, now!"

I firm up my hold on Danny's arm. "Wait till you see what I got you."

"Sydney, please," Matt says.

"I'm fine."

"My mother said you bolted from the restaurant and disappeared."

"Your mother's a fucking cunt!"

Another jump cut and Danny is gone, out of my grasp, across the kitchen, down the hall, up the stairs. Blood rushes to my head. I see myself in the stainless steel of the dishwasher, a Sydney-cloud, a blob of flesh on a silver page.

"What is wrong with you?" Matt is yelling. He never yells. My throat goes tight. He's standing over me, looming, bending over to get in my face, to see me up close.

I scramble backward. "Don't do that."

"I just want to talk to you." He reaches for me. "Will you please get off the floor."

"I like the floor." It occurs to me, distantly, that *I like the floor* is not something I would say after coming home on a normal night, the night I was trying to force into existence.

The edges of my high are being filed off. Its core begins to burn away.

There is no more coke.

Ride it out.

"Fine," Matt says, and sits down on the floor with me. "I think, for Danny's sake, it would be best right now for me to go put him to bed, and for you to sit at the table and have some tea. Then we can talk."

Judy's voice, buried in powder and drowned in alcohol, springs free. *These things are prone to manifesting in the teen years.*

I get to my feet and wait for the room to right itself. "I have to say goodnight to him."

Matt is up next to me. I remember a flat-topped rock with the view of a mountain lake and a distant blot of sandy beach.

"I think it's best if you let me get him tucked in," Matt says.

Something in me crumbles. "I love him so much."

"I know you do."

This time I let Matt escort me to the table. He gets me a glass of water then leaves the room. At my feet are the shopping bags. Numbness competes with a tight ball of tinfoil unfurling in my guts, sharp pain tied to the mounting tension in my head. I'm going to have to answer for this. No more riding it out and no going back.

Eight years clean.

I reach down into one of the bags and retrieve Danny's present, a plush Donatello. He's got several already. I'm not sure why I bought him another one. It seemed like a good idea at the time. I sit the Ninja Turtle up on the table, legs out straight, shell against the rim of a bowl full of apples.

Time passes. Matt comes to take me into the living room. He sits with me on the couch. He doesn't yell, or lecture, or press me for an explanation. Dullness takes over, a low-hanging cloud in my brain. I let it claim me.

What was the point of it all, white-knuckling through eight years then letting my discipline slip one random afternoon because of Judy Fucking Melford?

"Do you hate your life?" he asks me sometime later. We have both been crying.

"No," I answer. "I love it. I never thought it could be this good."

He takes a sip of tea. "This can't happen again. I mean, if it was just you and me, if we were working through things... but with Danny." Matt takes my hand. "This is so scary for me; I can't imagine what it's like for him."

They're going to take him away...

"I don't want to be like this ever again," I say. "I'll do anything."

He's quiet for a moment. "You know my cousin Wynn?"

"Man bun," I remember, from the first and only time I met him. "Just got engaged."

"Yeah. He's a hotshot research biologist, like a nerd among nerds. Anyway, he's consulting with one of those Big Pharma giants right now, and they're developing an experimental treatment for situations like yours. It sounds pretty revolutionary. *Absolutely beautiful*, he called it."

"I'll do it," I say with no hesitation.

"It's in beta right now, I mean still pretty early. You'd essentially be testing it. But I trust Wynn, and he swears by it. It's like nothing he's ever seen, apparently."

"Yes," I say. "Please. Anything." I squeeze Matt's hand. "Yes."

THE FINAL
VISITATION

(now)

A lark plunges from the top of a pine tree beside the highway. What a plunge, lark!

I don't really know if it's a lark. I don't know what a lark looks like, I just know it's a bird, but the words come together in my mind, unbidden, and make me smile.

Everything is injected with a manic pulse. My face hums with a lack of feeling that's somehow more pronounced than the actual feeling of my face. My heart pumps with furious glee. I breathe in angular, harmonic gasps. My teeth dance in my mouth, clacking lightly to the same rhythm I'm tapping out on the steering wheel.

Trevor's coke is speedy and buzzy. My addict muscle memory identifies the cut: amphetamine and talcum powder. It'll never fling me too far skyward, no matter how much I do, but for now—I glance at the rearview mirror—it's keeping the swimmer at bay, clearing the air around my face.

My eyes fire inquisitive queries at the world at large. There's a gorgeous expansiveness to Interstate 87 in the morning, where even commuter traffic is sparse, and the October sky glints off the guardrails and signs. This stretch of highway is mostly evergreens, but every so often a shock of honey-colored leaves pops through the pine.

I'm halfway to Matt's parents' house. Twenty minutes to go, two more exits north on 87. Then, from the Melfords', it's three hours to our campsite at Cedar Valley Park—Danny's favorite spot in the state, a secluded place where we can reconnect, sort things out, lay the groundwork for this new path we're traveling together.

Just like that, the hierarchy of my life presents itself to me fully formed, and the clarity and precision is astounding. The lowest tier is my time with Trevor, when all my energy was spent in efforts to know myself less and less. The next tier up is my Matt period, when I was much more in touch with the person I wished to become. And now I'm embarking upon the swimmer's stage, and the swimmer is a companion I don't need to set myself off against or define myself by because it is, essentially, me.

The conclusion of this little dissertation on Sydney Burgess presents itself in such grand array it might as well be written across the sky: the swimmer isn't a man. That was the problem with the two lower tiers of my life. I didn't need Trevor to reflect my own degradation, just as I didn't need Matt to reflect the discipline and grace of my recovery. I slap the steering wheel and laugh out loud.

The radio is playing classical music, hundreds of syrupy strings dipping and swelling in unison. I scan through the stations, but nothing feels right. Matt's parents' exit comes on faster than expected, and as I ride the sharp curve off the highway and into their Catskills postcard of a town, I feel the slight mental tickle of those first three lines beginning to burn themselves off. I kill the radio and focus on the street signs until I get to Calico Lane, home to Judy and Owen Melford's stately Colonial.

I park just behind the row of pines that flanks their mailbox and check my face in the mirror. It might be my imagination, but I swear I can see that sheer curtain rippling in its nonexistent breeze. I take the key from the ignition and dip it into the ziplock. Two, three, six key bumps later, my face is fixed, and the world's pulse is once again surging through me. The edges of the mailbox are crisp, the light on the pine trees perfect. I do my makeup in the rearview, put on Professional Sydney. Then I sit and entertain a thousand wild notions of how to proceed.

Ring the doorbell? Toss pebbles at their upstairs guest room window? Drive the fucking Outback straight into the living room?

But then Danny, sweet Danny, decides for me. My windows are closed but I can hear his muffled voice coming from the driveway on the other side of the trees. I get out of the car, shut the door quietly, and peek around the edge of the mailbox. Blood rushes pleasantly through my head and sings in my temples. Judy, in a preposterous fur stole, is ushering Danny to the Cadillac parked in the driveway. Owen locks the front door behind him and steps lively after his wife.

With no real plan in mind, I dart past the mailbox. I'm halfway up the driveway before anybody notices me and it's Judy who does.

"My God!" She stops short and puts a hand to her heart like a startled actress from a silent movie.

The world softens as I meet Danny's eyes. I flash to the hierarchy that came to me on the highway, and I know that the two of us will emerge from this changed for the better—that we'll finally both be home. Judy and Owen are mere shades to me now, already fading into gray smudges.

"Hey, Danny-tello!" I smile. "You ready to go?"

"Mom?" Danny blinks, then looks up at the fuzzy blur that's ostensibly Judy Melford.

"I'm fine now, kiddo!" I tell him. "Come on, we gotta go." As I close the gap between us and Judy tries to pull Danny away from me, the Owen-blur moves faster than I thought possible for an old-before-his-time man like him. He posts up in front of his wife and Danny and comes back into focus.

"Sydney." Sheer puzzlement on his face. He looks over my shoulder. "Where's Matt?"

How long before they find out, I wonder.

"She's here alone, Owen," Judy says sharply. "And she's *high*." Judy turns to lead Danny back toward the house.

I decide not to say another word. What's the point? Moving quickly, I feint one way and sidestep to get past Owen. Then I sprint to the porch where Judy's fumbling with her key. Danny opens his mouth, but nothing comes out.

"Call Matthew!" Judy yells to her husband as I catch them at the front door.

I take Danny by one arm while Judy, back in focus, grabs the other.

"God, you guys, *oww*," Danny says, trying to wriggle away.

"You're in no state to take him anywhere," Judy says. "And certainly in no state to be driving a car!"

Just like that, I break my vow of silence from a moment ago, and words I can barely control come out of my mouth.

"He's my son, you haggard old bitch."

Is that a smirk I see threatening to break out? "Then you ought to care about his well-being."

"Like you did a bang-up job with *your* fucking kid."

"Matthew?" Her brow furrows at the idea that anyone would malign her son's character.

I get right in her face. "You know what he does to people?"

"Stop!" Danny yells.

I tighten my grip. "We're leaving."

"My son has only ever tried to help you! Again and again! But you're beyond help!"

"He's not answering!" Owen reports from the driveway, holding up his phone.

"Call the police!" Judy yells back.

Danny manages to shake Judy but I'm too strong for him. "You're hurting me!" he says.

"We just have to get to the car," I say firmly, turning to take us both off the porch.

"Jesus Christ, Mom!"

"He doesn't want to go with you!" Judy Melford lays a hand on my shoulder and tries to spin me around. "Owen, goddammit!"

Holding onto Danny, I strike out blindly to swat Judy away, and my elbow connects with her nose. There's a sound like a snapping celery stalk and a cry that turns into a wail. I don't look back. Blood drains from Owen's face. He drops his phone and rushes up to the porch.

"Judith!" he cries, and then calls after me, "My God, what have you done?"

Danny glances back. "Mom, Nony's bleeding."

"She shouldn't have tried to hit me, she tried to *hit* me, Danny. I had to defend myself. Anyway, I barely touched her. We really have to go. I'll explain everything in the car, I promise."

"We can't just leave!"

My heart swells with love. I have raised a kind boy with good instincts and a boundless capacity for empathy.

"It'll be okay."

I've never heard Owen raise his voice before but now he's hollering after me. "This family is finished with you! We're pressing charges!"

We round the corner past the mailbox, and I deposit Danny into the front of the Outback before getting into the driver's seat.

I take a moment to ask my heart to kindly stop jackhammering. The blood rushing through my head sends me into a woozy fit and I take a few deep breaths before I start the engine and pull away. Danny turns and cranes his neck, but the wall of pines hides the Melfords' porch. At the end of Calico Lane, stopped at the stop sign, I lean over to give Danny a seatbelt-contorted hug. The gangly contours of his little frame make me light-headed all over again.

"Where's Matt?" he says. There's a flatness to his voice that disturbs me. I'm afraid he's withdrawing into the shock of the moment.

I turn out onto the main road, past a white-steepled church holding a flea market in its yard.

"It's been so long since it's been you and me, I wanted this trip to just be us. Danny and Mom, Mom and Danny." I'm aware that I'm speaking very quickly and make an effort to slow down, but the words keep flinging themselves out. "Things have been so intense lately and I've been doing a lot of soul searching." My thoughts feel like they begin in my belly, not my brain, and rush up through my throat to my tongue. "Do you know what soul searching is? It's when you look inside yourself for answers about who you are and why you do the things you do and how you might want to be in the future."

I follow the signs for Interstate 87 North. A cloud slides across the sun and dulls the silver of the guardrail.

"Nony and Pop were taking me to the diner for breakfast," Danny says.

"Are you hungry? There might be some granola bars in the back. I can stop and check. You know what, if I'm gonna stop, I might as well wait for a gas station. Then we can stock up on snacks. We're gonna need food."

"Where are we going?"

"Camping!" I grin. "We're going to Cedar Valley."

"Isn't it kind of cold for camping?"

I blink. When was the last time I even noticed the weather? "I don't think so." And then, more confidently: "No way. It's totally fine. That's what fires are for. We'll just bundle up."

"I don't have any of my clothes."

"I brought some for you!" I pause. Did I remember to do that? "We can stop at a Kohl's on the way. So, listen. I know it's been a little weird at home since I got hurt"—I flash to what the swimmer has given me, the memory of last year's relapse—"and maybe before that, too, but I'm better now. I've got things in perspective." I put on my blinker, glide into the middle lane, and then drift into the fast lane. "For the first time in maybe forever I feel like I'm in control of our future. See, the control I thought I felt before was a lie. It was fake. But now we're gonna be okay. We're gonna be one hundred percent more than okay."

I check my face in the rearview. Situation normal.

"You fell in the kitchen," Danny says. "You said the F-word to me." I can hear the dam break in the fragility of his voice. I'm brightly attuned to its quaver.

"I remember," I lie. "And I am so sorry."

"You told Matt to 'F' himself and you told me to—"

"It's never going to happen again!" This comes out louder than I want it to, like I'm yelling over music even though the radio is off. "Never. I promise."

"That's what you said last time."

"I wish I could make you understand how different things are now. I wish I could open up my head for you to see inside. The only thing that's *not* different is that you are the most important thing in my life and you always will be. I love you so, so much."

At this, the swimmer stirs, and the side of my mouth begins to twitch. Another glance in the rearview. Professional Sydney glances back, unaltered.

I keep talking to drown out the swimmer's petulance. "Do you remember when you were five?"

"Not really."

"When you were five and the heat went out on the coldest night of the year, it was below zero—remember that apartment was such a dump, the one with the crazy hole in the wall by the boiler, the hole of *doooooom*—anyway, the heat went out and we made a blanket fort and put the space heater inside. Henry!"

"Oh yeah."

"That night I tried to stay awake because I was afraid of the blankets catching fire, but at some point, I was so tired I zonked out for a few hours. And I had this dream. I never forgot it. Hey, do you want to put some music on?"

"I don't care."

"Okay, so, the dream. I never told you this before, I don't think. It was one of those dreams that starts in the exact place you're sleeping, because the exact place you're sleeping is so weird and out of place to begin with that it messes with the wiring in your head or something. So, the dream starts and I'm in a pillow-and-blanket fort with you and it's super-hot. We're both sweating buckets. By the way, you're *you* but you don't look like you, if that makes sense."

"I know how dreams work." He pauses. "I think we should call and make sure Nony's okay."

"She's fine. Listen to this dream."

"Can we call Matt? I can do it and put it on speaker since you're driving."

I flick my eyes to the speedometer. I'm pushing eighty-five. The last thing I need is a cop pulling me over. I slow down a little. Seventy-five should be safe.

"No phone calls," I say. "We're having a conversation. In the dream, the Danny-that's-not-quite-Danny says to me, *Mommy's in the soft spot.*"

I pause to let that sink in. It seems to capture his imagination, like I knew it would. During the brief silence, my gaze pings like sonar across a bridge abutment, a tractor trailer, a circling hawk, a half-felled pine.

"Mommy's in the soft spot?" he says, finally. "Hmm. Maybe because the fort was made of pillows."

"Maybe! So, what happened next is, I peeked outside the blankets and I realized that we were in some kind of cavern, and that the cavern was supposed to be the inside of your head. I don't know how I knew that, I just knew. And I was so happy to be able to live inside my son's head, because I loved him so much."

"Like, you were shrunk down, or I was huge? And why was I in my own head?"

"I don't have the answers to those questions. But listen to what I did when I figured out where I was. I held your hand

and we walked outside the fort to the wall of the cavern, which was super squishy, and we started to *nggghhhhh*—"

A guttural wail escapes in place of the words I was trying to say. The swimmer is getting restless, or fed up with the way I've cast it aside for the time being. My hands flop bonelessly against the steering wheel and the car begins to slip into the middle lane. My foot is a block of lead weighing down the gas pedal.

"Mom!"

Stop! I admonish the swimmer. *You're going to kill us!*

It relinquishes its brief yet total hold on my body. I feel it retreat, sense its raw hurt. It's almost like a teenager stomping down the hall to his bedroom and slamming the door.

I straighten out the car between the lane lines and let up on the gas.

"Sorry about that!" I smile at Danny. "Brain fart."

He looks back at me, wide-eyed and silent, and I check my face in the rearview. Was that a fleeting hint of the sheer-curtain shimmer? I can't be sure.

"So anyway, we're at the squishy wall of your cavern-head and you, um..." I blink. My fierce and shining clarity, the sense that I was heading for a perfect interweaving of theme and message, suddenly deserts me. A momentary fog descends that has nothing to do with the swimmer. It's as if a glimpse of the impending comedown has revealed itself, the wrung-out befuddled mess I'm going to be pretty soon. What am I getting at with this dream story?

When I launched into it, the sense that I was lifting the veil on some great mystery of life for my son was like a mild electric current running through my body. Now it's vanished, leaving me lost in a thicket of vagueness. I tighten my grip on the steering wheel and shift in the seat. I glance at an onrushing road sign. We've been driving for much longer than I thought. I could swear we just left the Melfords' town, but here we are seventy miles up the highway. How long ago did I fall silent? What have I been thinking about this whole time?

Did you do this? I ask the swimmer, well aware of its power to steal snippets of time. I look over at Danny. He's asleep with his mouth half-open, head nearly wedged in the gap between the side of the seat and the window.

Rearview mirror check: I am decidedly not myself. The swimmer is seeping back to me like water through a hairline crack. Quickly, I maneuver a house key off its ring, leaving the car key in the ignition. I pull the ziplock from my watch pocket and hold it up for a quick look. My heart sinks. There's only a little bit of powder left, less than I'd anticipated. I must have done too much back there in front of the Melfords' house. The sickly clawing at my brain begins, the looming certainty of the comedown, the facing-up to what I've done.

The swimmer doesn't try to stop me. Perhaps it knows that I'm only delaying the inevitable. Keeping an eye on the road, I dip the house key into the baggie and do a bump. One more for the other nostril and the bag's just about empty. I rip it open, making it into a flat rectangle, and then drag the plastic across my gums. The residual powder numbs the front of my jaw and makes my teeth feel isolated when I clench them. The upsurge floods my brain and I ride it out smoothly. Another glance at Danny, my sweet sleeping boy, makes my whole body go warm and tingly.

My dream story snaps back into place and contentment settles in my bones. I crack the window and let the wind take the empty ziplock. Then I roll up the window, wipe my nose, and nudge my son's shoulder.

"Danny!" He stirs and mumbles something. "Danny, wake up!"

He rubs his eyes and gapes at me.

"So, we're standing at the edge of the inside of your head, and you point to this one section. To me it doesn't look any different than the rest of the squishy wall, but hey, it's your head, you know what's going on there, right? So, I sort of push my way through the wall. It feels like goo, but it's also light and airy. And inside that section of the wall, I come to a place where there's all this nice soft light, like reading-lamp light. And there's one thing in there, sort of painted in the air, or on a thin invisible piece of glass. It's the most beautiful painting, it's almost overwhelming. I can't describe it. But I knew it was sort of percolating in your head, living in there fully formed until it was ready, when you were older, for you to show it to the world. Then I woke up in our little fort and I was so happy. Because I knew that you had greatness in you. Not necessarily painting, or even art, but the kernel of *something* inside you that was going to change the world. And I knew that I'd made the right decision, that you were my one right decision in a life of pretty bad ones. And I loved you more than ever at that moment."

I blink away tears until I can't fight them anymore and then I'm weeping, right there at the steering wheel, while the Outback eats up the miles.

Danny's quiet for a while. Then he slides toward me in his seat, squirms out of the shoulder belt, leans over the center console, and kisses me on the cheek.

"I think I'm gonna put on some music now," he says. He fishes in the glove compartment for the ancient iPod we use on car trips and hooks it up with the aux wire.

He puts on *Abbey Road* and we both sing along. I feel like

the world is moving at a million miles an hour while we're insulated in our bubble, my son and I, outside of time. Then the bubble bursts somewhere around the opening piano chords of "Golden Slumbers."

The swimmer sends jealous little scents floating through the atmosphere of the car, weird potencies that remind me of my obligation to it. I turn down the radio. The comedown fog begins to descend again, but this time I can't keep it at bay. There's nothing left. I'm going to have to ride it out.

"Danny, there's something I have to talk to you about." My plan is to be as plainspoken as possible. To introduce the swimmer like I'm introducing a new friend. "I know you've noticed something different about me lately. This is what I was getting at earlier in the drive. You're absolutely right, something is different about me."

I shoot him a look to see how this preamble is coming across and find that he's already closed his eyes.

"You don't have to do that. I want you to look at me."

"I know what you're talking about. I don't want to see it."

"It's nothing to be scared of! I promise."

But he won't open his eyes. I decide to let him have a moment to acclimate. The Cedar Valley exit comes up fast and five minutes later I'm easing the Outback through a tunnel of sun-dappled branches, the venerable old trees that line the entrance to the park.

"I was scared of it at first, too," I tell him. "But it's shown me again and again that it only wants to help me. To help *us*."

I stop at a tiny booth, forward progress blocked by a red-and-white-striped barrier. I buy a camping permit from the ranger-hatted man inside the booth. He shows me where our campsite is on a printed map of Cedar Valley. I try to avoid his eyes and say as little as possible, remaining in the shadows of the driver's seat. The half-life of the drug is diminishing my high by the minute and the sickly dread of the real is gnashing at the edges of my vision.

Ah, but the swimmer eases the transition, bearing me up with its impossible limbs, its otherworldly murmur...

"Ma'am?" The park ranger is staring at me. Hurriedly, I take the permit and the map. "Is everything okay?"

"Fine," I say, "thanks."

He narrows his eyes slightly. Then he gives an imperceptible shrug. "Okay, then. Enjoy the park. Whatever you take in, you take out."

"We know the drill. Thanks."

Our site is deep within Cedar Valley's verdant southern tier, and my ears pop as the road winds up through a stunning density of ancient earth: mulch and loam, unbound and shot through the towering trees in bark like armor plating and patches of birch. I share my sense of wonder with the swimmer and it hums like a well-oiled engine deep within my heart.

"Almost there, Danny-tello. You're missing all the pretty stuff."

When he doesn't reply, the swimmer urges me to try a different tactic. I'm heartened to know that it's as invested as me in these introductions.

"It's like we were saying about dreams—when you know your friend is your friend even though they don't look *exactly* like your friend."

I assess myself in the mirror. There's a slight corruption, an unnatural wavering, but my features are intact. It's more of a mood, a tweaked perception, than a rearranging of form. I think he should be able to get used to this fairly easily.

"Danny," I say, adding a bit of motherly command,

"you're going to have to help me set up the tent. And you're going to have to open your eyes for that or you'll fall flat on your face."

I pull into the gravel parking space adjacent to our site. We're all alone in a small clearing, and through the gaps in the trees I can see the crags of an outcrop that looks out over the park's central valley. Flanking the overlook are massive rock formations mottled with rich veins of moss. It's perfect.

I kill the engine and unbuckle my seatbelt. The swimmer, in its eagerness and desire to connect, wrenches me across the center console. I find myself grabbing Danny's chin and tilting his face toward mine while a protest rises inside me: *no no no no.*

Caught by surprise, Danny shuts his eyes even tighter.

There's no going back now. "Look at me," I say. "Look at me right now and then it'll be done."

His breathing comes in frightened gasps. He screws up his face and I feel his body clench. And then, abruptly, he opens his eyes. For a split second he goes perfectly still. Then he twists away from my grasp, opens the door, and tries to run out into the forest. But in his haste, he never quite gets his footing, and he tumbles into the gravel. I'm out of the car and upon him before he can right himself and make for the trees.

"It's not so bad!" I say, helping him to his feet. He doesn't look at me, but he also doesn't try to make another break for it. I consider that progress. I slide the bundled tent frame out of the Outback's hatch and together we make our way to the site. There, in the tamped-down grass and dirt of the clearing proper, next to the remains of the last campers' fire in the cinder block pit, I set down the frame and try again.

"You know, people can get used to anything," I say to his

back. Then I pause, listening. Danny's not simply turning his back on me, he's searching the tree line for something. After a moment, I hear it, too—amplified by the swimmer, it's like they're standing right next to me: a group of people, talking and laughing, gathered at the next campsite. Cans pop open, a fire crackles, a softball thwacks a glove.

The swimmer surges. It knows what's going to happen and nearly knocks me off my feet with its flailed warning. But I'm not fast enough. Before I can grab him, Danny is running down a slight incline, leaping over fallen branches and decomposing logs, kicking up dirt in his wake.

"Help!" he calls out. "Somebody help me!"

No no no no no

I'm off and running. I can hear the stunned pause in our neighbors' revelry at the unlikely sound of a nearby child in distress.

"Over here!" he calls again—and then I've got a hand around his belly from behind and I'm pulling him back to me and never letting go. He struggles but the swimmer reinforces my grip.

I kneel down in the underbrush and hold him. When he realizes he's not getting away, he starts screaming again.

"Help me help me help me help—"

The swimmer clamps my hand over his mouth. *Be gentle*, I admonish it. *Please*.

Our campsite neighbors are scrambling toward the distress calls. "We're coming!" someone yells.

Danny bites my hand, but the swimmer takes the pain away. A brutal wave of nausea nearly blinds me. The pit of my stomach is boiling, the fire spreading up into my throat and out into each arm. I'm curled like an invertebrate hunter around my son, gripping my prey with alien strength. *No*, I tell the swimmer. *Let him go.* But it's too late. My impossible biology asserts itself and tiny holes bloom up my forearms, cluster at my knuckles, and spread to my palms. Danny's cries become shrill and he kicks his legs in the air. When the swimmer passes between us, I'm senseless with love. Danny goes limp in my arms and I'm entirely spent. I want to collapse and sleep for a week. At the same time, *no no no no* is thudding through my skull and pure hysteria's not far behind. I can see five men from the neighboring campsite hacking their way through the underbrush. They're burly and fleece-clad.

"Hey!" one of them calls out.

Summoning the last of my strength, I stagger to my feet with Danny in my arms. I still have time to hide. Somehow, I manage to run. I sprint past our site with its tent frame still bundled and make my way toward the outcrop. The boulders are massed higher than I'd seen from behind the trees, and in several places they're not boulders at all but inlets of eroded stone that appear almost ocean-formed.

The men are sprinting through my campsite in pursuit. Quickly, I head for the natural shelter of a moss-covered overhang, a jutting piece of stone layered like shale. As soon as I duck underneath, I realize that I've just discovered the mouth of a cave. Crouching, I carry Danny inside to the edge of daylight's reach and lay him gently on the floor.

"Come on, Danny, *wake up.*"

I give him a rough shake. He doesn't stir. I lean close to his half-open mouth and listen to his shallow breathing. He's not dead. He's comatose.

Just outside, the men are holding a frantic discussion. We've eluded them for now, but it won't be long before they stumble upon the entrance to the cave.

"Come on, come on, come on."

I'm shaking my son with methodical urgency, rocking him back and forth, back and forth. At last, his eyes snap open. He sits up. And speaks.

"Do you love me?"

I'm lost in the precious face. The sheriff was right: it *is* beautiful.

Godhead.

To see, now, in Danny what everyone has been seeing hints of in me. Bequeathed from mother to son: not a foul bloodline but a timeless gift. His eyes shine with knowledge. The air around him is alive with sensation. What had struck me, once, as corruption now appears as natural as aging— lost teeth, body hair, crow's feet.

Danny sits up, trailing the boy he used to be, inhabiting fully the boy he is now. I have given him more than I ever could have imagined. The air around my son steals density and shape from the walls of the cave. The swimmer delights in his youth. He is capable of so much more than I ever was.

"Yes," I say, and the word fills the cave with its profound rightness. "Yes."

Danny swims past me to the mouth of the cave. Soon the men come, and it isn't long before their voices turn to screams. Eventually, all is quiet. I sit in the dirt with no particular expression on my face, awaiting the return of my beautiful boy.

ACKNOWLEDGMENTS

Sincere thanks to:

Cameron McClure, an amazing agent, listener, and advice giver, not to mention all-around funny and smart human being. Thank you for your guidance and encouragement.

My editor, Bradley Englert, for his empathetic and insightful perspective on this story and its characters, his thoughtful commentary, and his fondness for Canadian prog metal. Thanks also to the entire team at Orbit/Redhook for believing in this book and working on its behalf.

Readers of various drafts during this book's evolution—Matt Lambert, Lauren O'Reilly, and Victor Pineiro. Reading an early draft of someone's novel is no small thing—it's not like, "check out this song I wrote, it'll take three minutes of your life"—and I truly appreciate you sharing your time, talent, and perspective.

Mike Jada, who introduced me to Fulci, Bava, Argento, and the inimitable Hugo Stiglitz, and whose impeccable film curation has been both influential and outrageous. Long live the Italian Horror Society. No talking please.

My family, for their unwavering love and support.

Mark, Chris, and Dan, for their enduring friendship.

Anne Heltzel, whose words changed everything.

MEET THE AUTHOR

Photo Credit: Stan Horaczek

ANDY MARINO was born in upstate New York, spent half his life in New York City, and now lives in the Hudson Valley. He works as a freelance writer. This is his first horror novel.